For my friends
Mary Coady and Richie Ball

Acknowledgments

Thanks to Leonard Cohen for permission to quote from his song 'Night Comes On' from the album *Various Positions*.

Thanks to Thomas Lynch for permission to quote from the documentary *The Undertaking*.

Thanks to Sgt Tony Timoney for help with my research.

Our children are always beautiful to us.

Thomas Lynch

JOHN MACKENNA was born in 1952 in Castledermot, County Kildare. His books include *The Fallen and Other Stories* (1992), which won the *Irish Times* First Fiction Award, *A Year of Our Lives* (London, Picador, 1995), *The Last Fine Summer* (London, Picador, 1998), *Things You Should Know* (New Island, 2006) and *The River Field* (New Island, 2007).

part

●

one

LATE ONE OCTOBER AFTERNOON, seventeen years ago, the doorbell rang and, when I answered it, I was met by two men in police uniform. I knew one of them, a middle-aged man, to see around the town and he seemed to know me, or perhaps years of doing this kind of thing had given him that aura of familiarity, that ease that the younger man, who was in his mid-twenties, didn't have.

'I didn't do it,' I said, laughing, but neither man smiled and, intuitively, I knew it was the wrong joke in the wrong place.

'Do you mind if we come in?' the familiar man asked.

'Not at all,' I said, and I ushered them ahead of me into the kitchen where Jane was sitting on a beanbag, watching some cartoons. They seemed to become uncertain at the sight of a three-year-old, as though she wasn't part of the plan. She smiled at them and went back to watching TV.

'Maybe another place,' the familiar man suggested, nodding at Jane.

'Sure,' I said, and I led him into the sunroom.

'You work at home?'

'I'm an architect.'

'Oh, yeah. You did that new surgery, the one at the mill?' the familiar man said and smiled.

'Yes.'

'You might like to sit down,' he said.

'This must be bad news.'

'It is. I'm afraid it is.'

I sat at the wicker table and he sat opposite. The other guard knelt in the kitchen, chatting to Jane, asking her about the cartoon. I heard him say that he had a little boy at home. He said the boy was five. He asked her how old she was.

'Three and a big bit, that's what my mammy says.'

'I'd say it's a really, really, really huge, big, enormous, monstrous bit,' the young guard said.

I heard Jane laughing and then he put his cap on her head and she saluted.

'It's about your wife,' the familiar man said. 'But I have to check.'

He read a registration number and make of car from his notebook.

'Would that be her car?'

I nodded.

'And she has blonde hair?'

'Yes.'

'There was an accident on the main road,' he said. 'Her car and a lorry. It was bad.'

'She'd have been on her way home from work,' I said. 'I was expecting her in the next twenty minutes or so.'

He nodded.

'How bad?' I asked.

'Very bad.' He shrugged and I knew, by the way he glanced at me and then looked away again, that he meant the worst.

'Put it on backwardses,' Jane was saying from the kitchen and I saw the young guard swivel his cap on his head, the peak tilting down his neck, his teeth protruding like a chipmunk's as he made a face to amuse her.

Jane laughed uproariously and the young man looked up, suddenly, caught my eye and blushed.

'I'll need to identify her or something,' I said.

'Yes,' the familiar man said. 'When you get things sorted – it doesn't have to be immediately. It'll be fine when you're ready. We'll bring you to the County Hospital. That's where your wife, where Beth is. That's where they brought her.'

'Right.'

'We'll drive you there.'

'You'll have to,' I said. 'She has the car.'

'Yes.'

'Had. Stupid. Had. I need to ask someone to keep an eye on Jane.'

'Is there anyone we can organise for you?'

'I'll ring,' I said, getting up from the table. 'I'll ring our friends, they live up the road. Kate will take Jane. I'll do that. And I'd better ring Beth's parents.'

'It might be best to wait until, you know, until you've identified her. I'm not raising false hopes but just, you know, it's always best to be sure before you go telling people, before the pool widens, so to speak.'

I nodded.

That night, while Jane slept soundly in her room, I lay awake and I thought about the hours. Fifteen hours earlier, I had stood with our daughter at the front door and watched Beth get into the car and drive away to work. Thirteen hours earlier, I had cycled to the playschool with Jane. Ten hours earlier, I had collected her and we'd had lunch together. Seven hours earlier, I'd begun preparing dinner. Six and a half hours earlier, the doorbell had rung and the familiar policeman and the young policeman had stepped into the hall downstairs. An hour later, I'd identified Beth's body. And an hour after that, I'd started making phone calls – to her parents, her sisters, my mother, my brother, friends, colleagues of hers from the office. And then I'd carried Jane, smiling in her sleep, down the avenue from Kate's house and put her to bed. And the phone had started ringing, and Brian and Kate had come down to see what needed doing. And, after they'd left, I'd switched off the house lights and the telephone and come up to bed, seen cars turning in the yard, heard voices, listened to people assuming I'd gone to stay elsewhere for the night.

And then I counted the hours that remained before the house would begin to flood with Beth's family and my family and friends and neighbours, all wanting to help, all wanting to be of comfort, all wanting to assure me that I wasn't alone. And I lay back, treasuring the hours I still had to myself, the only hours of privacy I'd have for weeks to come.

And I also thought of the other hours and days that stretched back through the summer that was long gone, back before Easter, back to the start of the year. The hours and days and weeks and months of unhappiness, when Beth and I had tried to find a way out of this marriage that wasn't working properly for either of us, and wasn't working for me at all. I remembered the intensity of our quiet fights, neither of us wanting Jane to overhear what was being said. And, after weeks of that, the tiredness of the long summer days when we were both at home and even the thought of each other's company was a bleak and dreary prospect.

The previous year, we'd gone on a holiday to Amsterdam, a city Beth had always wanted to see. We'd done all the things she wanted to do, visited the Rijksmuseum where she spent twenty minutes *oohing* and *aahing* over Jan van Huysum's *Still Life with Flowers and Fruit* while I kept Jane entertained. And then it was on to the Tropenmuseum and the collected plunderings of a colonial power.

I made the mistake of saying this aloud.

'I thought you'd possibly left your politics at home,' Beth said.

'No, they were the first thing I packed.'

'This is culture,' she said.

'Ah, I thought it was just things that had been stolen from other people.'

'The closed mind, always the closed mind.'

We did agree on the Van Gogh Museum and spent what might have passed for an idyllic afternoon, by our standards, wandering from room to room while Jane slept in a sling on my back.

But the following morning, the Anne Frank House was another cause of disagreement.

'It's hardly the most uplifting experience,' Beth said when I suggested it. 'I'm sure Jane won't find it interesting.'

'Considering the fact that she slept through the Van Gogh experience that won't be too surprising. I'm sure she'll survive it.'

'Unlike Anne Frank. Why are you consumed with these depressing things? There's so much life and colour and beauty in this city and yet here we are, visiting a mausoleum.'

From the moment we stepped into the house, everything was wrong. There really wasn't anything to see, and the house was too hot, the queues were too long and they were moving too slowly. It was claustrophobic.

'I think that's the general idea,' I said. 'I think claustrophobia is part of what it was all about in here.'

'You're just being smart-assed,' Beth hissed. 'You know damn well what I meant. It's stifling. I really don't want to be here.'

'Well would you rather wait outside for me?'

'I'm not standing on the footpath for an hour like a hooker.'

'I think you'll be safe.'

'Predictable.'

'Oh, for God's sake, Beth. It's the middle of the bloody morning, the streets are full of people and, anyway, this is not a hooker area. Not at this hour of the day.'

The following evening we ate at a restaurant in the Museum Quarter. The wind was warm, the food was good and everything was right with the world.

'Have you enjoyed the break?' Beth asked.

'I have, yes. Thoroughly.'

'It's only when I'm somewhere like this that I realise how much I miss city living.'

'It's difficult to judge a place by a holiday, isn't it?'

'Of course, but some things you just know. Well I do, anyway. I know I'd love to live in a place like this. It has such a buzz, so much energy. It has life.'

'And hookers.'

'Very funny. Wouldn't you like to live here, even for a while, for two or three years? You could do some work here, get new ideas, get you out of the routine of small-town Ireland. Could be the making of you, could be the move that gives you the grand design.'

'I'm not interested in producing the grand design.'

'Course you are. All architects are. I've never met an architect who didn't want to produce something that made the world stand back and admire.'

I laughed.

'Why are you doing that?' Beth asked, her eyes darkening. 'You're laughing at me. Why do you have to do that?'

'Because you're telling me what architects want.'

'And?'

'And I'm telling you not all architects want that. I'm certainly saying that I don't. I'm telling you something but you don't believe me. You're not really listening. That's why I'm laughing.'

'So you're saying you don't believe a move to a city like this would give you a broader canvas, a more sophisticated view on life, a greater chance of designing something that makes your name.'

'Yes, I am saying that.'

'Rubbish.'

'It's not rubbish. I work on a small scale, I work with the landscape I know, I work from the people I grew up with. That's how I work.'

'And that's why your buildings have the same … I don't know … the same …'

'Prices?'

'Not what I was going to say,' Beth said. 'That's why you end up working for the same kind of people, doing the same kind of work. It's why you haven't made the breakthrough to the mass market. It's why you don't get asked to work with builders in Dublin. I mean, are you seriously saying to me you wouldn't like to see your next design on the cover of a magazine in the bookshop in Amsterdam airport? Seriously?'

'Of course I would, but only if it was the building I really wanted to work on.'

'So you don't have ambition?'

'Depends on what you mean by ambition. I have ambitions to design good buildings and then better buildings. I have ambitions to do work that people find interesting and challenging and that people like. I have ambitions to go on working –'

'That's the process you're talking about,' she interrupted. 'I'm not talking about the process. Every architect has to do what you're talking about. I'm talking about the bigger picture.'

'Thinking outside the box?'

'Yes.'

'Being focused on the endgame?'

'Yes.'

'Identifying a market going forward?'

'Yes.'

My sarcasm was missing the mark or being ignored.

'Bollocks. That has nothing to do with design.'

'Of course it hasn't, not if being asked to present prizes in the local school or draw the plans for the local football changing room is what 'focus' and 'market' mean to you. If you limit your context, you limit your possibilities. Living here, in this city, with its history and culture and sophistication would have to change your point of view.'

'But it doesn't interest me,' I sighed.

'There comes an occasion in everyone's life when the time is right to let certain things go.'

'And, equally, there are things in our lives that we don't want to let go of – ever.'

'I think you're afraid of the world,' Beth said. I knew by her eyes that she was serious. 'I think you feel safe being the medium-sized fish in a tiny pond. But what happens if another fish appears in that pond?'

I shrugged my shoulders. I knew she believed she was right and nothing I could say about roots or background or my belief that the things that are relevant anywhere are relevant everywhere would have the slightest effect.

'If I'd settled for being a small-time solicitor in a small-time town, where would that have led me?' Beth asked. 'To frustration, to bitterness, to thinking a Saturday-night rumpus on the town square was the height of what I might aspire to dealing with. If I had been prepared to settle for what I knew, what I imagined was comfortable for me, then I'd still be there, swimming around in circles, fooling myself into thinking this is all life has to offer in the way of work. That's what you're doing. You're confining yourself unnecessarily, through fear, through a thought process that hasn't grown in confidence.'

'I can't be you,' I said.

'No, but you could be a different you. You could be someone you haven't even dared to meet yet. If you never try, if you never test yourself, if you never put yourself under pressure, how will you know what you have inside or who you really are?'

'That sounds like something from a self-help book.'

Beth put her fork down loudly on her plate.

'There you go again. Anything you don't agree with you feel the need to criticise and to be sarcastic about.'

'But it does,' I said. 'It sounds like a recipe for "a life well lived" or some shit like that.'

'Are you afraid of failure?' Beth asked.

'No,' I said. 'According to you, I've been living with it all my life.'

'I didn't say that. I simply asked you a question.'

'Right,' I said. 'Let me ask you one. If I were designing buildings that were being built in Dublin or London or Amsterdam, would you be happier?'

'I think you'd be happier.'

'What makes you think that?'

'The human condition is to want more. I see it every day in work. Sometimes it comes out as greed and sometimes as ambition, but it's there.'

'Maybe I fail the human condition test, then. Would you be happier if I were more successful?'

'Yes, for you.'

'And for yourself?'

'Of course. I'm happy for anyone who reaches his or her potential.'

'And I haven't?'

'I think you haven't allowed yourself to. I think you haven't stretched yourself. What was the first design you worked on? A house for someone you grew up with. What are you working on now? A shop for someone you grew up with. The house was a peak when you began; you're still on the same peak but other people are climbing higher and higher. People you were in college with. You don't see that.'

'I've kept my clients.'

'So has the grocery store down the road. But it's not the same clientele that the supermarket gets.'

'But it's a select clientele.'

'Or a failing enterprise.'

'Well,' I said. 'That puts me in my place.'

'No, you decide on your place and you accept it or you look for another place. I can't put you there and I can't move you. All I can do is encourage you. I know I find my work a lot more satisfying since I moved companies. I know I was willing to take a risk. I know there were many people who'd have been happy to see me fall on my face, many who thought I had ideas above my station, but they don't matter and I never gave them a moment's thought. I did what I knew was best for me. Not what I was comfortable with but what would push me. That which tests me makes me stronger, even if I fail.'

'Who said that?'

'I did.'

'Well then,' I laughed. 'It must be true.'

The last conversation we'd had about us, about our lives, was ten days before the accident. We were in the kitchen, washing up after dinner.

Beth was telling me, for the tenth time that month, that I should buy a car.

'I don't need a car,' I said. 'I have the bike.'

'And when the winter comes, when you're cycling through the rain with Jane, when she's going in to playschool drenched and cold, will that satisfy your ego? Does the fact that you're putting your daughter's health at risk, just because you're too stubborn to let me buy a second car, not cross your mind?'

I laughed out loud.

'I am not putting Jane's health at risk. I walked to school in winter, you walked to school in winter, you're being melodramatic and unreasonable. She's a normal, healthy child and she enjoys the bike trips.'

'Says who?'

'Says I. Ask her if you don't believe me. Just ask her.'

'I'm not dragging her into this squabble,' Beth said.

'Well, then, you'll never know, will you? If you don't ask the chief witness.'

'Why are you always so eager to take the piss out of my work? I don't do it to you.'

'It was a joke, m'lud,' I said.

'And why is it that you put so much energy into negativity when it comes to my opinions? If you wanted a car, I wouldn't say you can't have it, I'd say buy it.'

'If I needed a car, I'd get a car,' I sighed. 'The notion that Jane is in any danger from being out in the fresh air is ludicrous. It's not something that'd stand up in court and even you wouldn't try to defend it. I wrap her up well, I cycle carefully, I look after her and to suggest anything else is totally unfair.'

'There you go again, everything you say is meant to undermine me. Court, witnesses, judges. All that stuff.'

'I didn't say anything about judges,' I said lamely.

Beth crossed the kitchen and stood in front of me, her eyes glaring into mine. What I saw in them was frustration and anger and distress.

'Why do you hate me so much?' she asked.

'I don't hate you at all.'

.

13

'Dislike me, then. Why do you dislike me so much?'

'It's not a question of dislike, more of disappointment.'

'In me?'

'Not in you, in us. Disappointment in what we are, how we are. Surely you're not happy with how things are between us?'

'No, but I'm trying to make them better.'

'Well, it doesn't seem to be working, then, does it?'

'And what do you suggest we do about it?'

How often had we reached this point where one of us had put that question to the other? And how often had we waited for the answer, wishing we could hear the other say what we were thinking. Yet, neither of us had ever had the courage to speak our mind. Instead, we'd skirted round the issue, looking for the half-truths that might make things easier, allow us to slip out of accepting the responsibility for the sham our marriage had become.

And so it was this time. I took things away on a different tangent.

'Money and cars and things don't buy better lives.'

Beth turned and walked away from me, stopping in the doorway.

'That's a cheap, nasty, lousy jibe,' she said. 'I have never used my money to try to buy your affection and I never could. Even if I wanted to, I wouldn't earn enough in a lifetime to do that.'

She stepped out into the garden and, as always, the argument remained unresolved.

Lying in bed, I wished her peace and I wished her a home in paradise, if such a place exists, and I recalled the good years and I was shocked at how few there had been. The year we met, the year we married, the year that Jane was born and that was it. Twenty-eight months out of almost six years, not enough to make me sad, not enough to make me cry, not enough even to keep me from sleep.

I woke to total darkness. I was alert, the way you're alert when you're sure someone has walked into the room or the way a phone ringing in the dead of night brings you totally and instantaneously to your senses. For a second, I imagined I had heard Beth open the front door. She must be getting home late from a meeting or some work 'do'. But then, as quickly as that thought came, it was followed by the realisation that she was dead, that I had seen her body on the mortuary slab, that the nurses or morticians, or whoever does these things, had ensured the body was as presentable as it could be.

So I lay there, listening to the darkness outside my open window. The little noises and the louder bellowing of cattle from two fields away and then the little noises again, of creatures about their business, of the house settling and reset-tling, of a dog barking once and then the quietness as his growl fell back into the night.

And, lying in the darkness, slowly putting shapes on the things that grew out of the pitch-blackness, I felt relief and then guilt seep through me. Relief that the months, years if I were honest, of pretending I had some interest in resur-recting *our life together* were over. Relief that fate had provided the answer that neither of us could – or would. I thought of Beth lying here, imagined my own body in the hospital mortuary and wondered if she'd have felt this same strange feeling of liberation if it had been me who'd died.

But there was a sense of guilt, too, that I had never found the courage to say what had been on my mind, to be straight with Beth and tell her I had no interest in that life any more. And there was remorse at the release I was experiencing, the ease with which I had escaped from something that, only twelve hours earlier, had seemed inescapable. Culpability that she had been the one to pay the price of my freedom.

And, immediately, I was sleeping again and I was dreaming of a woman I'd gone out with in college. We were sitting in the narrow seats in the cinema of my hometown and she was kissing me, and then we were walking the long empty main street and there was music trickling out of a pub on the corner but we turned down a lane, into the darkness of the mediaeval graveyard. We pushed through the gateway, the hinges singing a rusty song, and crossed between the graves to a flat table of stone that leaned into the lie of the land, the names and dates of its sleeping dead long gone. And I lay down on this memorial table and the woman straddled me and, as she bent to kiss me, I kissed her breast through her T-shirt and then I was awake again, hearing Jane's voice from her room down the landing.

'It's backwardses,' she said and then she laughed, a warm giggling laugh, and I knew she was talking in her sleep. I smiled and closed my eyes again but the woman from college was gone and the gravestone was empty and I knew it was time to get up, to do the things that needed doing, to prepare the house for the days ahead.

It was still only half past six but I cleaned the bathroom and washed the kitchen floor and baked bread and made coffee and stood in the kitchen, watching the sky begin to crack above the blackthorn hedge.

And then I turned the phone back on, sat at the kitchen table, a mug of steaming coffee in my hand, and checked the messages. There were eleven. *Are you all right? Devastated to hear. Can't believe the news. Are you ok? If there's anything that needs doing. What is there to say at a time like this? Will you be all right? Are you there? See you tomorrow. We're thinking of you. Things will be all right.*

And Jane was in the doorway, her teddy tucked under her arm, sleepy eyes, frowning.

'Is it today or yesterday now?'

'Today, sweetheart, it's today.'

'And is it early?'

'Yes, it's early.'

'Where's the funny man with the cap?'

'Gone home to his own house, to his little boy.'

'He was funny.'

'Yes he was.'

'Will he come back?'

'I don't think so.'

'He was very funny.'

My brother, Robert, and I were standing in the garden, surveying the empty plot that had been that summer's vegetable patch. Two drills of leeks were all that remained of the season's work. It was the morning of Beth's burial.

'How were the crops?'

'They were good,' I said. 'Good.'

'And how are you?'

'I'm fine. I will be, when today is over. When everyone has gone.'

'And Jane?'

'Jane's just excited about all the visitors, all the attention. You know yourself what kids are like.'

He nodded and we walked farther along the path, into the fruit garden where the late raspberries were still clustered in golden bursts on the canes.

'She thinks it's great that her mammy is in heaven. She reckons that she only has to ask and Beth will send stuff down to her, she reckons it's like having two Santa Clauses looking after her. I know there'll be other days when she'll really miss Beth but I'm the one she's used to having about the place.'

Robert smiled.

We walked to the end of the garden and turned to look back at the house.

'Do you mind if I say something to you?' he asked.

'Not at all.'

'It might seem a strange time to say it but, once we go back in there, there might not be a better time today so I thought I'd say it now.'

'Sure, fine. Go ahead.'

'You remember when Amy went?'

His wife had died of cancer four years earlier.

'Of course.'

'I learned a lesson then and I just thought I should pass it on.'

'Shoot.'

'This might seem macabre but what I found out then was that a woman's corpse attracts other women. It's like they can sense it from a hundred miles away. Like they have this drive that makes them want to feast on it, not literally of course, but like they have to travel to see what the pickings are like. Suddenly, there's a man who's totally available and they come like a pack of coyotes across the world. They come with all this, I don't know, all this sympathy and smiles and blouses opened that extra button or two and short skirts and they'll be calling to see that Jane is ok – but they'll be calling when they know she's asleep. And they'll run into you in the super-market and again at the school and they'll turn up in the places you least expect them, totally by chance, of course! The less subtle ones might even be hovering after the funeral today but it's the ones who are more devious that you have to watch for. They'll take their time – you won't necessarily see them coming. That's what I found. That's it.'

He looked at me and shrugged.

'I hope you didn't mind my saying that. It might seem insensitive but I was thinking about it last night, driving up here, so I thought I'd just say it.'

'I don't mind at all,' I laughed. 'But I may be disappointed if it doesn't happen. It could severely damage my ego, you realise that?'

'It'll happen.'

'Well, at least now I'm prepared.'

'Course we didn't have kids, so it might be slightly different but it'll happen, in some shape or form.'

We began walking very slowly, back towards the house.

'Did you love Beth?' Robert asked suddenly.

'No.'

'Did she love you?'

'She said she did. She loved the three of us together. She loved this place. I think she was in love with an idea of what we could have been or might have been. She'd say that's bullshit if she were here but that's how I saw it.'

'The tangled web and all that.'

'Very tangled.'

'Was there anyone else?'

'Not for me,' I said. 'I didn't have the energy. Not even the desire. Just keeping away from being sucked back into something that was bound to be a compromise took every ounce of energy I had. And I have no reason to think there was anyone else in Beth's life either. I couldn't see any way of getting out, but I was damned if I was going to pretend things were hunky dory. It was like living in a waiting room, expecting every minute that someone would open a door and give a diagnosis – and then being disappointed when they didn't. Truth is, I knew the diagnosis all along, certainly for the last couple of years. That's why, when I got the news, apart from the shock, I felt like I could breathe easy, for the first time in a long time. Isn't that a fucking awful thing to say about the death of my wife?'

Robert shrugged.

'It's just that when I say it out loud it sounds cold and clinical, cruel even. I've been thinking it but that's a different thing to saying it.'

'I've long ago given up on judging people,' Robert said quietly.

'We talked about going our separate ways. No, let me correct that. I skirted around the possibility and Beth ignored it. Maybe because she really wanted us to stay together but I was never sure about that either because neither of us could ever find the courage to come out and say. If I'd been as honest with her as I'm being with you, things might have been clearer.'

'I'm sure, if she had the choice now,' Robert said quietly, 'she'd have chosen that kind of separation over this kind.'

'I'm sure she would,' I said.

Late that night, long after midnight, while Beth's parents and my mother were still chatting in the sitting room, I walked Robert to his car.

'How long are Beth's folks staying?' he asked.

'Don't know, didn't feel I could ask them.'

'And Mam?'

'Day after tomorrow I think, not any longer I hope.'

'Right. Well, if you feel like a break, you know where I am. Just hop in the car.'

He coughed, realising what he'd said.

'Sorry, sorry, sorry, sorry. Fuck, sorry.'

I laughed.

'It doesn't matter.'

'Get on the train or I'll come up for you.'

'Thanks,' I said. 'We'll see. I'll probably try to keep Jane in a routine with playschool and all, but we'll see. Maybe some weekend in November or before Christmas. Or whenever. You know.'

Robert nodded.

'The thing is, I'm going to have to get a car now. That was another bone of contention.'

'You probably will.'

'Anyway, thanks for everything,' I said. 'And I am all right. I'm fine about things. Once the menagerie of parents has gone, I'll be even better. Back on an even keel.'

'Good. But there will be an absence, you know. No matter what was said or done, no matter how roughly things were going, there will be that sense of absence. Just be prepared for it. You may not be expecting it.'

'There's been an absence for a long time,' I said.

'Yeah, I know, but this will be something different. You just need to be prepared – it took me unawares.'

'Thanks.'

Robert sat into his car.

'I'll look out for you brother,' he smiled. 'Keep the faith.'

During the second summer after Beth's death, on Jane's fifth birthday, Robert told me he was moving to America.

'It's something I've been thinking about for a long time,' he said. 'Making enquiries, sussing the situation out. We'd talked about it, Amy and myself, and then she got sick and it went on the back burner for all this time. I think it's the right time to go now. I'm thirty-three – if I don't go someone may crucify me!'

He laughed but I knew he was waiting for a reaction.

Brian and Kate were sitting with us. It was midafternoon, midsummer's afternoon, and the sun was hot on our faces. Jane was playing with her friends in the sandpit at the end of the lawn. Their laughter was infectious. Every so often, we'd stop our conversation, just to listen to the rising giggles and the belly laughs that followed. Five children lost in the sunshine, having a good time. We were all happy for them, made happy by their joy.

'I think you're right,' Kate said. 'Go for it. Why not, you're young, gifted and, if the summer goes on like this, you'll be black by September. I've been trying to get Brian to up sticks and go to Australia. It has to have more going for it than this place.'

'Have you mentioned it to the old lady?' I asked.

'Not yet,' Robert said.

'And when would you go?'

'They want me in October.'

'Where?'

'Flagstaff.'

'Where's Flagstaff?' Brian asked.

'Arizona.'

'Mountains, desert, sun, snow, heat, skiing, long hot summers. Will you have a guest room?' Kate sighed.

'I'm sure I will.'

'What she means,' Brian laughed, 'is will you have a bedroom? I'm losing her! Single man with Arizona apartment wins out over married man, two kids and dead-end job.'

'Too true,' Kate smiled.

'So, what do you think, brother?'

'I think you'd be a fool not to go for it.'

'Do you?'

'I do.'

'Really?'

'Absolutely, really.'

'Good,' he said, and I could see the relief in his eyes.

Later, while he and I were cooking and Kate and Brian were playing with the kids, I asked him why it mattered what I thought.

'It matters,' he said. 'Life is short, we both know that better than most. You're my brother. What you think matters to me. A lot.'

'Thanks,' I said and I hugged him.

'Do you think the old lady will be as understanding?'

'Are you joking?' I asked, laughing and shaking my head. 'She'll have a canary, but only because she knows it's expected of her. It's tradition, isn't it? I can hear her already. "I'm losing one of my sons to a place thousands of miles away. I'm getting on. I may never see him again." And, come October, there'll be tears and telephone calls asking you to reconsider. And by next summer, she'll be out there and loving it and then she'll be back home telling all her bridge buddies how fabulous it is and inviting them to come out with her the following Easter. You'll have Kate in one room and the old lady and half a dozen grande dames in the other.'

'I heard that,' Kate said from the open kitchen door.

'You're supposed to be outside.'

'I bring a query from the small people as to when the burgers and chips will be ready because, Jane says, they're "starveded".'

'So the old lady and friends will be out there watching you living with Robert. They'll be scandalised.'

'All the more reason for you to come and live with me, Kate,' Robert laughed. 'It might keep them away.'

'Thanks. Thanks very much,' Kate grinned. 'But I'm not sure I can drag myself away from your beloved brother. I mean, having him as a neighbour is like living down the road from Paul Newman. My heart would break if I didn't have the chance to peep through the curtains in the hope of seeing him cycle by every morning. This is a hard call.'

She slid the grill pan from the cooker and turned the burgers.

'I'm doing that,' I said.

'No, you're not, you're thinking about doing it and forgetting to do it. I'm ensuring the kids get fed. Robert, the thing you should know is that if I wasn't around, Jane might die of starvation.'

'He needs a woman,' Robert said.

'See,' Kate laughed, poking my arm. 'Have I or have I not told you the same thing?'

'You have,' I said. 'But you haven't offered yourself and you're the only woman for me. If I have to wait fifty years for Brian to move on, I'll wait.'

'Bullshit,' Kate said, suddenly serious. 'I've had this conversation with him, Robert, half a dozen times since Easter. Not pushing him to think about walking down the aisle, just to go out with someone, have a meal, talk to someone, hug someone, kiss someone.'

'But I have you,' I said.

'Joke over,' Kate said quickly. 'You need to think of you. Not just of Jane. In fact, I think Jane would benefit from another woman in her life – apart from me and your mother.'

'I think she's right,' Robert said.

'Hark to this fellow,' I laughed. 'You've been single for six years. Talk about people in glass houses!'

'I don't have a daughter.'

'So?'

'So it's different.'

'Bullshit.'

'Would you not like to go out with someone?'

'Not particularly.'

'Would you not find it exciting, challenging, whatever?'

'It hasn't crossed my mind.'

'It must have.'

'It hasn't.'

Brian came in from the garden.

'Food is required, very urgently or we'll have a rebellion on our hands.'

'Brian,' I pleaded. 'Rescue me from this pair. They're telling me I need a woman, a girlfriend and a mother figure for Jane. Tell them you're happy to share Kate with me.'

He laughed.

'I thought Kate was going to live with Robert in Arkansas or Arizona or wherever. Don't tell me she's staying here with you and me, now?'

'I haven't decided.'

'But, if we're being serious about this,' Brian said, cornering me, 'I think it would be good for you to see someone, just to get out, to socialise. It's almost two years since the accident. I think you'd be surprised at how much you might enjoy the experience.'

'If anything happened to me, this fellow would be out the following night, if not the night I was brought to the church,' Kate said, nodding at her husband.

'I'm calling the kids for food,' I said. 'It's the only way I'm going to escape this inquisition.'

A week later, Kate came for coffee. Jane had gone to a sleepover with one of her friends.

'Are you working?'

'No, too sunny,' I said. 'I spent the morning weeding the vegetables.'

'I brought some scones,' Kate said. 'I'll put the kettle on.'

We sat in the garden, in the shade of the broom.

'How the hell do you keep this place so well, so productive, so ordered?'

'I'm an ordered person, that's how buildings get designed, order and discipline.'

'Wish I could do that,' she sighed.

'You have two kids to look after.'

'Three,' she said.

'Congratulations!'

'I meant Brian. Three when you include him.'

'Right, right. Just for a minute there …'

'No, thanks. I've done my labour.'

We sat and drank our coffee and a robin came and perched beside us, picking fallen crumbs from the table.

'Jane sometimes says that's Beth, come back as a bird,' I whispered.

The robin ate its fill while we watched and then flitted to a branch on the crab tree.

'That's not necessarily a good thing,' Kate said.

'What isn't?'

'Jane, thinking that, saying that.'

'I think it comforts her. It keeps her mother's memory alive in some way for her. She hardly remembers Beth as a person, just snatches of things, something to do with her last Christmas, the colour of her car, that coat thing with all the colours.'

'But she needs living people, too, and not just me. I love her dearly, I adore her, I think of her like one of my own. And your mother loves her but I'm her friends' mother, the neighbour three fields away, the aunty figure. And your mum is her granny. That's different to someone she can see as a ...'

'A mother figure?'

'No, you're trying to lead me down a dead end here, like you always do with this. All I'm saying is that Jane might benefit from another woman in her life, someone who hasn't got her kids to look after and someone who isn't an elderly lady. And so might you!'

'But I can't just go out with someone because you and Robert think it might be good for Jane.'

'Oh, you're so frigging infuriating,' Kate sighed. 'All we're doing is asking you to look beyond your current condition and to be open to possibilities. I am not setting myself up as a matchmaker. Have I ever invited you to dinner with another available woman?'

'No.'

'Have I ever tried to hook you up with someone without your knowing?'

I shook my head.

'Have I ever suggested that you get over Beth?'

'Come on,' I said. 'You know how close I was to the end of my time with Beth.'

'Yes, I do, but my point is that I have never tried to arrange your life in any way, much as I'd like to try. There are at least half a dozen friends of mine whose company I know you'd enjoy but I have never landed them on you or landed you into a situation with them. Now I'm telling you it's time to open yourself to possibilities. That's all.'

'But why?'

'Because you're my friend and I don't want you becoming a reclusive gardener whose daughter knows three women – her granny, her teacher and her aunty neighbour – and who thinks a robin is her mother reincarnated.'

'Lots of kids think stuff like that.'

'You're right,' she said. 'I know that. Maybe it's more that I worry about you.'

'Why?'

'Because I love you, I care about you. You've been a good friend to me … to us.'

'I thought you were going to say you'd like to shag me,' I laughed.

'Maybe I would, but that's not the point.'

I looked at her, searching for a smile, a hint of irony.

'Well it kind of is, if you're not winding me up. It is an issue, if you'll excuse the pun.'

I wanted to keep things light, I still wasn't sure whether what I was hearing was meant to be funny or whether she was telling me something that was going to change the nature of the relationship between us.

'That's something I have to deal with.'

'Come on, Kate,' I said. 'You're sitting here telling me, bang out of the blue, after five years of being neighbours, that this is how you feel about me and then, with the next breath, you say it's something you have to deal with. It might just involve me, too, you know.'

'It can only involve you if I let it,' she said. 'And I don't intend to. If Beth was still alive, I might consider it, but not now.'

'What do you mean by that?'

'I mean there'd have been some balance in my going behind Brian's back and you going behind Beth's back, but that doesn't exist now. So! Anyway, I'm making a big assumption here, that you'd be interested. And you don't have to answer that because, either way, it won't happen. So let's get back to what we were talking about. Or not.'

She laughed and poured some more coffee.

.

'Right,' I said. 'But you drop a bombshell like that and then move on as though nothing had been said. Why didn't you say this when Beth was alive?'

'Because I was too nervous, because I might have had to put my money where my mouth is, if you'll excuse the expression.'

'I don't know what to say.'

'I don't want you to say anything. I should have kept my thoughts to myself.'

'Well, I think I'm glad you didn't.'

Kate smiled, a shy smile. 'Thank you, I think.'

'It's not necessary to thank me. I mean it. You've been a pillar to me in the past two years but maybe I'd forgotten that you've been more than that. And don't ask me to put that into words.'

We sat in silence. Birds sang, a wasp hovered over the unfinished food and the unhurried, low, drumming sounds of the summer garden rose slowly and swallowed that silence. I reached out and put my hand on Kate's. She looked up slowly and smiled but what I saw in her eyes was almost despondency, and it frightened me.

'Life seems to be a series of secrets we carry around with us, doesn't it?' she asked.

'Sometimes.'

'Not that you have any secrets, I suspect.'

I shrugged.

'Have I fucked things up between us? Metaphorically?'

Her smile was suddenly uncertain.

I squeezed her hand.

'Far from it,' I said. 'You've made me feel closer to you than I've ever felt to anyone.'

'That's a nice thing to say.'

'Can I hug you?' I asked.

She nodded and we stood in the shadow of the broom and hugged, as we had done a hundred times before. But this time there was something different, a closeness that kept us apart or an uncertainty that brought us nearer. I kissed her hair and she tightened her arms around me and wouldn't let me go and I knew she was crying.

'Do you know what I'd love to do?' she asked when, finally, she had stepped away from me and I could see the tear stains on her sunburned face.

'What would you love to do?'

'I'd love to spend one night under the same roof with you. Just that. I think that'd be enough for now. And now you know that and all the other secrets of my soul. I want you to go in and make some fresh coffee while I wash my face. And then we're going to come back out here and sit down and take up where we left off.'

'And that's it?'

'For now, that's it. That's all I can say or do for now. Don't ask me any questions, don't try to explain anything, don't do any of those things, ok? If, and when, I'm ready to talk to you about this again, I'll do it. And, yes, I know it's unfair to you and the last thing I want to do is be unfair but I've said more than I ever intended, probably more than I should, and I'm asking you to just leave it. Please.'

The weekend before Robert left for America, he came and stayed with me. I made dinner for him and invited Brian and Kate to join us. We laughed a lot and Brian kept reminding Kate that she had booked a place in Robert's bed in return for life in Arizona.

'I'm not getting involved in this, beyond issuing a general invitation to all of you, *mi casa es su casa*.'

'Impressive,' Brian said. '"International, multilingual, single man seeks uninhibited woman for interesting conversation – or something."'

'Very funny,' Kate said. 'I'll talk directly to you, Robert, when the time is right.'

'Well that leaves you and me out of the loop, Brian,' I said.

He nodded and then, without pausing, he went into a game he and I often played.

'Pick a year,' he said.

'Seventy-eight.'

'"Oh Carol".'

'Too easy. Smokie.'

'"Dreadlock Holiday".'

'Oh come on: 10cc.'

'"If I Can't Have You".'

I thought for a moment.

'*Jesus Christ Superstar* singer … ah … Yvonne, Yvonne Elliman.'

'"Stay".'

'Jackson Browne. The man.'

Brian paused, thinking hard.

'"Don't Cry out Loud".'

'A hit in seventy-eight? You sure?'

'Top twenty, almost made the top ten.'

'In seventy-eight?'

'Yes.'

'Yes,' Robert and Kate chorused.

I trawled the back catalogue of my brain but that song was missing.

'Going … going …' Brian said.

I shook my head.

'Elkie Brooks.'

'Bugger!'

'Well,' Robert said, raising his glass. '"Here's to the few who forgive what you do and the fewer who don't even care."'

'Good line,' Kate said. 'Your own?'

'I wish. Leonard Cohen. Now name the track or the album or the year?'

'Come on,' Brian laughed. 'We're singles men, chart men. You older guys had the money to buy the albums.'

'"Night Comes On". *Various Positions*. 1984,' Robert said quietly.

'Great line,' Kate said. 'I'll buy it.'

'The album?'

'And the line. Here's to you, Robert. Bon voyage. Bon chance.'

'Bonnie Tyler,' Brian interrupted. '"Lost in France". What year?'

'So things are going all right for you?' Robert asked.

We were sitting in the darkness that had grown around us through the evening as the dinner candles burned out one by one. Kate and Brian had left an hour earlier. Jane was sleeping on the couch, a rug wrapped snugly around her.

'They're fine. Working away – I'm in the middle of doing a fairly major piece of work for a shopping centre, bigger than I've done before. Much bigger. I hope to have it with the clients by Christmas.'

'And you're happy with it?'

'As happy as I ever am. You never can tell, you know. Something that you worry about can connect with people and something you have faith in can just pass them by. It's like any job, the customer is always right, but the customer isn't always kind.'

'Well, I hope you'll come and see me at Easter. I'll be well settled, the weather will be warm but not too hot for Jane to enjoy it. I was talking to her earlier about school. She likes it.'

'She loves it. I think she's a bit of a handful, in the sense that she's used to talking on a one to one with me. The principal says she thinks Jane is miffed that she hasn't been asked to have her lunch in the teachers' room.'

Robert laughed.

'Well her mother will never be dead while Jane is alive then.'

'More or less.'

'Do you see Beth in her? I see Dad every time I look in the mirror now.'

I thought about what he'd asked. Did I see Beth in our daughter? Not really, but perhaps that was because I had never looked for her. I had never looked for Beth anywhere. There were things of hers in the house, things she had bought. The rooms were still the colours she had suggested I paint them. There were ornaments that I looked at, that reminded me of places we'd been or particular days, but there was nothing that made me think immediately of her as a person. There was nothing of her that haunted the house. I had kept some of her clothes, a long multicoloured coat, some dresses, her wedding dress and a jacket, but only because I imagined there might come a time when Jane would want to have them as mementoes of her mother.

'I don't,' I said. 'No, I don't.'

'Her hair is different, colour-wise I mean, and her eyes. But there's something about her, something in the way she smiles.'

'That's because you know who she is,' I said. 'I honestly don't see Beth there. If you look at pictures of Beth as a child, there's very little resemblance.'

He nodded.

'Does Jane ever ask about her? Talk about her?'

'Sometimes. She looks at her picture every night before she goes to sleep and kisses it. She prays for her. Says goodnight to her. For a time, during the summer, she thought one of the garden robins was Beth come back to see her. She asks if Beth is happy and I tell her she is and then she rings Beth's mother and tells her not to worry that Beth is happy in heaven. But most of the time she doesn't talk about her. It's almost half her life ago.'

'That's good, though,' Robert said. 'That she talks about her, sometimes, that she's still a certain part of her life.'

'Oh sure. I'm not certain how she'd feel about another woman stepping onto her turf: I think she might have the wit to resurrect Beth at that stage, as an important part of her life, as a tool in the war for her house, her space, her daddy. She can be quite protective of all that. Like, when Mam comes to visit, Jane is always welcoming but she's always glad to see her go, too. Same with Kate, though I think she sees her more as a sister-cum-friend.'

'Kate's a good woman.'

'Yes she is. She's been a great help. In lots of ways.'

'Is she happy?'

'Why do you ask?'

'Don't know, just … you know.'

I shrugged.

'I'm sure if she's not, she'll take up your offer of a room in Flagstaff.'

'I doubt that. I think she might like to be closer to home.'

'Meaning?'

'Meaning, I think she likes you, a lot.'

I laughed.

'And is there someone else in your life?' Robert asked.

'What's this "else" about?' I said. 'That's making an assumption that Kate is somehow a part of my life, which she isn't. At least not in the way you seem to be suggesting. Where the hell did you get that idea? Are you becoming a pop-psychologist in your spare time?'

Jane turned on the couch, pulling the rug closer about her.

'I'll bring her up to her room,' I said. 'You make some coffee.'

Carrying Jane up the darkened stairs, I laid her in her bed, keeping the warm blanket wrapped about her. She turned when I pulled her duvet over her and half-opened one eye, smiled and fell fast asleep again. Then I turned on her bedside light and the landing light and went back downstairs.

Robert had thrown some logs on the fire and was spooning coffee into the percolator.

'So,' I said jovially. 'What is this theory you have about Kate and me?'

'Are you going out with anyone?' he asked

'No,' I said. 'I'm not.'

'Have you seen how she looks at you?'

I frowned and shook my head. I thought he was talking nonsense and I told him so.

'Maybe I am, but the last few times I've been here, I've noticed that wherever you go, her eyes follow. You can tell, brother. There's something in the way people look at each other.'

'Well,' I laughed. 'If you've noticed I'm sure Brian has noticed so I'm up the creek!'

'I don't think Brian notices much. Brian's world is mainly other things, work maybe, stuff.'

'Jesus, you have us all analysed and you've been here, what, three times in the last twelve months.'

'The outside eye,' he laughed.

We pulled the couch closer to the stove and sat there, mulling over our coffee. The last of the candles flickered and seemed to die and then flickered again before, finally, going out. The light from the burning timber lit the room in streamers that fluttered and fell and rose and hovered and dodged and fell again.

'This is good,' I said.

Robert nodded and sipped his coffee.

'It is.'

'You don't have that Cohen album?' he asked.

I shook my head.

'I'll send you a copy from the States. And I'll send one for Kate.'

I turned and saw that he was grinning.

'Muckraker,' I laughed.

He shrugged in a melodramatic gesture of shock and surprise. 'Well, I'm just telling you what I see. Or what I think I see.'

'All right,' I said, and I recounted the conversation Kate and I had on the summer morning in the garden. 'But she hasn't mentioned it since and nor have I. I think it was one of those moments, like when someone has a skinful and then regrets it the next day.'

'But she hadn't had a skinful!'

'No, but neither has she mentioned it again. So fifteen-all.'

'Well, all I'll say, and I'm not being flippant,' Robert said quietly, his face serious in the full firelight, 'is that I don't believe it has gone away, maybe for you, if there was anything there in your head. Not for her. It's still in her heart.'

'Well,' I said. 'I promised not to raise it and I won't.'

'We obviously inherited that trait from the old man,' Robert smiled. 'Certainly not from the old lady, ever!'

·

Again we sat in silence. The night outside was calm and quiet, no wind knocking against the back door to creak the loose lock, no sound of sighing leaves as they fell from the chestnuts, nothing to dent the tranquillity of two brothers sitting together as they seldom did, two men who separately and reciprocally valued these minutes and hours of shared conversation and shared silence. Two men who had learned enough from life to know the value of such times and their fragility. I think it may have crossed both our minds then that, when the morning came and Robert left to see our mother, nothing could or would ever be the same again. Our lives would change, gradually but inevitably, as lives always do. And so we valued this time of not being the people we would become but, rather, savouring who we were at that moment.

A lifetime of growing together as young boys, a period of change – first for Robert and then for me – as we matured into young adulthood and, finally, the mutual sorrows that seemed to me to have given us a glimpse of the fact that we might only ever have each other to share the feelings we could never divulge to any other breathing person.

'I like my life,' I said quietly. 'We get along, Jane and me, things are good for us. Maybe there are experiences that are passing me by, excitements as well as disappointments, but, for now, I don't feel those are the things that are paramount. What I need at the moment is a steadiness. I need to know where and what and who and how I am. Call it routine if you like, but I'm happy with it. I do like my life.'

'That's good,' Robert said.

'And if Kate came back here tomorrow and said she wanted to do something about us, something open or something surreptitious, part of me would be flattered and excited and part of me would be thinking this is not the time.

It's not a moral quandary, it's a comfort thing. And, yes, I know, some psychologist would tell me that's a sign of depression. But I'm not depressed, Robert. I am actually happy and I enjoy my life and I'm waking up in the morning full of energy for Jane and enthusiasm for my work.'

'That's good,' he said again.

'And you?'

'I'm running. Still running.'

'Away from what?'

'Not away – after. I'm still running after Amy. Or something that makes me accept that she's gone. Not a replacement. I just want to see if there's something or some place or someone that can persuade me that I can and should get on with my life. That our life, as in Amy and me, isn't going to go on just because I want it to. I actually need to go somewhere that isn't a place we lived or visited or stayed in or even passed through. I still find myself doing that, I drive through some village we visited when Amy was alive and I remember – or imagine I remember – what she said or where we had a coffee. It's crazy. We were married for two years, I only knew her for four years and she's been dead six. The balance is completely wrong. She's everywhere and I know that's not good.'

'"You're everywhere and nowhere, baby,"' I said.

Robert nodded but I was sure he wasn't really listening.

A month after Robert had left for America, a package arrived from him. Inside were two copies of Leonard Cohen's CD *Various Positions* and a brief note.

> As promised. One for you, one for Kate. All great
> here. Hope things are going well with the work.
> Love to Kate. R.

He had already phoned me three or four times to tell me that he was thoroughly enjoying his new life. That the job was really interesting, the people he was working with were welcoming, that he was looking at houses, that the scenery around the city was spectacular, that the place itself was my kind of place, arty but not pretentious, that he'd found a vegetarian restaurant, that he thought he was really going to like living there.

On my way to collect Jane from school, I called to Kate's house with the CD.

'God, isn't he great,' she said. 'He must have had enough on his plate over there without searching this out. I'll drop him a line and say thanks. Will you ring me with his address?'

'Sure.'

'Have you time for a coffee?'

'Of course.'

She filled the kettle and plugged it in.

'Have you listened to the songs yet?'

I shook my head.

'Right.'

'The parcel just arrived this morning. I will. Later. When I'm working.'

'How is the job going?'

'Ok, just ok at the minute. Just a bit stuck on something. Maybe the answer is in the CD!'

'How do you mean?'

'Well, it's a bit like overhearing a conversation. Something clicks and it gets me thinking and I find something in my head that I can use. It can be anything, even a song. You hear something and that reminds you of something else and you get an idea, and sometimes it gets you out of a sticky spot.'

'So that's how you do it.'

'Not always, not that often. It's like a conversation, you know. The way we pick up phrases, ideas.'

We sat at the kitchen table. Outside, the day was cold and still. All the colour had gone from Kate's garden. The bark of the silver birches was a smoky grey, frozen in the dusky afternoon. The hawthorns were spiked against the sky in a crown of winter thorns.

'How's Brian? It must be three weeks since I saw him.'

'He's fine. Working hard, but he's fine.'

'And you?'

Kate shrugged and then her shoulders sagged and I saw her eyes fill with tears.

'I'm fine. Don't mind this, time of the month, you know yourself.'

She laughed and snot bubbled from her nose. She wiped it quickly on the back of her hand.

'Fuck,' she said. 'What a lovely sight. Fuck. Sorry. And, of course, you don't know what it's like but you know what I mean. But I'm fine. I have two lovely children, a hardworking husband, a nice house, good friends who send me CDs from America and a guy who lives a couple of fields away that I'm in love with. Who could ask for more?'

'Which fields?' I smiled.

'You wish it was the other direction, don't you?'

'No, I don't.'

'But ...'

'But I don't want to be a disappointment in your life.'

'How could you be?'

'I was a huge disappointment to Beth.'

'I'm not Beth.'

'I know that. But, if, and I'm not even sure he is, but if Brian is a disappointment to you, there's no guarantee that I won't be, too. If we sleep together, what then, how long does that go on for before one of us wants more? What happens if one of us decides that it's time to live together? Do you move into my house? Do the kids move with you? Where does Brian come into the equation?'

'There are a lot of maybes and ifs in there,' Kate said.

'I'm just playing devil's advocate.'

'I'd settle for holding you,' she said quietly.

'But would you?'

'At the moment, I would, yes.'

I stood up and walked around the table, to where Kate was sitting, and put my arms around her, hugging her to me.

'I seem to be fecking crying every time you hug me,' she said, her voice muffled against my jacket.

'That's all right,' I said. 'Any excuse.'

'Anyway, it's not a good time for me to be talking about this, all these hormones racing around the place. I need to have my head together for these kinds of conversations.'

She pulled away from me.

'Sit down,' she said, brushing the tears from her face. 'Have your coffee.'

I did as I was told.

'What was it I said that day on the lawn at your house? That nothing was going to happen. So much for good intentions.'

'Nothing has happened.'

'True. But I was sure of myself that day, sure I wouldn't let it happen. Now I'm not so certain.'

'Well, thanks for warning me,' I laughed.

'Can I ask you something?'

'Sure.'

'When you finish your design, when will that be?'

'It has to be in by Christmas.'

'Ok. January. Can you and me sit down in January and talk about all this. That gives us eight, nine weeks. I know it sounds nuts, to be talking about something that's just a figment of my hormonal imagination, but I really would appreciate it if you gave this some thought. I know I'm not even clear from day to day about what I feel. Well I am clear but I may not be clear to you. So, if you could promise me that you'll think about things – us, you and me – and put your cards on the table, honestly tell me what you think after Christmas. Even if that means you saying, "Kate, I think you have great tits but I'm not in love with you."'

I laughed out loud.

'I never said you had great tits.'

'No but you think it.'

'True.'

'So, is that ok with you?'

'Yes.'

'And no bullshit, no pretending, no trying to be nice, just the truth?'

'Yes. That goes for you, too.'

'Absolutely. Now, I'd better go and wash my face. I can't appear at the school gates like this.'

'I can pick the girls up,' I said.

'Thanks but they like me to be there.'

'Well we can travel together then. You get cleaned up, I'll wash the mugs and away we go.'

'It might get tongues wagging, if we arrive together.'

'God, I hope so,' I said. 'It's time they had something new to gab about.'

The following morning, I had just got back from dropping Jane to school when the phone rang. It was Kate.

'Three things,' she said. 'First, I knew you wouldn't be working yet so I'm not disturbing you.'

'True.'

'Second, do you have Robert's address? I wrote to him last night and I want to post it today.'

'Just hold on,' I said. 'It's here.'

I opened my address book and read it to her.

'Thanks. Third thing. Have you listened to the CD Robert sent?'

'Not yet,' I said. 'Jane and myself got into a discussion on the meaning of life last night, well, actually, it was about why snow is white and why rabbits' tails are short and why flowers are different colours and why different animals make different sounds, and, by the time that was over, I didn't have the energy to do anything other than fall asleep.'

'Well listen to it. It's brilliant. That guy is a genius. I've fallen in love with him, instantly. The voice and the way he writes about love and people and heartbreak.'

'He's a better writer than I am an architect?'

'Yes. And better looking. And that voice.'

'So am I yesterday's man?'

'Shut up and go and do some work. And listen to the CD, ok?'

'I will.'

'Don't just say it, do it.'

'I will, boss.'

My mother came to stay for Christmas. I would have preferred for Jane and I to have the house to ourselves, as we'd had for the previous two Christmases, but, with Robert in America, the other options were for her to spend it alone or with friends, and that wasn't something I could inflict on anyone. I had warned Jane that we both needed to be on our best behaviour, that Nana would be here for a few days.

'I like it when Nana is here.'

'I know you do, but sometimes you get fed up with her being here. So do I, but she'd be alone for Christmas if she didn't come here. You wouldn't like that, would you?'

She shook her head, very gravely.

'I feel sorry for Santa,' she said.

'Why?'

'He goes all over around the world with presents and then he has to go home and he's all on his own on Christmas Day.'

'He has Mrs Claus.'

Jane shook her head.

'No?'

'No, she's dead. Like Beth.'

'Is she? How do you know that?'

'He told me.'

'Who told you?'

'Santa's robin.'

'Did he? When?'

'One time.'

'Right. Well, then, I suppose he spends it with the elves, the same way Nana is spending it with us.'

'But we're not elves.'

'No, not yet.'

My mother arrived in the early afternoon of 23 December. We had dinner at six, the three of us, in the light of the Christmas tree.

'It's a little difficult to see what I'm eating in this gloom,' my mother said.

I got up and turned on the overhead light.

'I thought Robert might get home for a few days.'

'I don't think Christmas is quite the same there as here,' I said. 'It tends just to be a day off.'

She was determinedly unimpressed.

'It's a Christian feast.'

'True, but not all Americans are Christian.'

'Yes but Robert is, surely they need to respect all cultures.'

'I'm sure they do, but businesses over there have a different attitude, a different ethos, I suppose.'

'Well, I had hoped he'd be here.'

I nodded and went on eating.

'Have you heard from Beth's parents?'

'Yes, they rang on Tuesday. We'll ring them on Christmas morning. Jane rings them every Saturday.'

'I do,' Jane nodded. 'At lunch-time. They always have their lunch at one o'clock and I always ring them at ten to one.'

'That's nice for them,' my mother said starchily.

'We ring you at different times,' I said. 'We don't want to tie you down. Beth's parents are creatures of habit.'

'Mmm,' she said, unimpressed.

We ate in silence and then Jane put her knife and fork down carefully and turned to my mother.

'Nana, you know Santa's elves?'

'Yes,' my mother said, smiling.

'They help Santa with his presents.'

'Yes, dear.'

'Do you think they're little mad little fuckers?'

My mother choked and reached for a napkin. I spluttered and reached for a glass of water.

'Mike Weaver said it in school, he said all elves are little mad little fuckers. He said it at story-time.'

I managed to find my voice without laughing.

'Did he? And what did Mrs Ferry say?'

'She said it was bold, but I think she was trying not to laugh. Her mouth was all crooked, like yours is now. It was bold, wasn't it?'

'Very bold,' I said, nodding.

'I sincerely hope Mike Weaver is not a child that Jane spends any more time with than is necessary.'

'No, he's in her class.'

'I was at his birthday,' Jane added helpfully.

'Yes, well, you know, children say these things.'

'You never did. Robert never did. I'm sure Beth, God rest her, wouldn't have been amused.'

'No,' I sighed. 'I'm sure she wouldn't.'

'Did you ever see an elf, Nana?' Jane asked.

My mother shook her head.

'Were there elves when you were a little girl? Was there a Santa Claus? Was he alive then?'

'Of course he was, Jane. I'm not that old.'

'What old?'

'How old,' my mother corrected.

'How old what?' Jane frowned.

My mother had talked about going home on the twenty-seventh and then it had been the thirtieth and then she decided she didn't want to be alone on New Year's Eve. Finally, on New Year's Day, I told her I had to get back to work, that I had a deadline to meet and I was already well behind schedule.

'I'm going to visit Robert in February,' she told me as I was helping her with her bags.

'Good. Does he know?'

'Not yet. I thought I'd surprise him. I booked my flights in Christmas week. I'm flying out on the thirtieth of January. And back on the twentieth of February.'

'Three weeks?'

'Yes.'

'He'll be working.'

'I'm sure he can get time off.'

'He's only been in the job for four months.'

'He's well up the ladder, they need him. I'm sure they'd want him to have the time off.'

'And when are you going to tell him?'

'Next week. I'll ring him. It'll be a lovely surprise for him.'

I rang Robert that evening and warned him.

'Three weeks?' he asked. And then he repeated the question. 'Three weeks?'

'Afraid so.'

'Jesus Christ, what am I going to do with her?'

'Pack her a good lunch, a bottle of water and a map and drop her in the desert. That should take care of one week.'

'I won't be able to get more than four or five days off work.'

'I think she's hoping you'll fly with her to New York and San Francisco and Chicago, you know, show her the sights. Oh and Washington of course – DC and state!'

'Piss off,' he laughed.

'Well you had a peaceful Christmas.'

I told him about Jane and the elves.

'There's a woman who works with me, she has two kids. I might just rent them for the three weeks.'

'So how are things on that front?'

Robert was silent.

'A-ha,' I said.

'I didn't say anything.'

'The eloquence of silence. Who is she?'

'No one in particular.'

'Liar.'

'Well there is this woman. We've been to dinner a few times – but she has kids.'

'Ah, I'll bet she has two kids and they may be available to rent when the old lady is over.'

'She might have.'

'And her name?'

'Jennifer. Jenny.'

'So the change of air is working?'

'It's early days,' Robert said. 'Early days. I'm taking it one dinner date at a time.'

'Is there a husband?'

'Yes. Divorced.'

'What age is she? What's she look like? What does she do? Where does she live? Come on, Robert, I need all this information. It's not like it's not my business.'

He sighed.

'This call is costing you a fortune.'

'I got a huge tax-rebate cheque before Christmas.'

'Did you?'

'Yes. Sixty-four quid even.'

'Wow, you should retire while you're ahead,' he laughed

'Anyway, you're changing the subject. Tell me about Jenny.'

'She works with me, well in accounts in the facility. She's thirty. Two kids, boy and girl, six and five. Three years divorced. Husband lives in LA. She's very nice – and not pushy. I like her.'

'How much?'

'It's early days.'

'How much?'

'A lot.'

'Good. Well don't let the old lady feck it up for you.'

'I won't.'

'Good.'

The following afternoon I took Jane and Kate's two girls, Elizabeth, who was seven, and Susan, who was Jane's age, to the pictures. On the way to the cinema, all the talk was about the film. Afterwards, we went for something to eat.

Driving home in the warm car, Jane and Susan fell asleep.

'So did you have a nice Christmas?' I asked Elizabeth.

'It was a bit sad.'

'Oh? Why was it sad?'

'I think my mammy and daddy are sad.'

'Really? Why do you think that?'

'My mammy was crying a lot. I heard her. I saw her.'

'People often cry,' I said.

'And they were fighting on Christmas Day. My daddy said my mammy is never happy. He said he tries to be happy, but she'll never be happy. Are you happy?'

'Not always,' I said.

'I'd be happy if my mammy and daddy were happy.'

'Sometimes big people argue. It doesn't mean that much. Do you remember Jane's mum? Beth?'

'Yes.'

'She and I argued a lot.'

'Does that mean my mammy'll be killed in a car?'

'No,' I said. 'That's not what I meant. I meant that when big people argue, it often sounds worse to children.'

'Did Beth cry all the time?'

'Sometimes she cried. Sometimes I cry.'

'My mammy cries an awful lot.'

Kate came to the house the following Monday morning, after we'd dropped the children to school. We'd seen each other over Christmas but always when other people were about. This was the first chance we'd had to talk.

'So,' she said when we sat at the kitchen table. 'Are you going to fuck my brains out?'

I smiled.

'It's a serious question,' she said quickly. 'I've thought about it a lot over the holiday and it's what I want. I've thought about all the ways I might say it, all the fancy ways of dressing it up but that's just a cop out.'

'It won't solve things.'

'I'm not looking for solutions. I'm looking for sex. Do you know how hard it is to say that? Do you know how difficult it is to sit here, across the table from you, to sit looking at someone I love and to have to tell him that I'll settle for something a lot less than love, even though I know he doesn't love me back?'

'I do love you –'

'– in a brotherly way,' she interrupted. 'You're my friend, you're kind and calm and caring and concerned and you're there when I need a shoulder to cry on and I appreciate that, but I'm not looking for a shoulder. I'm married to a shoulder that I can cry on. And I'm there when you need someone. And so is Brian. So it could be one of us or the other.'

'That's hardly true,' I laughed.

'Don't interrupt me,' Kate said quickly. 'If you do, I'll lose my courage and I'll never say what I need to say. Just being your friend, someone you can call on when you need Jane collected from school, isn't enough for me. And I'm not content with knowing you'll collect my kids or bring them to the pictures or mind them when I have a doctor's appointment. That's what being a neighbour is about. That's not what loving someone is about. And I love you and whether you love me or not isn't the issue. I want you to sleep with me. I want to be fucked, I want to forget all the things that aren't working in my life and have one thing that is. I'm not asking you to live with me or run away with me or commit yourself to me. I'm prepared to settle for fucking you when you feel like it. I'm prepared to let you be the one to decide the where and when and how often. I'm prepared to grovel.'

There was a steel in her eyes, no tears, no uncertainty, no sense of humiliation, just a determination to be whoever she had to be in order to get what she needed. I admired her for that.

'So?' Kate asked and her tone was matter of fact.

I spread my hands on the table.

'Don't go silent on me,' she said quietly. 'Please.'

'I won't,' I said, and then I was silent.

Kate smiled a half-smile, her mouth crooked, her lips pursed. Suddenly, the certainty was gone from her eyes and she was simply a hesitant person again, waiting for news, waiting for the best she could hope for or the worst she should dread, waiting for me to be the bearer of a gift or a slight.

I told her about the conversation I'd had with Elizabeth after the film.

'And do you believe whatever you say will stop me from crying or make me cry even more?

'No,' I said. 'But I don't want your sadness to go on. I know the power of sadness. I know the way it can decompose from unhappiness to grief.'

'Do you, though? Do you really, truly?'

It wasn't a flippant query, it wasn't an attempt to puzzle me. It was a deeply serious question.

'Maybe not, but I have some inkling.'

She smiled again.

'That's like saying a cut on your finger gives you some inkling of what it's like to lose an arm.'

I nodded. She was right. I had no real idea what she was feeling. I could throw out an image or be an onlooker to her anguish, but I had never experienced what she was living through.

'If I sleep with you,' I said, 'I'll feel guilty. Not for myself and not for Brian but I'll feel guilty for you, about what I'm doing to you. Not the sex but the deceit.'

'And if I want to be deceived? If I settle for deception?'

'How long can anyone do that?'

'This is one way of finding out.'

'Kate, I want to tell you three things. I love you more than I have ever loved any woman in my life and I don't mean as a friend. I love you. And I fancy you. I would love to have sex with you, often ...'

'But ...'

'... but that would eventually lead to us going our separate ways because one or other of us would become jealous. You of my freedom or me of your husband and that would be the end of everything. And I know by saying what I'm saying I may already be condemning this friendship to death.'

She shook her head.

'But I'd rather we walked away from here with things damaged than that we took our chances, knowing that we'd be left with nothing in a year or eighteen months.'

'You're a very moral man.'

'No, I'm not,' I said. 'If I were moral I'd have better reasons for not fucking you. I'm a coward. I can't imagine my life without you. This is self-preservation.'

'But you'll have sex with me today, so we both know what we're missing?'

'Yes.'

'Now?'

'Yes.'

'And afterwards there won't be any guilt or recriminations. This ride won't be the epitaph for our friendship?'

'No.'

'You know you're contradicting everything you've just said?'

'Yes.'

She shrugged and smiled.

'You're a very strange man.'

'I know. And you're a very beautiful woman.'

She sighed and shrugged her shoulders again. We sat in silence, the kitchen table with its coffee rings between us. The winter sun lying like snow in one corner of the garden, the kitchen clock ticking towards ten in the morning.

'And I won't be back here next week saying, "If you could do it once you can do it twice." It won't be like that.'

'It may be very disappointing, of course. You may not want to come back, ever.'

She laughed, a short nervous laugh, and we fell back into silence. I heard the letter box clatter and the flap of envelopes on the hall floor.

'More bills,' I said.

She nodded, stood up, took my hand and led me upstairs. On the landing, she paused and waited for me to lead the way. I took her into my bedroom and we sat on the bed, then Kate turned and touched my face and we kissed, awkwardly. And then she stood up and undressed quickly, her jumper and blouse falling like leaves about her feet, heeling off her runners, wriggling out of her jeans and pants, standing naked before me.

'Not too late to change your mind,' she said, and the seriousness in her voice was frightening.

I kissed her breast, tasting her perfume and then her skin.

'Let's get into bed,' I said.

I turned back the duvet and she nestled into its coldness while I struggled out of my clothes and slid in beside her, the starch of the sheet against our goose-bumped skin.

I tried to think of something erotic to say but, before I could, Kate's mouth covered mine and her tongue slipped between my lips and her legs twined around me and there was nothing to say. The wetness of her cunt and the hunger of her mouth were more eloquent than any words could ever be, her body moulding itself about my own, her hands lifting my thighs so that she could take me into her, moving gently back and forth, rising and falling with me, pushing against the thrust of my cock. And her skin was flushed, beads of sweat on the back of her neck as I brushed her hair to one side, her eyes open but unseeing, her legs contracting about me, forcing me back against the bed, fucking me slowly. And then I felt her body tighten about me, really tighten, and her breathing was short and sharp, her body hard against mine, no longer moulded into me but working against me. She was gone from me, driven by her own desire to come, compelled by this need, her breath coming in gasps that were words, then sounds, then words again.

And then she was coming, her mouth in my ear, telling me that it was all right.

'Fuck me,' she said. 'Fuck me. I want to feel you fucking inside me. I want to feel your come in my cunt. Don't fucking stop, don't, not now.'

Her body tensed around me and I lay still while she rode me with all the desperation of someone who fears for her life, biting the side of my arm, her body a corkscrew, tightening and turning until it could tighten no more and she came again and then again.

'Now,' she said. 'Now.'

And I came inside her, every drop of energy flooding out of me, everything dissolving in that instant – lust, desire, concern, doubt – our bodies caving into each other, finding a sudden, unexpected comfort, reconciled to the sleepy ease of this impulsive familiarity.

part

•

two

IT RAINED THAT MORNING. Just as I was turning for home, the showers came sweeping across the woods, sheets of mist closing in from two sides so that, by the time I'd reached the small stone bridge that crosses the stream, the rain was thick enough to run everything into a blot and lose sight of my car in a haze at the other end of the road.

I sheltered beneath an elder, the dog at my feet, picking at the black fruit which hung even lower in the drizzling air, the branches pulled down by the weight of the sudden rain. In front of me, the lane was pocking as the raindrops rebounded off the hardened clay. And then the pockmarks began to multiply, the dry dust becoming a light sheen of mud, the surface of the laneway changing colour and texture before my eyes. In the shelter of the overhanging tree, about my feet, the ground remained dry, the branches protecting me from the falling rain.

Six feet from where I was huddled, a red squirrel and then another scampered across the open roadway and disappeared into the evergreens. Not grey squirrels, not wild mink but red squirrels. The first pair I'd seen on this laneway in over a year. The dog had missed them. And then, as though taking its cue from the squirrels, the sun broke weakly through and the rain began to lighten, rays of brightness brushing it aside, drying the ground almost as they fell.

It was a Tuesday morning, the last Tuesday in September, an ordinary day in a week that promised nothing of any greater significance than the appearance of this pair of wild animals.

Waiting for the bow of rain to clear my shelter, I watched the crows rising out of a stand of trees, turning against the clearing blueness of the sky. Ten minutes would get me to the car and another five would get me home to coffee and work.

Stepping back onto the laneway, my attention was caught by the smell from the small stream running under the low bridge. Afterwards, I would try to recapture it exactly, that smell you get on a particular day in spring and again in autumn, the scent that leaves you uncertain about whether it augurs a growth or a decomposition. It's as if the river and everything that feeds into it reaches a point, some time in March and again in September, where there's a perfect balance between progress and decay. It's not something that lasts but, if you catch it, you can gauge the turning of the year and the change of season by this particular smell. It may be there for a day or it may last as little as an hour. And then it's gone and the year has suddenly shifted from one phase into another.

I was aware of the smell that morning, the sudden dampening of the countryside after three weeks without rain, a freshness that tantalised the senses, suggesting that spring might be about to burst on the world again, though, of course, it wasn't. The nights were drawing in and, each day, dawn was becoming more and more hesitant. The swallows had already gathered and dithered and then taken off in a surge of wings and longing. The roads were a slow procession of hay lorries, drawing bales from the fields. Haws were lighting up and sloes were darkening in the ditches. This was definitely September.

I stood a while, leaning over the balustrade of the stone bridge, gazing down into the stream as though I expected a face to peer back at me from the cloudy bog water, as though the face of autumn might reveal itself to me. And then the wind lifted, and the rain was gone from the air and the sun was emptying itself out across the stubbled fields, running like a train along the tracks of headland.

From a crevice at the foot of the bridge, a blackberry branch straggled above the brown water. Whether it was the shelter of the bridge or some freak of nature, the leaves on this branch were a soft, almost lime green. They stood out against the darker foliage around them, as if the summer had poured everything it owned into them, every last drop of vibrant colour, every promise it had ever made. Their paleness was an olive butterfly poised above the dark water, uncertain in that moment about whether to stay or go.

And when I looked up from the water, the fallen mist was melting in the early sunshine and the road was reappearing, rolling out before me to the gateway where I had parked the car an hour earlier. And I knew this would be a good day, that the sun would continue shining and the montbretia in the ditches would be as dazzlingly orange as they had been for the past few weeks, flaming up against the passing of one season and the arrival of another.

A tractor lumbered between the pillars of a farm avenue, a trailer rattling behind it. The driver waved and I beckoned him ahead.

He gave me the thumbs-up, pointing to the sky.

Smiling, I saluted.

The tractor swung right, through an open gateway, climbing steadily up the hill and coming to a stop beside the only rick of hay bales remaining in the field. I watched the driver climb down from his cab and uncouple the trailer before starting to load the bales.

I walked on, whistling, reminding myself to tell Jane about the squirrels and the blackberry leaves and the racing sunlight.

The house was quiet apart from the sound of the dog's paws on the wooden floor. Jane was still sleeping, her last week at home before going back to college. Late nights and late mornings, sometimes early afternoons, before she surfaced, hair falling wildly about her face, smiling, calling Rostropovich to her, rubbing his ears, getting him to roll on his back so she could rub his belly.

The name had been her idea. She'd been doing something on Rostropovich in school when I'd brought him home for her fourteenth birthday, a black-and-white bundle of something akin to collie but not quite.

'Do you expect me to call him Rostropovich in public?' I asked when she suggested the name.

She laughed.

'Hardly. You can call him Ros for short, but Rostropovich is his name.'

And so it was decided.

And now he was five and the house was his.

Standing in the kitchen, I made coffee and caught the news headlines on the radio. Politicians disagreeing. Monks marching in Burma. Road accidents. Settled weather ahead, calm and sunny.

'Right,' I said to the dog. 'Time for work.'

He watched me walk into my study and I knew, once the door was closed, that he'd go and lie outside Jane's bedroom door and, when finally she appeared, he'd greet her like a long lost friend, jumping and barking and chasing his tail to impress her, delighted that she was there to talk to him, to rub his ears and tell him how beautiful he was. And he'd sit at her feet, under the kitchen table, and wait for chunks of buttered toast to fall his way. That was this dog's life while Jane was home.

When she was in college, he settled for a rug beside my desk and buttered brown bread and my conversation but there was never any doubt about whose company he preferred. I might walk him twice a day but I accepted myself for what I was, a poor second choice.

At the desk, I looked back over some sketches I had made that morning, before taking Ros for his walk. They were no better than they had been two hours earlier. I stared at them, walked around the desk, viewed them from the sides, mentally tinkering here, altering there, but they were still missing the structure I was trying to design. These were the days I dreaded. The times when walking away I hoped that either I'd come back to something that looked better than it had done when I left or that I'd bring something back with me that would unlock the angles and aspects to set the whole thing moving again.

Then I was rustling back through my sketchpad, back to what I'd drawn the night before, searching for something there, a place from which to start again. Turning on the computer, I looked over what I had there and pressed delete. No point in playing with something that was dead and gone. Let it go. Start again. Put the lot out of my head and go somewhere else, back to the photographs I'd taken of the site, hoping the empty space would lead me somewhere else. Perhaps up another blind alley but perhaps not.

I drew a line, another, an angle, a possibility. I didn't look back, I just kept drawing, sketching whatever the photographs suggested and the pages began to fill, forms starting out in one place and scratching across until they reached another. A potential beginning to unfold, an imagined angle, a window looking in, another looking out. I was like a guitarist picking out a tune. It all seemed so important then, to get the lines together, to finish the sweep on an arc, to breathe in and out the breaths of this building whose life was confined, for now, to what I thought and drew on these sheets of paper. These walls which would eventually include and exclude experiences unlike my own.

To design is to live vicariously, to fool yourself into believing that you are God and can create another person's life, inhabit their mind and body, instruct or allow them to see or not to see the things you permit or don't permit. And I was lost in that process for an hour, then two, then three so that lunch-time came and went and I heard Jane and Ros in the kitchen, heard the sound of cutlery being set and dishes and cups being laid on the table, and still I went on, drawing madly for fear that I would lose what I had found. Believing what I was doing was of value and might somehow change my life or someone else's because, for those hours, in that room, I had faith in what I was doing, had faith in the power of the eye and the brain, succumbed to the ego of the designer who thinks that what he envisages is important. The architect who knows that without that arrogance, he would never draw another column or imagine another view or describe another building from his assortment of outlines and figures and shapes. Without that arrogance, I told myself, the dancer would forget her steps, the sculptor would lose all sense of proportion, the poet would be redundant.

And so I went on working, delaying the knock on the door, postponing the moment when my daughter would come smiling into the room, a steaming cup of coffee in her hand, telling me lunch was ready, telling me it was time to put this work away, sentencing me to the return, which is never as filled with promise as the moment that is now. And the arcs bridged the screen, pushing my vision closer to the edge of something I would either forget or come to terms with, an outline that would blight this day of my life or give me the pleasure of creating something whose fragility and strength would stay with the people of this town long after they had forgotten my name or anything about me. And I smiled as I worked because I believed in what I was doing, for those hours I believed in the power of the idea and the possibility of rising to the challenge.

And then I heard the footsteps in the hall and Ros was snorting and Jane was tapping gently on my door, a knock that never waited for an answer and I pressed Save and turned to see her smiling at me.

'How's it going?'

'Well,' I said. 'Slow start, but it's beginning to get somewhere now.'

'Lunch is ready when you are.'

'Fifteen minutes,' I said. 'Give me fifteen minutes and I'll be there.'

'Fine.'

'Sleep ok?'

'Seems like,' Jane laughed and then she was gone and I could hear Ros *put, put, putting* behind her, across the hall and into the kitchen, and the ideas were central again, racing each other to find their place in my scheme.

Over lunch, I told Jane about the red squirrels.

'And you're sure they weren't mink? You know your eyes!'

I assured her that they were squirrels.

'I'll take Ros down the lane after lunch. I'd love to see them.'

'Well don't expect him to spot them for you. He didn't seem to notice them this morning and, if he did, they might as well have been leaves blowing across the road.'

'Ros is a pacifist.'

I laughed.

'We should talk about things, before you go back to college,' I said.

'Like?'

'All sorts of things. Money, what you'll need. Getting the new violin. Christmas. Us.'

'You love talking about things, don't you?' Jane smiled. 'You love analysing things, looking at all the permutations and combinations and possibilities. You should have been a writer or something.'

'I don't think so. But today is Tuesday and you go back on Friday. It doesn't leave an awful lot of time.'

'Well the money situation is fine till at least Christmas – I told you I'd save my summer wages and I did so there's money in the bank, more than enough to get me through this term. And I rang the music shop this morning, while you were creating art, and he said they wouldn't have the fiddle before Hallowe'en, so there's no immediate rush on that. Anyway, the other one is fine till then.'

'You're sure?'

'Yes, positive. And Christmas is fine. I'm dying to see Robert and Jenny again. So everything is hunky dory. You worry too much. It's bad for you.'

'And then there's us,' I said.

'Us is fine,' Jane laughed.

'Is it?'

'Absolutely. Are you happy?'

'Yes, I'm happy.'

'And so am I. Very. So let's stop looking for things that might come between us. Be happy, there's enough of the other stuff out there. If I allowed it, you'd analyse things out of existence.'

She swallowed a last mouthful of tea, jumped up from the table, kissed me and whistled at the dog, all in one easy, sweeping movement.

'Your turn to wash up, it'll get your mind off things. Physical labour is good for the soul.'

And then she was gone, running out the door, pulling on a jacket, racing Ros down the avenue, her hair blowing as she ran, her slim figure disappearing and reappearing between the trees.

I sat watching them through the window until they vanished onto the road and then I leafed through the newspaper. More politics, so little good news, house prices falling, negative equity, a man lying dead on a street in Rangoon, a body found in a house in Dublin, a murder trial. Maybe Jane was right, maybe there was more than enough of the other stuff out there. Or was I closing my mind to things, accepting her word on things because it suited me?

I told myself I'd think about it later, I'd bring it up again over dinner. In the meantime, there was work to be done, washing-up to be finished, a walk around the garden, windfalls to be picked, a computer screen still waiting for my attention.

It was after four when Jane and Ros got back. I heard his snuffling at the study door and then Jane came in with two mugs of coffee and plonked down in the armchair across from my desk.

'No squirrels,' she said. 'You're sure they weren't mink?'

'Did you see any mink?'

She shook her head.

'So there's no reason to assume they were mink.'

'Apart from the fact that there are always mink down there and we've never seen red squirrels.'

'I saw red squirrels last autumn.'

'Bit like UFOs,' Jane laughed. 'Only ever seen when you're on your own. Curiouser and curiouser.'

'I know what I saw. This is nice coffee.'

'It's real coffee. Properly made, taking time. Not just two spoons of shite in the bottom of a cup.'

'Well that was very thoughtful of you.'

'I know, but then I'm devoted to your happiness, as you well know,' she winked. 'By the way, I'm meeting Elizabeth for a drink tonight. She's heading back to Cork in the morning so I won't see her again till Hallowe'en.'

'Where are you going?'

'The New Place.'

'I'll drop you both in.'

'Ok.'

'Do you want me to collect you?'

She shook her head.

'We'll get a taxi or walk if it's fine.'

'Don't forget your key. And don't lose this one. I think half the country must have keys to this place, if only they knew it.'

'There you go again,' she said, laughing. 'I have lost two keys in, what, five years? Sorry, three keys in five years and one of those was stolen with my purse in college so that hardly counts.'

'Ok. Point taken.'

We drank our coffee and Ros lay under the desk and sighed.

'He's tired,' Jane said. 'Lots of exercise.'

'Good for him, he needs to lose weight.'

'You've lost weight,' she said. 'I can see it in your face.'

'Thank you.'

'But don't lose too much more, it doesn't suit you to be too thin. Makes you look gaunt.'

'Thanks very much.'

'It's true.'

I drank some more coffee, put the mug on my desk and looked at Jane.

'I do need to talk about us,' I said. 'I know you think I shouldn't, but I do. If only for my own peace of mind.'

She laughed, the steam from her coffee shadowing her face, making her look older than her nineteen years.

'This always happens with you at this time of year, it's like you need reassurance before you settle down for the winter,' she said.

'It does not.'

'We sat here in 2005, late October, and we talked for three hours and I told you what I thought and you told me what you thought and we had reached an agreement. And then last year, just before I went back to college we talked again. Honestly, it's like some kind of annual outing for your conscience or something.'

'It's important to me.'

'It's important to me, too, but I don't have anything to add. Nothing has changed in my mind. Have you changed how you feel?'

I shook my head.

'But it still worries you?'

'Sometimes. Not worry. Concern. It unsettles me sometimes.'

'And if I tell you it doesn't concern me? If I say that truthfully, how does that make you feel?'

'Better.'

Jane got up from her chair, put her coffee mug on the desk near mine and knelt on the floor beside me, her elbows resting on my knees. I ran my fingers through her hair and she smiled.

'Have you not had enough unhappiness in your life without looking for more?' she asked.

'Life hasn't been as bad to me as it has to others. It hasn't been bad to us, not when you look at what other people go through.'

'Ok. But you worry about all kinds of things. You cross bridges before you get to them and then you set them on fire when you're halfway across.'

'Your happiness is important to me.'

'I know that,' Jane said quietly. 'I've always known that. But you have to learn to take kindnesses from people, not just to give them. Even Robert has learned that, took him long enough but he's learned it. And you should, too. If I were unhappy, I'd tell you. If I were troubled, I'd tell you. I'm really, really happy, I'm enjoying my life, all of it. I want you to know that. I'm very, very happy.'

'Ok,' I said, and she put her head on my knees and we stayed that way for a long time, sitting in the silence of the late afternoon, the sun sloping in through the study window, the shadows of passing crows fluttering across the wooden floor, the day winding slowly down towards evening, darkness gathering out there somewhere in the fields to the east.

We made dinner together and ate it together and then Elizabeth arrived and she and Jane went upstairs to dress for going out, reappearing an hour later, two stunningly beautiful young women standing in the kitchen, laughing.

'Are you ready to go?' I asked.

'All set. And, by the way, I left a CD in your study. You should listen to it. I think you'd like it.'

'Thank you. I will. Might not be tonight but I will.'

We walked to the car while Ros sat morosely in the hall.

'Poor old Ros,' Elizabeth said, patting his head. 'No walk this time.'

'He's done well today,' Jane said. 'Dad had him out and then I had him out. He's fine.'

I closed the door and we sat into the car.

'So how's Cork?' I asked.

'It's good,' Elizabeth said. 'But I'll be glad to be finished there. I'm thinking of applying to do my Masters in Dublin. If I do ok in my finals.'

'Good for you. How are Kate and Brian? I haven't seen them for the past week.'

'Same old same old,' she laughed. 'Settled into their mutual animosities. I think they'd miss it if anything happened to either of them. Co-dependence.'

'God,' Jane laughed. 'You rattle out this social-work spiel like it's second nature to you.'

'It is.'

'But they're your parents.'

'Which doesn't necessarily make them perfect,' Elizabeth said.

'Bloody hell,' I said. 'Wait till you guys get to be where we are. See how co-dependent you are then. The certainty of youth is a wonderful thing.'

The traffic into the town was light and I stopped around the corner from the pub to let them out.

'Have a good one,' I said. 'And if you want me to collect you, just text me.'

'We'll be fine,' Elizabeth said.

'Good night,' Jane said and she kissed me.

'You have your key?'

She laughed.

'I have my key. Won't be too late.'

'I believe you,' I said. 'Enjoy yourselves.'

And then they were away, crossing the street, stopping to wave, disappearing around the corner.

There are those moments when you catapult from sleep, instants when you're immediately awake but you don't know why. It's not that the dog is barking or the phone is ringing or the doorbell is going, rather it's a response to something unheard, even something that's just about to happen that makes you instantly and totally alert.

It was like that with me, in the early hours of the last Wednesday in September 2007. For no reason that I could explain, I was awake and my bedroom window was filled with the bursting yellow light of the full moon, throwing shadows on the wall, a perfect cross of the window sash, a pattern of leafy branches from the silver birch. And then Ros was barking and there was the sound of tyres turning slowly on the gravel drive and a different light and different shadows moving across my bedroom ceiling.

The engine of a car murmured quietly for a moment and then fell silent. A door opened and closed and then another. Footsteps on the gravel, Ros barking, the doorbell ringing and Ros barking even more loudly.

I stepped out of bed, knowing the story. Jane had taken a taxi home, she'd forgotten her key and she didn't have the taxi fare. I smiled. Not the first and not the last time this would happen.

Pulling my dressing gown from a chair and wrapping it loosely round me, I went down the stairs into the hall that was a pandemonium of wagging tail, barking dog and semi-darkness.

'All right, Ros,' I said. 'It's Jane. It's Jane.'

My words had the desired effect. The tail became a propeller but the barking stopped. I switched on the hall lamp and opened the door. In the puddle of murky light that fell between the leaves of rusted Virginia creeper stood two guards, a man holding his cap in his hand and a very young woman whose eyes were shadowed by the peak of her cap.

The man cleared his throat and smiled but it was a tentative, uncertain smile.

'Sorry to disturb you at this hour,' he said.

I had no idea what time it was and, suddenly, it seemed important to know, as though the hour of the morning would tell me something about the gravity of the reason behind this visit.

'That's all right,' I said. 'Come in. I suppose. No, come in.'

I stood back and the man stepped into the hall, the young woman following, removing her cap as she did, blonde hair pinned up. Ros licked her hand and fussed about her. She rubbed his head and said, 'Good boy.'

Closing the hall door, I ushered them into the sitting room.

'It's warmer in here,' I said, as though I needed to explain something. 'Sit down.'

They sat side by side on the couch and I sat in an armchair near the fireplace. Ros lay at the woman's feet, watching her, occasionally flapping his tail on the wooden floor.

'You have a daughter,' the man said. I noticed that his eyes were a very deep blue and, somehow, I assumed he was therefore going to say something very profound.

'Yes,' I said. 'Jane.'

And as I said her name I realised that, in all probability, she was upstairs, asleep in her room. That she had been dropped at the top of the avenue and had walked down to the house. Ros wouldn't have barked. She'd forgotten to turn off the outside light.

'I think she's asleep in bed.'

'Would you mind checking?' he asked.

'Of course.'

I went upstairs, opened Jane's bedroom door quietly, not wanting to wake her. Her bed was empty and, immediately, my stomach cramped. I didn't want to go back downstairs; I didn't want to tell them what they already knew. But there was no choice.

'She doesn't seem to have come in yet but there's nothing unusual in that,' I said as I sat back down on the armchair.

The young woman glanced at the man with the blue eyes. He seemed to be avoiding my gaze; instead he was looking at a place somewhere around my knees. He coughed, looked at me quickly and then coughed again.

The young woman bent and rubbed Ros, who rolled on his back, tail slapping hard against the floor. The man looked me up and down.

'Would you know what your daughter was wearing when she left here earlier?' he said

I wanted to ask why, to ask what business it was of this man's what my daughter was wearing but I didn't.

'She was wearing a dark jacket, dark blue, maybe black. And blue jeans and a jumper, ah, it was blue, I think.'

'Shoes?' he asked.

'Of course.'

'No, I mean do you know what kind of shoes, what colour?'

'Ahhhm. Black. I think. Shoes or boots, I'm not sure, I'm sorry, I don't know.'

He looked me up and down again and looked quickly away, clearing his throat. The young woman looked past me, at a point on the wall. The man reached into his tunic pocket and took a card from it.

'Is this your daughter's?' he asked.

It was Jane's student card.

I nodded.

'I'm afraid we have bad news for you.'

I sat back in my chair. Whatever it was that he was about to tell me, I didn't want to hear it. The young woman glanced at me again, blushed and went back to rubbing Ros. The man coughed again. I wanted to tell him to clear his fucking throat, to say whatever he had to say. And at the same time,

I was racing through what he might say. Car accident? It couldn't be serious if Jane and Elizabeth were in a taxi coming from town. Taxis never got up speed on this road, unless some boy racer had hit the taxi. Walking home with Elizabeth? Had they been knocked down?

'I'm sorry,' the man said. 'We found a young woman, this card was in her purse and the clothes she was wearing fit the description you've given us.'

'Found her where?'

'I'm afraid your daughter is dead.'

Ros rolled over and wagged his tail. I looked at the young woman but she went on staring past my shoulder.

'You might make a tea or a coffee,' the blue-eyed man said to her.

She nodded.

'Is it all right if Jane makes us a tea or coffee?'

'What?'

'Is it ok if Jane makes some tea or coffee? If she uses the kitchen?'

Was this some kind of bizarre joke, black humour pushed to the ultimate, was I about to find that Jane had been hiding in the kitchen and these were her friends, dressed up and having me on?

Suddenly, the young woman seemed to realise what had happened.

'Oh, Jesus,' she said quietly.

The blue-eyed man glowered at her.

'We have the same name,' she said.

And then she apologised, as though it were her fault that she and my daughter had been christened Jane.

'When is your birthday?' I asked

'September.'

'What date?'

•

73

'The eighteenth.'

'Last week.'

'Yes.'

'What age are you?'

'Twenty-one,' she said.

'Jane is nineteen. Mid-summer day.'

'I'm sorry,' the young woman said. 'I'll make some tea. Or coffee?'

'Make some coffee,' the blue-eyed man said. 'Is coffee ok?'

'Yes,' I said. 'Milk, no sugar.'

As if it mattered.

Ros followed the young woman out of the room and I heard her say, 'Good boy,' again in the hallway.

The blue-eyed man coughed again.

'I'm sorry,' he said. 'I didn't want to say anything while my colleague was here but, ah, we can see your testicles and, ah, your private parts, your dressing gown is open.'

I looked down and laughed without knowing why. He was right, my dressing gown had fallen to the side of my leg. I pulled it back and covered myself.

'The tragic and the ridiculous,' I said, feeling, again, that I should say something.

'I am so sorry,' he said. 'So, so sorry.'

From the kitchen, I could hear the clink of cups and saucers and then the young guard reappeared, Ros trotting in front of her. She had three cups of coffee and milk and sugar and spoons on a tray. She must have some sixth sense, I reckoned, about where all this stuff is kept in the kitchens of people who have lost relatives in violent circumstances. I wanted to ask if this was part of her training.

The man took the tray from her, while she handed me a cup and poured milk into it. They were practised at this kind of thing.

'Thank you,' I said.

They sat opposite me, each of us cradling our coffee cup. I checked my dressing gown.

'I'm sorry about that,' I said to the young woman.

'It's ok,' she smiled.

'"The grace of the Lord".'

She nodded.

The blue-eyed man looked at her, frowning.

'It's what my name – our name – means,' she said.

'Jane was with her friend, Elizabeth,' I said. 'I dropped them into town, they said they were going to the New Place. They said they'd get a taxi home.'

The blue-eyed man sat forward.

'Elizabeth who?'

'Lawrence. She lives about half a mile farther out this road, beyond the bad bend, second house on the right after the bend. They were together.'

'You know the house?' he asked the young woman.

She nodded.

'You should go,' the blue-eyed man said quietly.

She nodded again and stood up.

'Excuse me,' she said. 'I'll be back shortly.'

'You can ring if you want,' I suggested.

'It's best I call to the house,' she smiled and then she was gone and I heard the car starting and the tyres moving slowly back down the drive and I closed my eyes, hoping that when I opened them again, in the silence that followed, there'd be just Ros and me in the room and everything else would have been in my head.

And then the blue-eyed man was talking quietly. I listened without opening my eyes, without even wanting to.

'I need to ask you some questions,' he said. 'I'm sorry that

I have to do this but it's something I need to do. I'll be as brief as I can.'

I nodded.

'What time did you last see your daughter and her friend?'

'Nine or so. Ten to, ten past.'

'Had they planned on meeting anyone?'

'Not that they said, no.'

'And after you left them, what did you do?'

'Came back here, did some drawing, watched the late TV news ...'

'There was no one else here with you? I understand your wife passed away some years ago.'

'Yes, she did.'

'And you had no visitors?'

'No. I rang my brother about one, he lives in the States. Talked to him for twenty minutes, half an hour. I was half expecting Jane to be home. Then I went to bed.'

'Thank you,' he said.

I opened my eyes. He was still nursing his coffee cup.

'I slept,' I said, almost apologetically.

'You didn't know,' he said.

'No. You think you'll know if something happens to someone close to you, don't you, but it's bollocks.'

'Yes.'

'Why aren't I crying now?'

'You're in shock,' he said simply. 'Is there someone I could ring?'

I laughed quietly.

'My wife was killed in a road accident,' I said. 'Two guards came to tell me. And one of them said just that.'

'Yes.'

'Elizabeth's parents will know, when your colleague tells them.'

'Yes.'

'They'll come down if ...'

Suddenly it struck me that I knew nothing about what had happened to Jane or where or when or if Elizabeth had been with her. All these things that I should have asked, all the questions to which I needed answers remained unspoken.

But there were no answers.

'I can't tell you because I don't know,' the blue-eyed man said. 'I was dispatched from the station. The report came from elsewhere.'

'Who found Jane?'

'I honestly don't know. I'm just a messenger.'

'Excuse me,' I said, jumping up. 'I don't feel well.'

Rushing to the downstairs bathroom, I vomited into the sink, coffee and bile, nothing solid, nothing I had eaten before the arrival of the news, nothing from the time when life was ordinary, predictable, routine.

'Are you all right?' came the blue-eyed man's voice from beyond the door.

'Yes,' I said and then another wave of nausea, another mouthful of bile, another retch.

I sat on the toilet and put my head between my knees. The sweat on my back soaked into the towelled dressing gown. I breathed deeply, deeply, deeply. So deeply that I felt dizzy. And then I sat up, ran the cold tap and splashed my face. The bathroom door opened and the guard stepped in, offering me a glass of water.

He sat on the edge of the bath and watched me drink.

'Would you like to lie down, even here, on the floor? I'll stay with you or I can wait outside. Or you might like to go up and lie on your bed.'

'What time is it?' I asked.

He glanced at his watch.

'Ten past four.'

'I'll be all right. I think I'll get dressed, if that's ok?'

'Whatever you want,' he said. 'The coffee was a bad idea. I'm going to make some tea. You take your time.'

I stopped outside the open door of Jane's room. The light from the landing fell like an axe across her bedroom floor, a shaft and triangle of brightness and then the darkness beyond, the space behind the half-open door, her bed still made, her clothes still tossed across a chair, her violin laid neatly and safely in its case, the CDs in an orderly array along the shelves, her diary, her letters, her bracelets, rings and clips, the pictures haloing her mirror, all the things that were a part of who and what she was and what she meant to those of us who loved her.

Could I step inside and touch the things she'd last touched? Could I breathe deeply and inhale the musk of her perfume? Flick the porpoise that dangled above her bed and watch it rise and fall on its rope of wire? Was I brave enough to be in this room that she'd left just seven hours earlier? And if I walked inside, would I have the courage to walk back out again?

I closed the door and went into my own room, stepped into and out of the hot shower, dried myself quickly and dressed. As I pulled on a T-shirt, I heard a car in the yard and Ros was barking again and then there was the sound of a second car and doors banging and the front door opening and quiet voices in the hall, then a voice from halfway down the stairs, Kate's voice.

'Can I come up?'

'Yes,' I said.

She came into my room, dressed in jeans and T-shirt, slippers on her feet. Crossing to where I stood, she buried her head in my chest and I could feel her tears through my shirt and her body shuddering and jerking. She tried to speak but the words wouldn't come and she clung more tightly to me. We said nothing because there was nothing to say.

Going downstairs, I caught a glimpse of Elizabeth through the open kitchen door and I waited for her to tell me that she could explain everything but her face was a washed-out grey, ploughed with tears. I wondered how she was still standing. It seemed as though every ounce of energy had been drained from her. Her cheeks were sunken, her eyes puffed, her hands shaking. She looked at me and her beautiful face warped into an ugly mask and a sound like anguish came from her throat and Ros backed away, cowering, whining, terrified.

In the kitchen, the two guards stood at the table; Brian came and hugged me. He started to say something but his mouth lost its shape and, instead, he shook his head.

The blue-eyed guard handed me a cup of tea and offered me a chair. Sitting at the table, I tried to think of something to say. But what? Should I tell Elizabeth that I was glad to see her unhurt? Did I thank them all for being here, even though I wished they'd go? Should I try, again, to find out where Jane was, who had found her and when? Could I ask Elizabeth what she knew? When had she last seen my daughter? Why wasn't she with her when she was killed? But I didn't have the energy to ask any of these questions.

'Would you like to say a prayer?' the young woman guard asked.

'Yes.'

So we knelt or stood or sat, six adults in a small room, and someone began to say The Lord's Prayer. The words coming out in disparate voices, some strong, some uncertain, coming in unsynchronised bursts.

'... Thy will be done on earth as it is in heaven. Give us this day our daily bread and forgive us our trespasses ...'

And all I could think of was that scene at the end of *Guests of the Nation*, the scattered figures in the boggy landscape, the sky opening out above them, the screeching water hens, the inevitability and the sadness and the irony of prayer and the hopelessness of hoping that words would bring any relief, make anything better.

'... deliver us from evil. Amen.'

And then silence. Elizabeth's breathing from the corner of the room, short and sharp and difficult.

'You're sure there's no one else you'd like us to contact?' the blue-eyed man asked.

'No. I'll do that later. What happens now?'

'Later, we'll ask you to come and identify Jane. But not till later. There are things to be done first. We'll be in touch later in the morning.'

'I can do that if you want,' Brian said. 'If you'd like. Or we can come with you.'

'Thanks.'

'We're going to go now,' the blue-eyed man said. 'We'll be in touch. Mr and Mrs Lawrence will stay with you. But we will be in touch. By the way, my name is Tim Roche and this is Jane Taylor. If you need to contact us.'

'Thank you.'

'We'll see you later, then.'

'Yes.'

'We might have a word with you, Mr Lawrence,' he said, and Brian followed the guards into the hall.

'What happened?' I asked.

Kate looked at me and then at Elizabeth but she was silent.

'The girls took a taxi back to our house,' Kate said. 'Elizabeth says they got back before twelve. We were asleep.

Jane left about half-twelve, she was walking, it's only ten minutes, they've both done it all their lives.'

'I know,' I said. 'I know that.'

'We've all done it, walked up and down from our house to here and back.'

'It's all right,' I said.

And then Kate was crying again.

'If she'd woken us and asked for a lift or rung you. Two minutes, that's all it would have taken. Two minutes. We'd have driven her home.'

I reached across the table and patted her arm.

'I'm so sorry,' Elizabeth said.

It was the first time I'd heard her speak since she'd arrived. Her voice was sharp and cold.

'We had a few drinks in the New Place and chatted and it was really quiet in there and then we got a taxi back home. Jane knew I had to be up early in the morning, to catch the train, so we just had a coffee and she said she'd head home. We'd arranged for her to come down to Cork in three weeks' time, for a weekend. And that was it. I walked with her to the end of our drive and we hugged and I went back in and went to bed. That was it. It was the same as we do every time Jane comes to our house or I come here. It never crossed either of our minds to think of asking for a lift. Why would it? We walked that road a thousand times. You know that.'

She looked at each of us in turn, seeking approval, agreement, an assurance that she wasn't to blame.

'If we'd come back here,' she said, 'I'd have walked home. That's what we did last Friday, you remember?'

'Yes,' I said. 'I know.'

Brian came back into the kitchen while, outside, car lights arrowed slowly down the drive.

'I'll make some more tea,' he said. 'Do you want toast? I know it seems an awful thing to ask but, fuck it, I can't think of what else to do.'

I nodded.

The four of us sat at the kitchen table and drank tea and ate toast, a bizarre, half-past-four-in-the-morning last supper, each of us finding our separate ways to Jane.

'They haven't told me anything,' I said. 'I don't know where they found her or how or when or any of that stuff.'

'They don't tend to,' Brian said. 'They keep that under wraps until they have everything they need, examinations and the like. For "operational reasons" is what they say. I think it's so there's no danger of anything getting out, any of the things that aren't public knowledge. They seal off the scene and all that kind of stuff.'

'Brian, shut up, please,' Kate said.

'Yeah, sure, sorry, sorry.'

'It's all right,' I said. 'None of us knows what to say or do.'

'I'll wash these cups and plates,' Brian said, and he gathered the cutlery and crockery and brought them to the sink.

'I think I need to be on my own for a while,' I said. 'I know you won't take this the wrong way, but I need to be here on my own for a couple of hours.'

'I don't think that's a great idea,' Kate said quickly.

'I'm not going to do anything stupid, Kate. I just need to be here for a while. I need the house to myself while Jane is still part of the place, before all the other crap starts to kick in, before the organising begins. I need the place to ourselves, honestly.'

'We should do what the man asks,' Brian agreed. 'We should get Liz back home, too. The guards want to talk to her later, she should get some rest for a while. We're there, you know we're there, whenever and whatever, you know that.'

'Yes,' I nodded. 'I know that and I appreciate it. I'll ring you later.'

Brian hugged me again and then Elizabeth hugged me and I said, 'It's all right, Elizabeth.'

She smiled weakly and followed her father out to the car. Kate and I walked behind them.

Standing in the front yard, Kate hugged me again, gently rubbing the side of my face, and then turned and got into the car. She was crying, her head shaking, her eyes glinting in the door light. Brian waved and then they were gone.

I stood in the darkness, after the car had disappeared, and waited for something to happen, something immense that would acknowledge the fact that my daughter was dead, some part of the universe that would concede to the horror of an event that had changed everything. But nothing did. There was, instead, this terrible gap filled only with the little knowledge I had of what had occurred, how little I knew and, most importantly of all, what I didn't know.

I had no idea where my daughter was or who, if anyone, was with her. I knew nothing of her condition. She had been half a mile from home when last seen alive. Was she lying somewhere along the roadside? Were there blue lights reflecting off plastic tape? Should I get into my car and try to find where she had been killed? Could I wait five minutes and ring Kate and ask if she had seen anything as she drove from her house to mine? I glanced up into the sky. What was I looking for? Light, a flashing blueness, God, hope?

Through the open hall door, Ros came ambling to find me, wagging his tail and shuffling past me, nosing the frozen grass and then lying down, his head on his crossed paws.

.

Above me, the stars were hardly visible through a light sheen of clouds that did little to veil the full moon, projecting its huge ring across the sky. Around me, the trees were still for a moment. Hoar frost had settled on the dahlias. And then the sounds came. A distant rumble of rolling metal bars, the whining of a dog, a car speeding along the main Dublin road three fields away, an ambulance siren. Too late for ambulances, I thought. I wanted that dog to stop whining. I shivered but I wasn't cold enough. I wanted to be petrified, to have my feelings blunted so as not to have to face what lay ahead. The moon was moving west, shadows lengthening; there was a slight breeze in the frozen leaves of the silver birch but not enough to clear my lungs.

And then Ros got up and rambled to the end of the drive. I saw the impression his body had left on the grass. And I felt the pain in my belly, knowing that Jane's body was lying somewhere, on a grass verge or a concrete footpath or a patch of tarmac, the frost on her hair, her face, her hands and her eyes. Settling around her dead body, leaving a shape on whatever piece of ground her killer had chosen. And I knew that somewhere out there, beyond the lights of the distant road, possibly somewhere beneath the glow from the town that garlanded the still, unbroken sky, was the person who had done this. And I had no idea who that person was. That was another question, another piece to add to the broken pieces that were to be my life from then on. And I couldn't think about him or them because I had nothing to focus on. All I had was this absence, the memory of my daughter, smiling as she stepped from the car.

Dressed to kill. That's what people said. And this is what it meant. Dressed for killing, for dumping, for throwing away like a piece of rubbish, consigned to some dark place to be found or not found as luck might have it. He or they might have thrown her somewhere else, some place that she'd never have been found. They might have buried her or burned her or hidden her in an out-of-the-way corner of some forest or bog, left her to wind and rain and time to annihilate. Instead, they'd pitched her in a place where she'd been found, where the certainty of death would be known in hours or days. Was that a mercy or simply a different kind of hell? I had no idea.

I was standing in my garden, our garden, at half past five on an autumn morning and I knew nothing more than I had known three hours earlier, beyond the fact that my daughter, whom I loved past words, was dead. That was all I truly knew and even that had not registered anywhere other than in my mind. The awfulness of the fact, the truth of what it meant, hadn't found its way into my heart. If it had, my chest would have burst, spewing out whatever ticking, heaving, over-wrought organs were held there.

I felt the stones beneath my feet and realised I had come outside without my shoes or socks, and I was glad. Walking the length of the drive, down to where Ros sat silent and passive at the wooden gate, letting the sting of broken shale and sharpened stones and icy pebbles work into the soles of my feet, I drew some tiny comfort from the fact that I was feeling pain. It was nothing more than a gesture of empathy with Jane. But I also understood that feeling had nothing to do with this, that my darling was beyond sensation, that every fibre that had ever felt pain or fear was numb now. And I found no comfort in that thought. To be without feeling, even the feeling of terror, was to be beyond anything that might bear any semblance of life. Death was awful because of its silent imperviousness to everything. Death was not some clean, clear word. It was not an image of an elderly man, like my father, laid out on pristine sheets, his work done, his life rounded out in the relative comfort of his home, in the

·

85

warmth of his family's care and loss. Death was a ditch or a dyke, a body violated and used, a human being reduced to flesh and blackening blood, to cuts and bruises and abrasions, a badly bent leg, a broken arm twisted back behind the head, hair clotted with blood. That was death.

What was that passage in the Book of Ruth? I tried to remember.

> Entreat me not to leave thee, or to return from following after thee: for whither thou goest, I will go; and where thou lodgest, I will lodge.

But I couldn't follow, I had no idea where Jane had gone. I had no way, perhaps ever, of finding her. And those who knew were bent on not telling me. This was now their case, their investigation, their mystery to be solved, a challenge to their intelligence, a game like all the other games they had played. The same rules and techniques would be applied. All that differed were the personalities involved. The killer, the policeman, the parent, the witness were stock characters. Change the names, alter the location and start all over again.

Bending down, I rubbed the dog's head and found I couldn't straighten up again. It was easier to sink to my knees and let them nestle into the gravel. Then my feet found places to lodge and I felt myself fold into the clay of the open gateway. And we lay there, the dog and I, two figures whose beloved would never come home again, two creatures close to the earth because we needed to be, because that was where we hoped we would find some echo of the one we had lost.

Pressing my cheek against the frosted stones I tried to catch a hint of the breathing earth, a consciousness of a place or state that stored things up, if only for a little while. A chamber somewhere at the earth's core where the lives and memories of the newly dead were sorted before dispersal. I envisaged a cave filled with all the waking dreams and the last thoughts and the recent memories of the dying. A place filled with voices and images and colours that separated and rearranged themselves, bringing some cohesion to the panic that must have set in as the inevitability of violence and confusion moved quickly from fear to fact. In this grotto, a benign presence descended, bringing order and calm to the confusion, reacquainting the lost with the wounded, the hoped-for with the desperate, putting pieces together again and allowing the scattered instances that pass for life to make some sense of who and what they were.

But it wasn't enough, and each time I thought of Jane's spirit there and tried to imagine a calmness descending on it, other fractured bits of bone and hope and skin flew from place to place, refusing to be identified. And I saw violins and knives and wire garrottes and bloodied stones and I knew there would never be a time when all these battered body parts and nightmares were silent. Each moment that threatened peace would be followed by a fresh incursion of blood and human offal, the dispossessed and useless, the derelict, discarded, forsaken remnants of the one I had adored and lost.

And I tried to cry, I tried to force some tears from my eyes but nothing came. Instead, I buried my cheek more deeply in the gravel, looking for some kind of pain to validate my anguish, but all I found was the warm clay beneath the stones, the softer dirt beneath the frost, the aggravation of my own inability to feel.

And then a bird sang out and another and another, cracking the darkness, responding to the threat of light in the eastern sky, telling me I must get up because I couldn't lie here all day, because there were things to be done, because somebody was already coming to look at Jane's body, to measure and assess and then somebody else would lift it from the ground and take it to be cut open, considered and sewn up again and I would be expected to be ready to take care of her from that point on. And because her grandparents deserved to know what had happened before they heard reports on the morning news and felt a tinge of empathy because some young girl who lived in the same town as their granddaughter had been killed. They deserved to be spared the further pain of realising when it was too late that brutality can come knocking on any door.

By then, the birds were singing out from all the trees above me and behind me and a pigeon fluttered down and settled on the grass across the drive from where I lay, picking and eyeing, picking and strutting. And so I got to my knees and Ros came and licked my feet and I held on to him, wanting him to take me back up the grey spectre of driveway that would never be welcoming again. But he was paralysed by his own sense of things being wrong and, in the end, I got to my feet and called him and the birds stopped singing and rose as one from the trees above us. We trudged together through the shadowy half-light to the open door of the empty house and, as we did, the birds settled again and went on with their singing.

Walking through the empty rooms, I flicked the light switches off – daylight had robbed the sallow bulbs of their use. In the kitchen, assorted mugs sat on the worktop, tea-rings tattooed the kitchen table, crumbs of toast in crescents, chairs drawn back like they were on Flannan Isle. For all the world, the room looked as it had done on a hundred other mornings that followed late-night conversations on philosophy and politics and life and death. But this morning was different. The time for speculation was finished. This was the day we never think about because we dare not imagine ourselves in this position and, anyway, we have no concept of how it really is, not even when it dawns.

I ran the hot tap into the kitchen sink and squirted a splash of washing-up liquid into the steaming water, dipping and wringing a dishcloth, wiping down the table and, as the heat soaked into my hands, I began to shiver and the dampness of the night air finally seeped through my clothes and dribbled down my skin. I was petrified.

I thought of a cross of artificial flowers that I had passed every day for three years on a country road. A garish arrangement that had changed colour through the seasons. It marked the spot where a boy of fourteen had driven a motorbike into a gatepost. Its gaudy pinks and yellows and purples had been refreshed by winter rains and unexpectedly lit by bursts of glaring spring. And then the constant summer sun had burned the colour from the flowers, day by scorching day, until the petals were nothing but discs of dirty, translucent plastic. And that's how they'd stayed for another year, the last vestige of colour disappearing with the seasons until, at last, the petals split and flittered into the grass and only the wire stalks remained, like cracks on the gatepost.

Was that what lay ahead, emptiness and then a complete lack of purpose? If I burned this house down, could I walk away and try to start something over? Could I be that man in the sad songs who carries his loss pinned well inside his soul, never speaking of it, doing his job, collecting his pay and retiring from the world till the world is ready to remove him from its numbers? That was what I wanted, to be clear of this day and this place and this horror.

The phone rang, its singing jingle at odds with everything. I picked it up, not because I wanted to but to stop its non-sensical cheerfulness.

'Are you all right?'

It was Kate.

'I'm all right,' I said and, as I spoke, I began to shiver.

'Are you sure?'

'Just cold. Shivers.'

'Get into the shower. Get warm. I'll be down in a few minutes. Leave the key in the door. Get into the shower.'

She hung up.

I hesitated a moment but I knew she was right. The shivering was becoming uncontrollable. I hurried upstairs and sat on the bedside, pulling off my shoes, trying to open my shirt buttons, cursing this epilepsy of loss. Rushing to the shower, waiting for the water to warm and then standing in the spray, shuddering, willing the heat to drive the bitter coldness from my skin and my bones, watching the water drain away at my feet, sucking the steam from the air, wallowing in something that wasn't loss and numbness, surprised that I was still capable of some feeling, welcoming the burning sensation on the back of my neck. And then the shower door was pulled back and Kate was standing in the steaming room, offering me a warm towel.

'Enough,' she said. 'Get dried off and get dressed and drink that brandy I've left on the locker.'

Turning off the shower, I stepped into the wrap of the proffered towel.

'I wish I could do more than this,' Kate said. 'But I'll do what I can.'

'Is Elizabeth ok?'

'I don't think it's really hit her yet. Nor any of us.'

'No.'

'I'm going to make something for you to eat. Not that you'll want it but we're going to eat something together and then we'll face whatever has to be done.'

'Thank you.'

She kissed my forehead and then she was gone.

In my bedroom, day had fully broken, the grey glow changing from a promise to a shining sunlight, which tilted through the windows in celebration of itself.

I pulled on the clothes that Kate had laid out on my bed. Jeans, a collared shirt and a thick jumper that Jane had given me for my birthday when she was twelve, a jumper that Kate had chosen with her.

Lacing up my shoes, I glanced out the window, down the avenue of falling golden leaves, to the gateway that yawned like something awful.

In the kitchen, Kate had set the table and hot food steamed on plates.

'Unless you absolutely can't eat this, I think you should. It doesn't matter if it has no taste. It's there for a purpose. Did you drink the brandy?'

I shook my head.

Kate smiled.

'I should have known.'

'I actually forgot it. That's the truth. Not that truth matters any more, does it? It won't ever change anything.'

'No. Probably not.'

Anyone looking in from outside the house might have seen a couple sitting at the breakfast table, lit by the early morning sun, eating slowly. They'd have seen something that might, once, have been a possibility. And if it had actually happened then who was to know whether Elizabeth and Jane would have remained friends, whether they might have been living under the same roof or whether we might all be living in different places. And, if even one or some of those things had happened, the chances were that Jane would not have been on the road between the houses in the first hour of this morning. So many things would have changed and to such effect.

All these things were going through my head, adding new instruments to the array of torture that I was just beginning to identify for my heart.

'There will be things to do,' Kate said, so quietly that I wasn't sure she had spoken.

'Did you say something?'

'There will be things to do. I don't know what they'll be, but things. Whatever I can do I will, but there'll be things you'll need to do. I'll be here with you, if you want, but only if you want.'

'Thank you.'

The tears came pouring down her face.

'Don't say thank you, please. What the fuck else would I do? I've lost Jane, not the way you have but I've lost her, too, and I just want to be whatever I can be ...'

Her sentence hung there, unfinished.

'For you,' she said at last.

I nodded.

We sat in silence and I could hear the birds singing outside, warmed by the early sunlight.

'When will you ring people?' Kate asked. 'Is there anyone you want me to ring?'

'No,' I said. 'It's best I do it myself.'

I thought for a moment.

'My mother, Beth's parents, Robert. Him first, I think, but he's seven or eight hours behind us.'

'That makes it just before midnight there. It might be a good time. If you leave it later, it'll have to be this afternoon and that'll make it harder for him to ... you know ... organise things to get here.'

I hadn't considered the fact that people might be travelling great distances but only because I hadn't truly had the time or the ability to comprehend that my daughter's death meant more than horror and heartbreak. It meant that the practicalities Kate had been hinting at would have to be faced.

'Do you think he'll come?'

'Of course he'll come. He loves her, he loves you, we all do. She was the centre of a lot of people's lives. Just the way you are. You need to prepare yourself for that, too. I don't think you realise how this terrible thing is going to spread out and hurt people and how they're going to do their best to bind up your wounds. And none more so than Robert.'

'I should tell him then. Now?'

'Yes, you should.'

'Hello.'

'Hi, Robert?'

'Hi. That's uncanny. We were just talking about you here. That's really funny. Can't be more than ten minutes since we were talking about you and Jane. Uncanny. Hey, either you're up early or I'm up really late. Which is it?'

'Both.'

'So, how are things?'

'Bad news, I'm afraid. Bad news.'

'Mum?'

'No, not Mum.'

'Who?'

'Jane.'

'Is she ill?'

'She's dead, Robert. She died last night.'

That was the first time I'd said it aloud.

'Jesus Christ. What happened?'

'She was killed. I don't know much. The guards came to the house sometime around four. They found her dead. I don't even know the details.'

'Jesus …'

'Yes.'

'Where?'

'Here. I mean here in the town. Somewhere between Kate's house and here. I don't even know where. They've told me nothing.'

'We'll be there as soon as I can arrange flights. Do you have any idea about, you know, arrangements? No, of course you don't.'

'No.'

'Is there someone there with you?'

'Kate is here. Brian and Elizabeth were here earlier.'

'Does Mum know?'

'No. You're the first person I've phoned.'

'Do you want me to call her?'

'No. I'll do that next.'

'Is there anything I can do right now?'

'No.'

'I'm going to book flights straight away. I'll call you as soon as I have flight information, ok?'

'Ok.'

'I'm so sorry, so sorry. Jesus … I don't know what to say, I wish I did.'

'I know.'

'I love you brother.'

'I know. Thanks.'

'I'll be back to you as soon as I have the flights booked.'

'Right.'

'And Kate is there?'

'Yes.'

'Ok. I'll be in touch as soon as I can. We'll be there as quickly as possible.'

And then a string of phone calls. My mother in tears. Beth's father incoherent with shock, his wife taking the phone from him and being practical. Alice, Jane's best friend from college, trying to breathe and then telling me everything would be all right, that she'd go into the college and tell them, that she'd contact the rest of their friends, that she'd be down the following day or as soon as she could. And then a plain-clothes detective at the door, while I talked on the phone, sympathising with Kate, assuming she was my wife and then apologising.

When I'd finished talking to Alice, I followed the detective into the sitting room. He introduced himself and commiserated with me and then began explaining things in as much detail as he deemed necessary, repeating the information that he thought I wasn't taking in.

'We're at a very early stage in the investigation,' he said. 'But we're confident that we can pursue a definite line of inquiry. There's a witness to the presence of some people in the immediate area where your daughter's body was found, in or around the time of her death. I'd like to tell you more but for operational reasons I can't. Suffice to say, we expect to make an early arrest. Not that this is of any consolation to you. But I did want to keep you informed about what's happening.'

'Yes.'

'I'm not sure whether you want to visit the scene where your daughter was found. I can take you there if you'd like to go.'

'Is she still there?'

He shook his head.

'She was taken away about half an hour ago. There will be a postmortem later today. You may not want to but, if you do …'

'Where was she found?'

He cleared his throat.

'There's a field just this side of the old forge, a long field that dips and then dips again.'

'We often walk the dog there on summer evenings,' I said.

'Your daughter's body, Jane's body, was found at the foot of that second dip.'

'It's only three minutes from here,' I said, as if he didn't already know this.

He nodded.

Over the detective's shoulder, through the window, I could see Brian arriving with groceries. I watched as he and Kate carried them from his car, cardboard boxes filled with the banal necessities for the coming days.

I laughed. The detective looked up from his notebook. I signalled to the figures outside.

'Life goes on,' I said.

'Yes.'

'In the middle of all this we're expected to carry on with the day-to-day things.'

'I know.'

'Of course you do.'

'So, would you like me to take you there?'

I shook my head.

'You're sure?'

'Yes.'

'Well, if you change your mind, just contact me.'

He scribbled a number on a piece of paper and handed it to me.

'I know the place,' I said. 'She was well away from the road. She should have been coming home along the road. That's how she always came home from Kate and Brian's.'

I heard the phone ring and then I heard Kate's voice.

'We believe she was walking home along the road,' the detective said. 'We believe she was taken from the road across the field.'

'It's a long way to the bottom of the second dip. A long way to take someone.'

'Yes.'

'Jane would fight.'

'Yes.'

'Did she fight?'

'I don't know. I wish I could tell you more. And I will, when I can.'

Again, the phone rang and then a car pulled into the yard.

'I'll let you know everything as it happens,' the detective said. 'Once the postmortem has been done, we'll be in a much better position. I think the investigative end of things will be resolved very quickly.'

'Good.'

He stood up.

'I'll be back to you. There will be the matter of formal identification. You might wish to do that. Or nominate someone else to do it.'

'I'll do it,' I said quickly.

'Depending on how things happen, that might not be until tomorrow. And, once that's clarified, I'll know when your daughter's body will be released to you. Again, I'm sorry.'

'Thank you.'

I walked him to the front door. Kate was still on the phone. Brian was standing in the yard, talking to Frank Morris, our GP.

We stood together, the three of us, watching the detective drive away, and then Brian went back inside.

Frank shook my hand.

'I just heard,' he said. 'I came straight out. How are you bearing up?'

'I don't know,' I said. 'It hasn't sunk in yet. The detective asked if I wanted to visit where they found Jane. It's only across the bloody road, in the long field. I could walk there in a couple of minutes if I wanted. But I don't want to.'

'Have you slept at all?'

'I was asleep when they came. That was about four or something.'

'Do you feel you need to sleep?'

'No.'

'I brought you some sleeping pills, if you need them,' he said, handing me an envelope. 'The prescribed amount is on the envelope. I'm in the middle of surgery but don't hesitate if you feel you want to talk or whatever. If you need anything, anything at all, ring me or get Kate or Brian to ring. Brian has my mobile number.'

'Kate already did,' I said. 'Obviously.'

He smiled and then he was gone.

Kate had a list of things to tell me.

'Robert called. He and Jenny will be arriving in Dublin late tomorrow evening. Brian will collect them. Your mother rang. She'll be here about three this afternoon.'

'Fuck.'

'Don't worry about it, we'll keep her busy. Beth's parents will wait to hear from you. Her mother rang and asked you to let them know what you wanted them to do.'

'At least they have enough sense not to come barging in immediately.'

'I think your mother believes she's doing the right thing but we'll keep an eye on her.'

'I know.'

'Now, I'm going down home to see how Elizabeth is doing and to have a shower. Brian is getting some stuff ready in the kitchen. Just to have things under way.'

'How is Elizabeth?'

'In shock. Frank was with her before he came here. Susan is with her now.'

'Give her my best.'

'Of course.'

'The detective said they're following a definite line of inquiry. He said he'd be able to tell me when I can have Jane back after they'd done a postmortem. That's what he told me.'

Kate nodded.

'Maybe you should rest now.'

'I'm all right. I will when I need to.'

My mother arrived before three that afternoon. Kate talked to her in the kitchen while I pretended, for as long as I could, to be doing things in the yard – chopping timber, putting coal in buckets, feeding Ros. When, finally, I had to come inside, I spent half an hour making up her bed in the spare room, anything to keep me from having to listen to the perpetual dolefulness of her voice.

In good times, I found her difficult company. In bad times, she was one of the people I least wanted to be with. Late in the afternoon, Kate offered to take her shopping.

'You should go home,' I said. 'You need to spend some

time with Elizabeth. And I have to spend some time with my mother, whether I like it or not.'

'Ring me if things get too much. Anyway, I'm sure there'll be lots of people coming and going. I've left everything ready in the kitchen. Food and drinks and stuff, you know, just things that you might need.'

After Kate had left, I made some tea and my mother and I sat in the dining room. She sighed a lot and cried.

'You seem to be cursed,' she said. 'One loss after another.'

'How do you mean?' I asked, pretending not to understand.

'First Beth and now Jane.'

'It's sixteen years since Beth died,' I said.

'Was killed,' my mother corrected. 'Both killed. Dying is one thing but being taken in the bloom of life, as they were, is another. Dying is natural, this is not.'

I nodded.

'Why do these things happen?' she asked. 'Why can't we live in happiness?'

'Laughter doesn't last,' I said.

She looked at me as though I were mad.

'What are you talking about?'

'Sadness is our true state of existence. That's why the things we remember are the moments of sadness. That's what I believe.'

'Well it's a damned strange thing to believe. It's almost like you're courting sadness, inviting it to make its home inside your heart.'

'No,' I said. 'That's not what I'm doing. It's just that I believe in the inevitability of sadness in our lives.'

'Sadness, yes. Murder and mayhem, no,' my mother said quickly. 'You're depressed and shocked. That's not the kind of talk a sane person comes out with.'

'You're probably right.'

I was too tired to argue any more. I just wanted to be quiet. I wanted to let my mind shut down.

The phone rang. It was Robert, reassuring me that the flight was booked. I put my mother on to him. She talked for thirty-five minutes while I went and prepared some food.

After we'd eaten, I kept waiting for the doorbell to ring, for someone to call, but the avenue was silent and dark. No car lights, no visitors trudging warily to the door. Perhaps, I thought, my mother was right and people shared her opinion and, by extension, believed there was something unnatural about me. Perhaps they were afraid of being stigmatised. Perhaps visiting the house of the dead was an acceptable thing but visiting the home of the murdered was something else entirely. Perhaps they feared some aura of contamination by association, something unspoken that would draw them in from the edge and make them more uncomfortable than they normally were with death.

'Did Jane have many friends?' my mother asked, as though she were reading my mind.

'Yes. Here and in college.'

'You'd think they'd be here, to pay their respects.'

'It's probably too soon.'

'People are strange.'

'Not just me, then?'

'That's a very flippant remark for someone who has just lost his daughter,' she said, sharply.

'If you say so.'

Brian and Kate arrived sometime after ten.

'I thought there'd be lots of people here,' Brian said.

'So my mother has been saying.'

'You should have rung us.'

'It's been all right.'

'I'll make some hot whiskeys,' he said, leading the way into the kitchen.

I listened to them talk for an hour. I had nothing to say.

'We should let you get some sleep,' Kate said, finally. 'Would you like one of us to stay?'

'No, not at all. We'll be fine.'

'You're sure?'

'Yes.'

I saw them to their car and when I came back inside, my mother was standing at the foot of the stairs.

'I've made up the spare room for you,' I said.

'And where will you put Robert and Jenny?'

'They don't arrive till tomorrow evening.'

'Yes but where will they sleep?'

'On the settee in my study.'

Had she thought I was going to put her in Jane's room? I was too tired to ask. Instead, I kissed her, wished her a good night's sleep and climbed the stairs to my own room, Ros padding behind. I passed Jane's door without a glance inside, too tired and too empty to face the further emptiness that the room held.

Brian was standing at the table, buttering bread, piling it on two big plates, when I came downstairs the following morning.

'You should be in work,' I said.

'Work is work,' he said. 'It's not life.'

Or death, I wanted to say but I didn't.

'Kate has taken your mother into town, to have her hair done. You slept.'

'Yes.'

'Good.'

'I can give you a hand.'

'Jesus, no. You have other things to do. Or just sit down, relax.'

'That's the last thing I want to do, Brian.'

He looked at me and he must have recognised the truth in what I was saying because, immediately, he pushed the tub of butter towards me and I took a knife from the drawer and we worked together, two men buttering bread for sandwiches, a mundane thing that we could do in silence, a chore that needed doing, something we could achieve without speech or communication of any kind and yet something that joined us for that time in a kind of union we had never found before.

Brian took a pack of cooked ham from the fridge and laid the slices on the squares of bread, folding another slice of bread over the meat and cutting each sandwich diagonally. I went on buttering the bread, a second loaf and then a third. Brian took some hard-boiled eggs from a saucepan on the cooker, ran them under the cold-water tap and then shelled them.

'I hate the smell of hard-boiled eggs,' he said.

'So do I. It's sickening.'

'Thing is, these'll be eaten before we know it.'

'Not by me. Or you,' I laughed.

I heard Brian chuckle from where he stood at the sink.

An ordinary moment in the midst of mayhem, an instant of forgetting what had happened and what lay ahead, a joke we might have shared at any get-together over the past twenty years. And then, as though we both realised what we had done, how we had breached the sacredness of why we were here, we returned to doing what needed doing. And Brian was mashing the eggs and spreading them on the bread and folding and

.

cutting and stacking. And I went on buttering and Brian took tomatoes from the fridge and washed and sliced them and the whole thing started all over again, the piled plates with their cling-film veils spreading across the worktop.

'Must be getting on for lunch-time,' I said. 'I wonder when they'll want me for the identification?'

'It's only twenty past ten,' Brian said.

'You're not serious?'

'That's all.'

'I thought it was one or two.'

He shook his head.

'I'll make some coffee. Are you hungry?'

'I don't think so. I don't know. I don't feel I have the right to be hungry. Does that sound crazy?'

'No. It makes perfect sense but it doesn't alter the fact that you need to eat. Do it as a thing that has to be done, like making these sandwiches, like phoning people, like … like … you know.'

We made a space between the crusts and crumbs and sat at the table, drinking strong coffee and eating scones.

'I wish to fuck I knew what to say,' Brian said. 'I'd love to be one of those people that knows what to say at times like this. They exist. They can put their finger on things and say something right. It mightn't heal anything but it comes out the right way. I'm here for the past hour trying to think of something better than sorry. Something that means something but I can't.'

'You made a few mountains of sandwiches.'

'That's easy, that's avoiding the real issue, that's hiding from the fact that Jane is dead and that I need to be able to talk about her to you.'

And then he started crying. The tears sloping down his face like rivers, his voice breaking and getting swallowed in the gulping breaths he couldn't take. A crumb caught in his throat and he began to cough and the tears of coughing and the tears of crying welled up and spilled over and his face was red and blotched and he held on to the edge of the table, spluttering and crying so that I was afraid he was going to choke.

Finally, slowly, he caught his breath. I brought him a glass of water and he sipped it, breathing deeply, regaining his composure, the high colour fading from his face.

'I'm sorry,' he said. 'You'd think I was the one …'

'We're all the one, Brian. It's not like sorrow turns back at the border.'

'No.'

I poured some more coffee and we sat there in silence, sipping from our cups, dark rings overlapping on the table. Neither one of us had the energy to get back to the things that needed doing. Ros came and lay across my feet, his nose muzzling warm against my leg.

I saw the post van moving slowly up the drive and a few seconds later the doorbell rang.

'I'll get it,' Brian said.

'No, it's ok. Might be something that needs signing for.'

The postman was standing three feet from the doorstep.

He proffered his hand. I reached to take whatever it was he had for me but, instead, his hand closed around mine.

'I'm terrible sorry. I just heard. I'm terrible sorry.'

'Thanks, John.'

'I know I bring bad news and good news to people every day but it's not this raw, not this awful kind of thing. I just wanted to say I'm sorry.'

And, then, as though he felt the need to justify his visit, he said, 'There's no post for you today. I just called.'

'Would you like a coffee or something. Brian and myself are having one.'

·

105

'No, no but thanks. We'll talk again.'

'We will. And thanks, John.'

He backed away, sitting heavily into his van, pausing before turning on the engine. And then he was edging the van slowly back down the drive. I stood at the door, watching him go, breathing in the warm morning air, wishing I were tired, wishing I could sleep the hours away but knowing I wouldn't.

Just before midday, Kate and my mother arrived with Elizabeth and Susan.

'I've spoken to the guards and the hospital,' she said. 'They'll be ready for you to identify Jane anytime after three. It doesn't have to be you. I can go or Brian can go.'

'I'll do it,' I said.

'Then I'll come with you.'

'That would be good.'

'There are other things. We need to talk to an undertaker. Again, I'll do that if you like. Or I'll come with you.'

'Ok. When?'

'Whenever you like. Before lunch-time?'

'All right.'

'We can go now if you want. I'm not rushing you, I just think it might be good to be doing things.'

'Yes.'

'You're sure you want to? I can do it.'

'No. I'll do it. But I'd like it if you came along.'

We drove to the other end of the town, to where the undertaker had his offices and workshop. Kate had rung ahead and he was expecting us. He met us at the door, friendly but efficient. That was what I wanted. He told me what he needed. A choice of coffin, funeral times, church, cemetery, cars, music.

'I'll leave all that to you,' I nodded.

'She was a music student,' Kate said. 'I think her friends might want to play.'

'Yes, yes, you're right. Of course, they might.'

'You can let me know when you know,' the undertaker said to Kate, and he jotted something on a pad.

'Jane would want a plain coffin,' I said.

'I can show you what we have. Or I can show you photographs. Whichever is the easier?'

'I'd like to see them.'

I knew that, later, I'd have to see her body. Seeing her coffin would be some kind of preparation.

He led the way through a second office. The woman working there glanced at us, smiled and went back to her computer. Through another door and we were in a showroom. Coffins, metal trims, artificial wreaths, lining fabric.

'There's nothing here that's particularly plain,' the undertaker said. 'If you don't mind following me into the workshop, I can show you other caskets. Plainer. It is a workshop, not as peaceful as here.'

Again, we followed, along a short corridor and into an open, airy workshop. Three men were working there. One of them was whistling along to a tune that blared from a radio. When he saw us, the man turned off the radio and stopped whistling.

The undertaker led us down to a corner of the workshop where unvarnished coffins stood like oversized kennels.

'These are how they begin,' he said. 'These are the plainest we have.'

I looked at them but I could see no difference between one and another.

'It depends on how plain you want it to be.'

'Plain,' I said. 'As plain as possible.'

'Unvarnished?'

'Yes. Just wood. No handles. None of that stuff.'

He moved two of the coffins aside, lifting them lightly, and I saw that there were others stacked behind.

'This is the plainest we have.'

Kate nodded and looked at me.

'Yes,' I said.

'And nothing on it?'

'No.'

'A cross?'

I shook my head.

'Just as it is,' Kate said.

The undertaker took the pad from his jacket pocket and jotted again.

He handed me his card and then handed one to Kate.

'Call me when you have details on times and so on,' he said. 'And I'll collect your daughter from the hospital.'

He said it so casually that it sounded like a boyfriend arranging to pick his girlfriend up from work.

'Would you like to have Jane at home overnight or would you prefer it if she was here with us? The funeral home could be open as late as you wish, all night if that's what you'd like.'

'Home,' I said.

Another note jotted on the pad.

Outside, we sat in the car. I waited for Kate to turn on the engine but she seemed to be waiting for something to happen. Cars passed on the road beside us, speeding in and out of town. In the top corner of the windscreen, I followed a jet trail across the open sky. Kate turned and looked at me.

I realised she expected me to say something but I was mesmerised by the white line speeding west towards America. And I was thinking of Robert, driving to the airport, getting on a plane, speeding east across the Atlantic, all that way to be here, in this town, because of something someone had done.

'Are you sure you're ok with identifying Jane?' Kate asked.

'Yes.'

The jet had disappeared from the windscreen and the trail was beginning to fluff out into a narrow feathered cloud, floating down the glass, dispersing slowly as it reached the rim of dust left by the wiper blades.

'Do you know anything about biology?' I asked.

'Not a lot, beyond having two kids,' Kate said.

'About what happens to us, to the human body, about how it begins to disintegrate?'

'Jesus Christ, no.'

'I've been watching that jet trail, it's breaking up, dissolving across the sky, a few minutes and there'll be nothing left. But that's physics I suppose. Is it?'

'I suppose.'

'We're biology. The way we dissolve. I just wonder how quickly it begins. I'm sure the undertaker might have known.'

'There's something nice about the way it just fades, isn't there?'

'Yes. I suppose that's how we're supposed to go too, to fade gently. I haven't been able to think about what happened to Jane. Not about the way she was ... dealt with. I feel I should be thinking about it, I should want to know who and what and where. I should be raging with anger. I should want to kill.'

'This is probably not the time for that. The time will come when you're ready for those feelings.'

'But this isn't about me, Kate. This is about somebody dragging my child across a field and butchering her, leaving her there like a sack of drowned pups. I should want to turn him on a spit. I should be out there looking for him. But I haven't even thought about it. It's like I have no interest. Almost like I don't care. But I do care. You know I care, don't you?'

Kate reached out, her fingers touching my lips.

'I care more than I can tell you,' I said. 'I know I'll never be able to tell anyone how much I care, how deep the wound cuts.'

'It doesn't all have to happen today or this week or this year. Give yourself time. It's not even thirty-six hours since you heard. Give yourself a chance.'

'It's like in there, in the undertaker's. I forgot about Jane's music, about her friends, about what they might want to happen. I can do, Kate, but I can't think. I had no problem making the sandwiches with Brian. But I can't think. I can't put one coherent thought after another. If you said, let's sit here and watch the sky for the rest of the day, I'd be happy. Or if the undertaker had said the only coffins he had were varnished, I'd have offered to sand one down by hand and I'd have done it and not thought there was anything strange about it. Just to be doing something. But I can't get myself beyond the physical. I can't feel.'

'Maybe you should be glad of that. For now. There'll be lots of time to feel, too much time, too much to feel about. Be grateful for the space. I can't stop thinking. About the what ifs. What if it had been Elizabeth? What if she'd been walking from your house? And then I feel guilty for making this seem like some kind of competition, for putting one girl's life above the other. And just now I was thinking what if I'd had to choose between Elizabeth and Susan. And I felt guilty about even thinking that. Jesus, I don't know what to think. But I keep thinking, I can't stop it. I wish I could but I can't. So be grateful for whatever it is that's keeping thought at bay. It'll come soon enough.'

'Will it? What if it doesn't?'

'It will. I know you.'

I wanted to tell her she didn't really know me but that would require an explanation and I didn't have the energy for explanations, or even lies.

'What about driving up, getting a bite of lunch there and then going to the hospital?'

'What time is it now?'

Kate turned the key and the dashboard clock lit up.

'Just after one. Or would you rather go back home?'

'No. AMAAC, as Robert used to say.'

Kate frowned.

'Avoid Mother At All Costs.'

Smiling, she started the engine.

We drove through the town, moving slowly, caught in the lunch-time traffic from the factories. I kept my head down. I didn't want someone knocking on the car window at the traffic lights, leaning in to sympathise, asking how I felt.

What would I say? I don't feel anything.

My eyes were heavy. Closing them, I let the sunshine pillow my face, drifting quickly into a light sleep, only vaguely aware of passing voices, the stopping and starting, the speed of the open road and the steady plainchant of the engine as we slipped onto the motorway, the miles sliding away behind us. And then we were slowing again. I opened my eyes. We were edging between the bollards of roadworks on the outskirts of a town.

'I'm sorry,' I said. 'I slept.'

Kate jumped in her seat.

'Fuck, I was a million miles away. You frightened me. I was lost.'

'That's ok.'

'The traffic is slow. We'll be fine once we get through here. We've got lots of time. We're doing fine.'

'Should you ring Brian? Tell him where we are.'

'No, he'll know. He'll know what's happening.'

'He's a good man,' I said.

'Yes.'

'Are you happy, you two?'

She shrugged.

'Happier than you were?'

'We settle for things, don't we? We reach a point in our lives where it's easier to settle for what is than to look for something else. That's what kids do, isn't it? Anaesthetise us against the pain of our mistakes.'

I said nothing and Kate mistook my silence for hurt.

'Jesus, sorry. Sorry.'

'It's all right. Don't take every word out and look at it. Be you. The you I'm used to, the you we're all used to.'

She smiled.

'When we get past the army barracks, we'll be ok, it eases off from there.'

The car moved forward, fifteen feet, and then we stopped again. Funereal pace, I thought, but I didn't say so. Between two cars, I caught a glimpse of a traffic light. Red. Then green and we were moving again, pushing clear of the roadworks. Moving as the traffic eased, past the turn for the hospital, down into the main street and into a car park.

'Would you like me to get something for us, bring it back here to the car?'

'No,' I said. 'We'll eat somewhere.'

The thought of sitting in the car, eating a sandwich, balancing coffee on the dashboard, watching the windscreen mist, looking out at the passing schoolgirls in their uniforms, the men hurrying to and from work in the ESB office across the road, was suddenly frightening. All this life, just out there. All this loss, trapped like a bird in a small space.

'There's a really nice coffee shop just down the steps.'

Kate led the way, edging between the tightly parked cars, walking quickly down winding steps into a courtyard. I followed.

'This is it,' she indicated the shopfront.

'"Bad Moon Rising",' I read out loud. 'Creedence. Fantasy Records.'

She smiled and we walked inside and sat at the window.

Kate ordered the food. The shop was quiet.

'We've missed the worst of the rush,' she said.

I nodded.

'It doesn't have to be you, you know.'

'Sorry?'

'You don't have to be the one to identify Jane.'

'No, I know.'

'I could do it.'

'Yes.'

'Just so you don't feel there's any pressure.'

'Thanks.'

'See how you feel when we get there.'

'Yes.'

A woman brought the food.

'Everything all right?' she smiled.

Kate smiled back and nodded.

'Just call me if you need anything else.'

'Thank you.'

The woman moved away again.

.

We ate in silence.

'This is good food.'

'Yes.'

'You ok?'

'I have to identify her,' I said. 'It doesn't matter how I feel or what it's like. I have to. I need to talk to her.'

'Of course. I think that's good. I think you're right. I just wanted you to know.'

I smiled at Kate, a very small smile.

'I'm just feeling my way with all of this,' she said. 'I have no idea if what I'm doing or saying is right or wrong. I'm just trying to get it right. Sorry if I keep repeating myself. Sometimes I'm not even sure whether I've said things to you or just thought them.'

'That's ok. You're doing well. We're both doing well. I'll be fine if I stay numb.'

'Will you?'

'I think so. I'll function.'

'That's probably enough for these days.'

And then we ate again, slowly, while the shop filled and the tables were quietly crowded and newspapers were opened and folded and closed.

'Jane will be in there tomorrow,' I said.

Kate looked at me, not understanding.

'In the paper.'

'Yes,' she said, her eyes damming with tears.

Kate's phone rang. She foostered in her bag while the ring grew louder. A woman at the next table scowled. Kate found the phone but it stopped ringing just before she answered.

'It's Brian,' she said. 'I'd better ring him.'

Kate stepped outside the door. The scowling woman shook her head and returned to her conversation. I ate some more of the food and then Kate came back inside.

.

'Everything's fine. Robert rang just to confirm that everything's in order. And there was a call from the hospital. We can go up whenever we're ready. The detective guy will be there in the next ten minutes. But he told Brian there's no hurry, that he'll wait. That's it.'

'Thanks.'

'Would you like another coffee?'

'No thanks. You?'

She shook her head.

I stood up and walked to the counter. The woman who had brought the food came and took my money.

'I hope everything was all right,' she said.

'It was fine, thank you.'

The cash register rang and she handed me my change.

'Enjoy the rest of your day.'

I had no idea what to expect. But driving along the quiet, tree-lined street on the edge of the town, my head kept filling with the architecture of death. A gleaming white room. A dark and grimy room in the Victorian wing. An isolated block set well away from the main hospital. A quiet, fridge-humming room off a busy corridor. Blisteringly cold steel. White light. Tiled walls and floors. Metal cabinets with drawers that slide quietly in and out, keeping one dead neighbour from the next, the old from the brutally young, the damaged from the simply dead.

The hospital car park was full. Kate trawled for a space, circling and circling till a man waved us to follow him. As he backed out past us, Van Morrison was singing 'Here Comes the Night'.

'Another song we'll never want to hear again,' Kate said, swinging the car into the empty space.

The engine died but neither of us moved. Instead, we sat watching the dry leaves of a chestnut parachute onto the car bonnet, landing softly and then sliding to the grass beneath the bumper.

A man tapped gently on Kate's window. It was the detective I'd spoken to earlier. Kate opened the door and he hunkered down beside her.

'I saw you driving in,' he said. 'I thought I'd come and meet you. Just to take you inside, to make things that bit easier.'

'That's good,' Kate said.

'Simpler,' he corrected himself. 'Not easier. Simpler.'

'Sure.'

'There's no hurry, take your time. Can I get you a coffee from the hospital cafeteria?'

'We've just had some,' Kate said. 'But thanks.'

'I'm really sorry, I don't remember your name,' I said. 'This is Kate, a neighbour and a friend.'

'We met at the house,' he said. 'I'm Larry.'

'Yes, of course, you did. I'd forgotten.'

'I think we should go in,' Kate said. 'I really think we should.'

She took her handbag from the floor. The detective stood up and stepped back, holding the door for her.

'We can just go round here,' he said, as we crossed the car park.

Guiding us past the main entrance of the hospital, he led us down a narrow path between some prefabs.

Was this where they kept the bodies now, I wondered?

I tried to remember where I'd viewed Beth's body but I couldn't. It hadn't been in a prefab, that much I was sure about.

'Just round here and watch the pipe.'

He stepped over a small white pipe that jutted from the wall to our left.

·

116

'How often do you think he comes down this path?' I whispered.

Kate smiled but said nothing.

'And here,' Larry said, turning sharply left and opening a door that took us into a corridor of the hospital.

We followed him, our shoes soft on the quiet lino. Somewhere, at the end of this corridor or another, a tea-trolley rattled its muffled clatter.

Larry stopped and Kate and I stopped behind him.

'This is it,' he said quietly, indicating an unmarked door.

Kate looked at me.

I nodded.

'I just want to say that this is simply an identification. It's not the last time you'll see Jane. I can't begin to imagine how difficult this is for you and it's not too late to change your mind. I'm sure Mrs Lawrence would do this or her husband or someone else. It doesn't have to be you.' Larry smiled a gentle smile.

'It does have to be me.'

He nodded and quickly opened the door, holding it for Kate and me to step through into a small, carpeted room with chairs around the walls. At the other end was another door, with bevelled glass panels, and beyond this, I knew, was Jane.

'I'm just going through, to let them know we're here. Take a seat. I won't be long.'

He slipped through the doorway and Kate and I remained standing in the middle of the waiting room.

'I'm thinking about the night before last,' I said, before Kate got to ask how I was feeling. 'About dropping Jane at the pub. And Elizabeth. Just about that. It seems like it was a hundred years ago. And, at the same time, it seems like I could reach back now, if I wanted, and touch her hair or kiss her face. Like I could tell her to stay in the car and come back home with me. Like I could save her life.'

.

117

Tears were running down Kate's face and I put my arms around her.

'Isn't that an awful thing, to imagine you can undo the worst thing that has ever happened to the person you love most in the world, to believe it's in your power to save your daughter's life and, yet, know that it's not, that it's just imagination, that you can't really do a damn thing? Nothing.'

'Ssshhh,' Kate said but she was talking to herself, trying to still her tears, to regain some composure before we went into the morgue.

Even thinking about that word, *morgue*, without ever saying it aloud made me shiver. It spoke of cold days, bitter days, wet days, sad days. It smelled of chloroform and soap and shit and blood. It sang of disappointment, loss, thievery, betrayal. And then, for no logical reason, I remembered a book I'd had published in my early twenties, my only venture into literature, a slim volume of poetry. I had bought sixty copies from the publisher and put them into grocery shops and chemists and pubs in my hometown, hoping they might sell over the Christmas season. In January, I'd gone back to collect them. Seven had sold. In the last shop, the five copies I'd left with the owner were still on the counter.

'No joy,' she laughed. 'But I read them. They're a bit on the heavy side, hard to understand. Not the kind of thing people want. You should try a comedy book, that's what people want. There's enough sadness in people's lives. Or stick to the architecture business.'

Only outside had I discovered her tottings of a number of bills on the back cover of one of the books.

Kate pulled away from my embrace, snuffling loudly, wiping her nose on her sleeve.

'I'm sorry,' she said. 'I might have been here to identify Elizabeth. That's what I was thinking. Fuck, how could I be thinking that, how could I be so self-centred? I feel like shit for thinking that and I feel like shit for telling you. Sorry, sorry, sorry, sorry.'

'It's all right,' I said. 'I was thinking about a book of mine that someone did sums on, years ago. Isn't that just as bad? Just as absolutely illogical and crazy?'

The glass door opened quietly and Larry filled its frame.

He nodded and we followed, mesmerised it seemed by what lay ahead.

The morgue was a large, well-lit room. Sure enough, a fridge was humming and water was running in a large metal sink. A young woman stood near a trolley on which a sheet had been drawn over a shape that must be my daughter.

'Just here,' Larry gestured.

'Thank you,' I said.

The woman at the trolley came and shook my hand.

'I'm so, so sorry,' she said.

'Thank you.'

'Whenever you want, when you're ready, you can see Jane.'

'I'm ready.'

She turned the sheet back quickly. It was like watching someone turn over an examination paper, wanting to see the worst. And there was Jane, her eyes closed, her skin pale, the summer colour gone from it, as though she had been sick for a long time, as though death was a release, a relief, an escape from something far worse. And then I thought, this is how it should be. Death was a release, a distraction from the whoever and whatever had been done to her.

'I'd expected it to be different,' I said, turning to Larry and the young woman. 'Her face is still … the same. I'd expected something, I don't know, something far worse.'

They nodded.

'I'm sorry but I have to ask you to formally identify Jane. Is this your daughter?'

'Yes,' I said. 'This is my daughter.'

'Thank you,' Larry whispered.

Looking again, I saw that Jane's lips were set in a line, something I had rarely seen before. Her mouth closed, silent, serious. Reminding me.

'Is she all right?' I asked. 'Is her body damaged? I'd like to know.'

The young woman shook her head.

'No,' she said. 'It's not. Just the bruising round her throat.'

'Yes.'

'Would you like to spend some time here, just you and Jane?' Kate's voice came from behind me.

'Yes. I would. Just a few moments.'

The three withdrew quickly into the waiting room. Through the bevelled glass, I could see the outlines of their bodies, Kate and Larry sitting, the young woman standing, waiting to get back to her work, the tending of the dead.

Looking, again, at Jane's face, I willed her to smile but I didn't will her to open her eyes because I knew there'd be no light in them. I'd be looking, instead, into a flat and cloudless sky that had no depth, no hope, no life and I'd know with the terrible certainty of something that is forever, that will not and cannot change, that my girl was gone beyond recall.

Lifting the side of the sheet, I touched her hand. Its frozen wax had nothing of the music she had made. I couldn't imagine how these fingers had pressed the strings of her violin, couldn't fathom how they had ever held a bow or lifted the fiddle from its case. These were useless blocks of crayon, incapable of anything, and that realisation came almost as a relief. These were not the fingers I had watched chasing

.

music, tying back hair, holding biscuits, tapping out e-mails, curling around my own.

Closing my hand around Jane's, I held it tightly, the heat of my palm melting the ice of her skin and I thought of her small hand in mine, holding on for dear life as we walked the path leading down to the Cliffs of Moher; her tentative hand in mine as she left for her first day in secondary school; remembered the casual touch of her hand one night as we were laughing. And then I let go, allowed her arm to slip back onto the trolley, released the inflexible fingers and walked away without looking back.

In the car park, Larry shook our hands and told us he'd see us soon. Kate and I stood in silence after he'd gone, not wanting to leave and not certain why. And then she ran her fingers through my hair and I felt an extraordinary sadness seep through me, so cold and so bitter that I couldn't tell if it was coming from outside or in. All I knew was that I had never felt so alone or so broken, and I understood what it was like to approach the gates of death and have no choice about whether to stay or to continue.

All afternoon, people appeared and disappeared. My mother and Beth's parents, Jane's friends, neighbours discreetly delivering cakes and bread and soup. And, as they came and went, Kate asked me a hundred things without asking anything. The questions came in the form of suggestions and ideas, about the funeral service, about appropriate readings and the offerings that might be brought to the altar to précis Jane's life.

'Her violin,' I said.

'Yes, of course. And perhaps something else?'

'Whatever you suggest, Kate. I'll leave that to you.'

'I'll talk to Alice when she gets here. She'll have something in mind.'

'Yes.'

'And the music. That's something we can talk about with Alice, too. She's bringing four other girls from the class. Did I tell you that?'

'I'm not sure.'

'There'll be a quartet and a singer.'

'That'll be nice.'

'Yes.'

And then someone was standing beside my chair, a woman whose daughter had been in school with Jane. I rose and shook her hand and her mouth opened to say something but no sound came out. She tried a second time and, again, there was nothing but silence. She patted the back of my hand and then I could hear a deep, guttural catch in her throat. She shook her head and we stood, neither one capable of speech. She went on patting my hand, her shoulders rising and falling as she gulped for air.

The back door opened and I saw Larry step in to the kitchen. He saluted me but crossed the room and spoke quietly with Kate. I saw her mouth tighten and then she came and told me I was needed outside.

'Why not get yourself a cup of tea,' I said to the crying woman. 'I'll be back in a moment. I need to talk to the detective.'

She nodded and I followed Kate and Larry into the yard. Outside, the afternoon was sliding into night. The three of us stood in the grey light beyond the kitchen door. As yet the moon had not appeared.

'There's never a right time to tell someone this,' Larry said. 'But I thought you should know, before anyone else does. We've arrested two men and they're being questioned about Jane's death. They'll be charged later tonight. With murder.'

I said nothing.

'Are they local?' Kate asked.

'No, not very local. They're from the north of the county.'

'And you're pretty sure it's them.'

'I can't say too much but we have a witness who saw them in the field where Jane was found. He took the number of their van. I can tell you more when they've been charged. But I thought it best that you know that much now, rather than hearing it on the news or seeing it in the paper or something.'

'Thank you,' I said.

'I'll see you at the church,' Larry said. 'Or you can ring me in the meantime, of course.'

'I'll text you later on,' Kate said. 'With the times for the removal and the mass.'

'Do, please.'

He shook my hand and then shook Kate's hand and then he was gone, walking down the drive, between the parked cars.

'Does that change anything for you?' Kate asked.

'What?'

'The fact that they think they've caught them?'

I shook my head.

'I'm sure it's an important piece of information but it makes no difference. It means Jane's killers have been identified, it doesn't mean she'll be coming home now. It doesn't alter the fact that she's dead.'

'Of course.'

'Not that I don't appreciate what Larry and his colleagues have done and maybe, in time, I'll be glad to look those bastards in the eye. But for now it hasn't registered. It's just another piece of information. Like mass times and coffin designs and the things people say to me. I hear them and I understand them but they don't mean anything. They're just words or figures or shapes. Nothing else, they have no consequence. They're not important to me because I can't feel anything beyond what's inside me. And, even then, all I'm aware of is the lack of feeling. It's like everything is an absence. It's not that I don't care. It's just that I can't care. These things are not important enough to think about.'

Kate nodded.

'Maybe I've said this to you already. I feel I'm repeating myself all the time, I can't remember what I've said or to whom.'

Brian collected Robert and Jenny from the airport that night. It was after ten when they arrived at the house. I saw Robert, another face among the procession of faces that had come and gone all day and it took me a moment to recognise him, to separate his features from those of all the other serious men who had traipsed self-consciously through the house and accept that this was my big brother who had always made things right for me when we were young. And then his arms were around me, bear-hugging me up out of my chair, and over his shoulder I caught a glimpse of Jenny hugging my mother and then my face was buried in the shoulder of his jacket and he was telling me how sorry he was, how much he loved me, how he wished he could think of something that wasn't trite.

'You don't have to say anything,' I whispered. 'You're here. That's all that matters.'

And he hugged me tighter to him and it seemed like I was ten again and it was September and he was leaving for boarding school and suddenly grown-up, telling me he'd see me in a couple of weeks, telling me I could listen to his records but to be sure I put them back in their sleeves.

'Whatever you need from my room, just take it. Don't leave stuff sitting there because I'm not here,' he'd said. 'But put the records back carefully, won't you? And don't drop the stylus on them.'

'I won't.'

'You can bring the record player into your own room if you want. And the records.'

'It's ok.'

'No, do it. That way you can listen to music when you're going to sleep.'

'Are you sure?'

'Course I'm sure. You'll have it for stormy nights.'

On nights when the wind was high, I'd creep, terrified, into his room and he'd turn the music up loud and David Bowie and Rick Wakeman and Elton John would keep the gale at bay. And, in that moment, I thought he might do it again, make everything all right, undo the harm and mend the damage and wake me to a sunlit morning where Daniel was leaving for Spain and nothing remained of the storm but the scattered branches that littered the lawn and a sky that had been cleaned and polished a bright and stainless blue.

I could feel his chest rise and fall. I knew he was crying and I envied him the capacity to give his sadness such expression. All day I had spoken and listened to people who were shedding tears, whose grief was palpable and all I could do was reassure them that I was all right, whatever that meant.

It was after one in the morning before Robert and I had the kitchen to ourselves. And when we did, we sat nursing two cups of coffee, talking about childhood and adolescence and the things we'd done and meant to do. It was the kind of conversation Jane would have loved. She'd have sat there listening, laughing, enjoying the relived victories and empathising with the disappointments of our teenage lives. And Robert and I knew this, we had no need to turn the conversation to Jane, no call to strain after her. We knew, without needing to define or analyse anything, that she'd understand and approve.

Sometime after three that morning, the back door opened quickly and Kate was standing in the kitchen. Ros crossed quietly to her, wagging his tail, sitting to have his head rubbed.

'Sorry to be coming back so late,' she said. 'It took a long time for Elizabeth to get to sleep. I think the whole thing is just hitting her now.'

'Of course,' Robert said. 'It'll take her a long time to come to terms with all of this. That's to be expected.'

'Sit down,' I said. 'I'll make some coffee.'

'You must be wrecked?' Kate asked.

'Who?' Robert and I said together and then we laughed.

'Both of you, either of you. All of you.'

'You've probably been on the go more than any of us,' Robert said. 'The brother tells me you haven't stopped all day. You've been doing everything.'

'Not really. I'm fine. It's the least ...'

Kate looked at me and, in that moment, I was reminded of just how much she loved me and I hoped she knew how much I loved her, even if those loves were stretched like railway tracks that could never meet.

'I stop and think about all this,' Kate said. 'It makes no sense. It seems unreal.'

'It's like she made her mind up,' I said. 'Like she decided she was going and there was nothing any of us could say or do to make her change her mind. That's how it feels to me now. It feels that cold. That final. That inexplicable.'

For that moment, it seemed, we were frozen, each one of us in our own circumstances, the space between us as close and as wide as it would ever be. A man standing by a cooker; a woman standing behind a chair, her hand on a dog's head; another man seated at a kitchen table. Three figures in a well-lit kitchen and, beyond this place, through the window, the light stretching away, across the dark late-autumn garden. But no matter how far it stretched, we each realised it would never light the darkness between the three of us and the young woman we loved in differing ways.

And then the singing kettle disrupted the stillness and we were about our business. I was making coffee, Robert was rinsing cups and Kate was unfolding a sheet of paper on which she had written all the things that day and the following day would bring.

'It's stuff,' she said apologetically. 'But it has to be arranged.'

We'd be driving the twenty miles to the hospital to bring Jane's body back home for one last night. Alice and her friends would be arriving. The music they planned to play at the funeral was listed neatly on the page as were the readings and the names of the people who might read them.

'Would you like to read or speak in the church?' Kate asked.

'I'd like to say something,' I said. 'If I'm able. I feel I am, but I don't know what I'll say, something that does Jane justice. And, if I can't, one of you might?'

Kate and Robert nodded.

I read down the page.

'Elizabeth will be ok for reading?' I asked.

'She wants to,' Kate said. 'If she can't, I will.'

'You should read anyway. Of all people.'

'I will,' she said. 'I'll do one of the Prayers of the Faithful, with your mother and Beth's parents. Robert, I've put you down for the Old Testament reading, is that all right?'

'My vintage,' he smiled.

'And Jenny for the second reading. Will she be ok with that?'

'Of course she will. But there may be others you'd rather have do that, Jane's friends? Jenny won't be upset if she's not asked to read, she's not expecting to be asked.'

'Jane's college friends are playing and singing. The music list is there. There are five of them – a singer, two violinists, a cellist and a pianist.'

'You've done a wonderful job,' Robert said.

'We'll leave here at half ten on Saturday morning. The mass is at eleven and then afterwards … And you want Jane buried, not cremated. Isn't that right?'

'Yes.'

'With Beth, of course.'

'Yes.'

'I didn't say no flowers. I mean, in the newspaper announcement. I thought she'd like flowers.'

'Of course. She'd want flowers, the more the merrier. Yes. You were right.'

'That's it, then. That's everything.'

I poured the coffee and we sat at the table.

'You should get some sleep. We all should. Tomorrow will be a long day. And tomorrow night, we'll be up for the night,' Kate hesitated. 'For the wake.'

'Yes. We should sleep,' Robert said.

We finished our coffee and I walked Kate to her car.

'Thanks,' I said. 'Thanks for everything, all of it. All you've done.'

.

She kissed me. Her mouth was hard against mine. And then she got into her car and drove away, her car lights unlit, and I went back into the house, Ros at my heels.

Robert was drying the cups and setting the table for breakfast.

'It's neither the time nor the place but I'm going to say it anyway,' he said. 'You should marry that woman.'

'Who?'

'Kate. It's so obvious that there's so much between you. A depth that's neither often found nor easily.'

'It's not quite that simple. There's Brian. And Elizabeth and Susan.'

'Unless they're blind, they must see what I see.'

'Sometimes we are blind, Robert, aren't we? We don't see what's coming down the line. And even after the train has hit us, we still don't know what happened. That's just the way of it. In life, in love, in death.'

Folding his arms, he leaned back against the sink and I knew he didn't believe me.

What do I write about the day that followed? It swims like a badly made home movie, in and out of focus. The second journey to the hospital, different from but no easier than the first; the prayers in the mortuary chapel; the cortège with so many cars edging out of the hospital gate and into the vanishing afternoon; crowds of people thronging the dark paths on the edge of town; the slow procession of mourners walking the last half-mile and gathering at the gate of the house.

And then the stream of people, late into the night, young men and women I'd known since childhood, words and silences as they stood in the sitting room, around the open coffin. The sound of crying, the hum of quiet voices, the occasional jingle of laughter as something was remembered – a school outing, the debs dance, a Christmas party.

Alice and the young women who would play in the church asked if I wanted to go over their choices of music.

'You know what she liked, what she'd have enjoyed hearing you play and sing.'

'You're sure?'

'Yes,' I smiled. 'It'll be like a concert, her last concert. It'll be a surprise, for both of us, if that doesn't sound too strange.'

'Sounds just like what she'd have said herself,' Alice smiled.

Much later, when the house was quiet, I stepped into the sitting room and found Ros lying at the foot of Jane's coffin. Looking up, he wagged his tail once, put his head back on his paws and sighed.

At midnight, Kate and Elizabeth arrived and I left them alone with Jane. This was the first time Elizabeth had seen her since they'd parted three nights earlier. After a long time, Kate called me to join them.

'I'm sorry,' Elizabeth sobbed. 'I'm so sorry. I wish Jane was still here, for all of us.'

'I know,' I said.

'I wish there was something I could do.'

'I'd like it if you'd do one of the readings tomorrow. If you feel you can.'

'Yes, of course. I will. But it's not what I meant.'

'I know,' I said. 'But it's all I can think of.'

My mother kept coming in and out of the sitting room, asking if anyone wanted tea, sitting down for two or three minutes and then going out again, only to return in twenty minutes with the same question.

'It'd be good for you, it helps keep the brain awake,' she said. 'I think you'll all be glad of it if you have it.'

'We're fine,' Robert said. 'Honestly. We're fine, Mum. Just sit down, relax. We can get it if we need it.'

'Well, I know when your father died it kept me going through everything. Milky tea with lots of sugar, it keeps the energy up.'

'Maybe in a while,' Jenny said quietly.

'I know Americans are not much given to drinking tea but it's actually better for you than coffee, despite what people say.'

And then she was gone again, cornering some unfortunate in the kitchen, pushing another cup of tea into their hand.

'Jesus,' I said. 'Can she not just leave things be? Anyone who wants tea can go to the kitchen and get tea. Why this constant question about bloody tea?'

'I think it's just her way of dealing with things, with all of this,' Jenny smiled. 'Jane is her only grandchild. That's a huge loss. Maybe we forget that.'

'I understand that but she really needs to consider other people and fit in, not try to run things simply because she thinks that's how they should be run.'

'Let it go,' Kate said. 'Jane would have laughed at it.'

'True. But it's still a bloody pain in the arse to listen to.'

By three o'clock that morning, there were just five of us left sitting with Jane: Robert and Jenny, Kate and Brian and myself. The house was night quiet and we had little to say.

From time to time, one or other of us went and walked in the garden for a few minutes, the rest drawing in the fresh, cool air as the front door opened and closed. Sometime after four, my mother came down from her room and we prayed together and then she went back to bed, if not to sleep.

Just after five, Kate and Brian went home and, shortly afterwards, I must have dozed off. When I woke again, it was half past seven. I felt like Peter, incapable of staying awake with the one I loved most in the world.

'You should have woken me,' I told Robert.

'You were both here, you were both sleeping. There was something appropriate about that. Something peaceful. I think it'd be good if you were to go and have something to eat, have a shower. I suspect there'll be a lot of people here by nine, Jane's college friends, school friends, they'll all want to walk with her to the church, the place could be packed.'

'Ok,' I said, 'I'll just grab some air first. Come on, Ros, let's take a walk.'

The dog wagged his tail once but refused to move.

In the garden, the morning was cold and crisp, the moon low in the western sky, dawn patrolling the edges of the fields to the east. I walked to the top of the drive and stood in the open gateway. I made a wish, not that Jane's death might have been a dream because such wishes are pointless. I wished for the power to feel again, for the numbness to fade, for pain to come into my arms and legs and head and heart. I wished for my lungs to find it impossible to draw in and exhale breath without my chest scraping in agony. I wished for desolation instead of remoteness, I longed for something to give, some part of my soul to break so that I would know that I was human, that I was truly alive. Only by being alive could I comprehend fully what it was like to have a child stolen need-lessly, senselessly, cruelly away.

Two hours later, as we carried Jane's coffin up the drive to the gateway and the open door of the waiting hearse, Ros lay, his head on his paws, in the shelter of a chestnut tree, unmoving, whining softly. I envied him that ability to feel and express the animal sensation for which I longed.

In the church, after the mass with its prayers and music and remembrance, I found myself standing at the lectern, Robert at my side, facing the congregation, suddenly aware that every pew, right to the back of the building, was thronged, that the aisles and porches were crammed and, beyond that, even out into the churchyard, a wash of people stretched into the cold, sunlit day.

I had no clear idea what I was going to say. I had written nothing down. I only knew that I must say something. And so I began.

'I was thinking, sitting here, during mass, about being a parent. About the fact that part of the ineffective parapher-nalia of being an adult is the naïve belief that you can fix anything for your children. I know I believed there was nothing that I couldn't and wouldn't do for Jane. I believed that no matter what went wrong in her life, I could fix it. Even if the world or life or love knocked the breath out of her, I believed I could breathe that spirit and resilience back into her heart and soul and body. I thought, foolishly, that this was what being a father is all about, helping when she needed help, picking up the pieces that were broken and, most of all, keeping bad things away, bad dreams, bad people.

It seemed that simple. But, of course, it isn't. It's much more complicated than that …'

I waited for another phrase to come, something by way of explanation, but I had only a scattering of words left in me.

'I realise this now,' I said, finally. 'And it's the saddest lesson I have ever learned.'

And then I was walking back to my pew, Robert still beside me, his hand on my shoulder, and the string quartet was playing and a voice was singing Stephen Foster's words above the precious, shadowed notes of the cello, a poignant song of deep, deep hope that became a desperate flood of deep, deep regret.

> 'Slumber my darling thy mother is near,
> guarding thy dreams from all terror and fear.
> Sunlight has passed and the twilight has come,
> slumber my darling the night's coming on.
> Sweet pleasures attend thy sleep, fondest, dearest
>   to me.
> While others their revels keep I will watch over
>   thee.
> Slumber my darling, the birds are at rest,
> wandering dews by the flowers are caressed.
> Slumber my darling I'll wrap thee up warm,
> pray that the angels will shield thee from
>   harm.'

And, while the music played and Alice's voice rose and soared through the echoing transept, I felt myself slipping away. Each word of the song was becoming separated from the next, as though isolated in space and time, and yet the whole thing made sense, the sentences had meaning.

I was aware of Robert's arm about me.

'Are you ok?' he whispered. 'Are you feeling weak? You look pale.'

'I must have been,' I stammered. 'I'm all right now. Thanks.'

'You're sure?'

I nodded.

'We can go outside.'

'I'm sure, it's passed.'

I breathed deeply, sat up straight, looked up into the vast, raftered church transept and the music lifted again but now the words were back together and Alice's voice was fighting to stay strong. One of the young women in the quartet put down her fiddle and went and stood with her, singing in harmony, maintaining the calmness.

> 'Slumber my darling till morn's blushing ray
> brings to the world the glad tidings of day,
> fill the dark void with thy dreaming delight.
> Slumber, thy mother will guard thee tonight.
> Thy pillow shall sacred be from the loud world's
> alarms.
> Thou, thou art the world to me in thy innocent
> charms.
> Slumber my darling the birds are at rest,
> wandering dews by the flowers are caressed.
> Slumber my darling I'll wrap thee up warm.
> Pray that the angels will shield thee from harm.'

part

•

three

I CAN DIVIDE THOSE WEEKS after Jane's death into phases.

There was that first morning of being alone again in the house, the first morning of pretending things were the way they used to be. It was twelve days since my daughter's death and no one was preparing food in the kitchen, there was no one on the stairs, no second and third and fourth car in the yard, no one ringing the doorbell and apologising for having forgotten their key, no one rushing to turn the TV off just because I had walked into a room. Nothing. No sounds from downstairs. Everyone had gone.

I lay and listened to Ros sleeping at the foot of my bed. I imagined Jane in her room. We were as we had been for as long as life had been settled. We were a family again and, in a while, when the light hinted in my window, I'd get up and step quietly along the landing, moving past my daughter's door, a man with his dog slipping softly downstairs, moving through an empty room, switching on a kettle in the grey light of the kitchen, watching the pigeons on the early lawn. Moving slowly, lifting a mug lightly from its hook, easing out the spoon drawer so as not to make a racket. Being quiet.

And I was thinking, this is our house and we look out for each other. When the dog barks in the night, it's to alert us. When we talk over the kitchen table, it's to make decisions. When things go well, we celebrate. When things go wrong, we find a way of dealing with them. When we sit together on the couch, we are as one. And, when one of us is snatched brutally away, I pretend for these few minutes that it never happened. I move tranquilly, I act as if my daughter is sleeping in her room, as if she will, eventually, appear at my side, smiling sleepily, telling me I should have woken her, touching the side of my face.

And, for that day, this was enough.

The previous afternoon, driving to the airport, I had asked Robert and Jenny when they thought I should get back to work.

'When you feel you want to open the door to your office,' Jenny had said. 'Work is not a betrayal but it may be a saving grace.'

And so, that night, eleven days after my daughter's murder, I opened my study door and switched on the light. The room spilled out like a badly wrapped parcel, everything appearing suddenly in the electric glare – my chair, my computer, the smell of stale fire-ash, the pictures on the wall, the bookcases, my own reflection in the bay window. And there, on the corner of the desk, two mugs like headstones, left as a reminder, the stagnant coffee gone green inside, like weathered copper.

Turning off the light, I closed the door again. Putting everything off until the following day, I went upstairs and got into bed and masturbated, knowing that if sex didn't bring pleasure it would, at least, bring sleep.

What did I expect from those days when everything was over and yet nothing had changed? Each morning, John the postman rang the bell or the letter box rattled open and fists of envelopes clattered on the hall floor. Mass cards, sympathy cards, letters, notes from people I barely remembered from college, from acquaintances of my parents, from Beth's old school friends, from people I had heard of but never met, from total strangers who put my name and the name of the town on the envelope and trusted their words of sympathy would reach me, even from a few lunatics who told me Jane had got what she deserved and would burn in hell.

I sat at the kitchen table and read them all, morning after morning, the sad words, the attempts at consolation, the efforts to fortify, the wishes for peace, for acceptance, for tolerance, for forgiveness. And, where there were addresses, I wrote back, short thank-you notes. That was my work for those hours.

And Larry stopped by. Asking how much I wanted to know. I shrugged and he talked in generalities because, I imagined, he believed I wanted to know something but not everything, because he wanted to keep me informed without distressing me. He came with information about the charges against the two men who had been arrested, with talk of DNA and the certainty of conviction. And I pretended to listen and nodded and made tea for him and probably said things that made him think I was listening and, after he'd gone, I went back and sat in my study and stared at the two mugs, still balanced on the edge of the desk, the last dregs of coffee now evaporated from them.

In the afternoons, I walked Ros, never taking the same route twice, avoiding the places where we had sheltered on showery mornings, the spots where we had picnicked, the places that were too painful because they were the public places we had made into our own private spaces.

And every day, Kate arrived with food and sat and ate with me or, if she felt it best, left me to my own devices. And every night she rang, *just to say good night*. And sometimes I resented her calling and sometimes I was happy to talk about the mundane things of the day.

And then Larry arrived at the house. Sitting uneasily at the kitchen table, turning and turning his coffee mug, squeezing the handle and talking bullshit. In the end, I came straight out and said it to him.

'You're beating around the bush, Larry. There's something you're not saying. Say it.'

'It's the guy who saw what happened. The guy who was in the field the night Jane was killed. Blackbird, that's what people call him.'

'I know. You told me.'

'He wants to talk to you.'

'Why?'

'I don't know. Well, I know what he told me. He told me he wants to meet "the beautiful woman's" father. That's what he calls Jane, "the beautiful woman".'

'She was.'

'Yes she was.'

'And this man? Blackbird.'

'He's … odd. No point in saying otherwise. Eccentric. But one of these guys who remembers every detail about every car he has ever seen and could tell you what someone was wearing and the colour of their hair, the ideal witness. No distractions or ulterior motives. Just facts. He says he'd like to meet you. That he has things to tell you.'

'Things I want to hear?

'I can't guarantee that. He won't tell me. That's the way he is. If he wants to tell me something, he tells me. If he doesn't, it's a waste of my time asking. I told him I'd talk to you and see how you felt. You don't have to meet him. I said you might not want to. All I promised was that I'd ask. And I'm doing it. No commitments.'

'I'll meet him,' I said.

'You're sure?'

'Yes.'

'You don't have to decide now. You can think it over for a few days.'

'I've decided. When does he want to meet? Can I ring him?'

'Blackbird doesn't have a phone. I'll contact him. What would suit you?'

'Tonight. Tomorrow. Whenever suits him.'

'I doubt his diary is full,' Larry smiled.

'That makes two of us then.'

'What if we say tomorrow. Eleven o'clock?'

'Fine.'

'I'll ring you to confirm that.'

'Where?'

'Can I let him decide?'

'Sure.'

An hour later, the phone rang.

'That's on,' Larry said. 'Eleven o'clock tomorrow morning. He said the path at the back of the old water mill suits him. You know where that is?'

'Yes. Thanks.'

I hardly slept that night. All the wondering about what to say and what I'd hear, what this man would be like and what he'd seen? How much? And how much he'd want to tell me? In some bizarre way, it felt like going on a first date, that same mixture of anticipation and fear. Wanting it to be worthwhile and, at the same time, knowing it might be a lot easier just to walk away from it all. And yet this man had some information about my daughter. He knew things about her that I didn't. He wanted to talk about her, so who was I to refuse?

I drove out to the mill and left the car on the roadside. It was a cold, bright morning with a blue sky above the falling leaves. The mill was down a lane and across a stone bridge. A path ran along from the back wall, curling its way onto the riverbank and following the waterline between the autumn fields.

A man was sitting on a windowsill of the derelict building. I had no idea whether this was the person I was due to meet. He nodded and I nodded but he said nothing. I walked slowly past him and stood on the bank, watching the river flow, following a broken branch as it turned in the twisting eddies. And then the man was standing at my shoulder, both of us staring out over the breadth of the rushing water, neither one looking at the other.

'You're the father of the beautiful woman,' the man said slowly.

'Yes.'

'I seen you at the funeral. I was at the funeral but there was a horrid lot of people there and you wouldn't know one off the other.'

'No.'

'The detective fellow said you'd be here.'

'Larry.'

'Him.'

'He said you wanted to talk to me.'

'Yeah.'

'Here I am.'

'I was in the field,' Blackbird said. 'I seen the beautiful woman there.'

'Yes.'

'They drove the van down the headland. It was a white Ford van. I was sitting on the low gate. The field was full of round bales, scattered hither and yon, and they had to weave in and out around a few of them. The bales were there two or three weeks at that stage, still waiting to be took in to the sheds. There was a clear sky and they had the lights on. I think they were afraid of getting stuck in the low part, if it was soft. They drove slow. I said to myself, "What's a van doing down the fields at this hour?" A tractor is one thing, a van is another.'

I nodded.

'There was two of them and they stopped at the butt end of the field and got out and went around and opened the slidey door on the side of the van and lifted something out and left it on the ground and then they closed up the door again and the lad that was driving got in and turned the van and the other lad looked around and then he got in and they drove off and at the top of the field they turned off the lights, just when they were driving out onto the road.'

'You saw the number of the van.'

'I did.'

He repeated a registration number to me.

'Thank you,' I said.

'When they were gone, I walked over to where they were after leaving whatever it was they took out and when I got there, I seen it was the beautiful woman they were after leaving lying on the ground. She was that pale.'

Blackbird indicated a tattered plastic bag caught on a willow on the riverbank.

'And she was getting cold. I touched the back of her hand. The warmth was going out of her. Then I seen her face. And I knew what was after happening and I sat down with her and talked to her. I done the same with my own father and him going. It takes people a while to go. You wouldn't like to think of someone going away by theirself.'

'What did you say to her?' I asked.

Blackbird was silent.

'You don't have to tell me if you don't want to,' I said finally.

'I said to her, "You're a beautiful woman. They had no right to do what they done but you won't be left on your own. I'll see to that." That's what I said to her. That was the right thing to say to her.'

'It was.'

'I picked daisies and put them there' – Blackbird pointed to his eyes – 'I think she didn't want to be looking out at the sky, not when she was that lonesome.'

'No.'

'I stayed with her until she was gone fierce cold. I wanted you to know that. Then there was a strange sound, like a lamb bleating. Like it was coming out of the ground somewhere under her. I thought it was the Lamb of God and then it dawned on me that it was her phone ringing in her pocket and so I waited. And then it stopped bleating. The silence was like no other silence. Then I went off and got me bike and went and told the guards. That's what I wanted to tell you.'

'And Jane didn't say anything?'

'Nothing. I listened real hard.'

'Is there anything else you wanted to tell me?'

'No. That's the all of it.'

Again we were silent, two men looking out across a river. We might have been waiting for a fish to jump or a boat to pass or a heron to rise out of the high grass along the banks. This might have been a morning in early spring with the summer laid out before us, just beyond the fields on the opposite bank. We might have been passing the time of day, Blackbird going about his business, me going about mine. Jane in college, everything well with the world. But the spring and summer were gone and, instead, winter was just beyond the river, hiding behind this sunny day.

'Can I give you lift back into town?' I asked, at last.

'I have me bike, beyond behind the galvanised sheets.'

'I could put the bike in the boot of the car, save you the journey.'

'I don't like cars.'

'Fair enough. Would you like to meet me in town for lunch or a cup of tea or something?'

'I don't go into them places.'

'Right.'

·

146

'I just wanted to tell you what I told you. So you'd know she was all right.'

'I appreciate that.'

Blackbird turned and started walking towards the galvanised sheets that were propped near the mill wall.

'Can I give you the price of a drink?'

He waved his hand dismissively. 'This wasn't about any of that,' he said over his shoulder, and I felt stupid for having asked.

He wheeled his bike from behind the sheeting and I watched him freewheel down the path, one foot on the pedal, without throwing his leg across the bar. And then he dismounted, lifted the bike through a gap in the hedge and cycled away across a field.

'So what was he like?' Kate asked.

'Ordinary. Eccentric but ordinary.'

'Would I know him to see around the town?'

'I doubt it. I didn't.'

'You wouldn't. You don't notice people much.'

'Don't I?'

'No, you don't. Not in that way. Not in the way I would. You don't tend to be interested in people in that way. I don't mean you don't care. I'll bet you can't tell me what this man was wearing.'

'A jacket, jumper and trousers.'

'What colour trousers? What colour jumper? What colour shoes? You don't know, do you?'

I shook my head.

Kate laughed and poured some coffee.

'It doesn't matter. How did you feel about meeting him?'

'Nervous beforehand and then afterwards, when I got home, a sense of, I don't know, anticlimax. I'm not sure what I expected from all of this. Maybe I thought he was going to tell me something that would change things, give me something new that made life easier. I think I was expecting something miraculous.'

'We all live in hope of that, don't we?'

'Do we?'

'I think so. I think everyone hopes for better things around the corner, mostly in little ways. The smaller miracles are the only ones that happen, of course. If they happen at all.'

'Yes.'

'Did talking to this guy help in any way or are you sorry you met him?'

'Not sorry, no. Just disappointed, I suppose, and I don't know why, there's no logic in that.'

'We're not living in a time of logic,' Kate said and then she frowned. 'Jesus that sounds pretentious.'

'That's because it is pretentious,' I laughed.

'Thank you for being so considerate of my feelings.'

And then we sat in silence, one of those easy silences that I associate with Kate's company. This was something I hadn't done since early summer, sat across the table from Kate and listened to the songs of the birds outside, the cackling of geese from over the fields, the rumble of cars passing on the distant road, all the echoes of daily life going on as usual beyond this house and this garden.

'I tried getting back to work,' I said.

'And?'

'Something depressing about going into the study. There were still two mugs on the desk from when Jane was last there with me. And it was night-time. Wrong time to try to begin, I suppose.'

'Would you like me to take the mugs out, open the windows, air the place?'

'Am I making it sound like it's beyond me?'

'No, but sometimes it's easier for someone else.'

'I'd appreciate it. Thank you.'

'Why don't you take Ros out for a walk? I'll have it done when you come back. That would be easier. For both of us.'

On the lane to the woods, a crow was barking, high up in a fir tree, its caw coming out short and sharp and harsh. It sounded angry, snarling at the world below and around, chastising everything for something that had or hadn't happened.

Farther along, where the trees were younger, on the edge of the woodland, a red squirrel followed me, skimming from branch to branch and tree to tree, just fifteen feet from where I was walking, taking a parallel route to my own. The dog nosed ahead, impervious to the company we were keeping.

I stopped for a moment, watching the squirrel race, seeing it dip and leap from branch to branch. I saw it hesitate to listen, to explore the possibilities of one tree or another. Suddenly, it disappeared between the rusted leaves, scuttling up a sycamore trunk. Leaving a wake of movement and falling leaves. And then it was gone. Only the wind-blown foliage and the wiry winter branches remained. The lane sank into stillness, again. A man standing motionless on a rutted track, a dog nosing in a gateway, branches easing back into immobility and a blue and empty sky above it all, nothing to show that anything had ever been different, nothing to remind that an instant before a wild animal had been careening through this place.

In the moment after its disappearance, nothing remained in this landscape to mark its existence. There was only memory and even that depended on those who had witnessed the animal's journey. If I hadn't seen the squirrel racing along beside the lane, the event would have gone unrecorded and once it slipped from my memory, or this memory went beyond recollection, the moment would be gone. And so it was with us. Our existence, beyond the experience, depended on the memories of others. And that made me smile because I knew Jane would be remembered by so many people – her grandparents, her friends, her aunt and uncle, me, Kate, Blackbird. Even the men who had killed her would never, I believed, forget what they had done or to whom. All of these memories would weave together to form the concept we describe and understand as a life.

From now on, I would be known more for my relationship to Jane than I would for my own life. I would be the father of the murdered girl, the father of the beautiful woman, that unfortunate man who lost his daughter. Jane's memory would spread out into the lives of so many people and when I talked with Kate that memory would be, for the most part, drawn from our separate and shared recollections of the girl we both loved. When Larry and I talked, it would be because of Jane. If and when I ever saw Blackbird again, I'd be seeing the man who had found my daughter, the man who had put flowers on her eyes to stop her from noticing the coldness of the moon, and there was consolation of a kind in knowing that.

And then, for no specific reason, I thought of Alice and her friends who had sung at Jane's funeral mass and I wondered where they had stayed. Had they paid for their own accommodation? I hadn't asked, had forgotten to offer them any money for playing and singing. I had hardly thanked them, beyond a few words in the cemetery and a few in the house. That was something that needed to be seen to.

Kate was at the sink and I knew, by the way she didn't turn around when I came in, by the way she didn't bend to rub Ros, that she had been crying.

'Are you all right?'

She nodded.

'What is it?'

'Just that I dropped the fucking mugs and broke them, on the way out of the study. They slipped from my hand and smashed on the floor.'

'They're just mugs,' I said.

'Yes but they were there because you had left them there, because Jane had left hers there.'

'And now they're gone and I'm glad.'

I walked into the study, the windows were open, the fire had been cleaned and set, things had been tidied, there were flowers in a vase on the desk, flowers that Kate had gone into town to buy.

'You shouldn't have cleaned out the fire,' I said, coming back into the kitchen. 'That was more than you needed to do. And the flowers!'

Kate was silent, still standing at the sink, her back to me, shoulders hunched.

'Thank you,' I said.

'You're welcome,' she whispered.

'As long as we're remembered, our lives are worthwhile. Our memory continues on.'

'Yes.'

'A lot of people will remember.'

'Of course they will.'

I put my arms around her and hugged her and told her about the squirrel.

'And I need to ring Alice, about the music,' I added. 'About paying her and the others. It completely slipped my mind.'

'I spoke to her. They wouldn't hear of taking anything.'

'But they travelled down and stayed overnight somewhere.'

'That's all been looked after.'

'By whom?'

'It's been done.'

'By you?'

'It's been done.'

'You can't just look after five people's accommodation and travel like that.'

'Why not?'

'Because it's my responsibility.'

'I'm not talking about this any more.'

'Where did the girls stay?'

'The Ritz! It's none of your business. And now I have to go. Susan will be getting in from school. I put some lasagne in the oven. Don't let it burn.'

She was gone, swinging out the door and then she was back, peering into the kitchen.

'And eat the lasagne. That's why I made it. Ok?'

'Ok.'

As I look back on it, the fortnight after Jane's death seems to have been a film that ran on and on, with garbled sound, one scene hurrying into another. Knocks on the door, bad news, practicalities, people – always people – about the place, those same people leaving, silence, other practicalities with which I couldn't deal, conversations, walks, further conversations, the knowledge that I wanted to get back to work – if only to keep myself on some track – but couldn't. And then, for no obvious reason, the film ran out, and my life suddenly became a series of photographs, each distinct from the next, each an occasion that seemed isolated from everything else that was happening in my world and from the world outside.

The numbness was no less, the threat of pain no smaller, but things changed and, instead of crossing an interminable pontoon bridge, I was in a small boat in the middle of a very wide river and each time the boat turned, I saw something and thought this might be the thing that was important and then the boat would swing again and something else came into view, and that seemed equally important.

I was walking the woods with Ros, up across the back of the hill that opened onto huge fields of newly ploughed earth when I caught the smell of a dead animal in the undergrowth, rotting tissue, skin and sinew breaking down. And I thought, immediately but unexpectedly, of Jane, how she might have been hidden in undergrowth, how her body might have been left for wild animals to scavenge on, how her flesh might have broken down into paste and trickled back into the earth, leaving only bones and hair and tattered clothes and how, in time, when the scent of death had cleared, they too might have broken down, been scattered by prowling animals, hidden in thickets, gnawed by creatures in search of winter sustenance. So I hurried away, leaving the dead to bury the dead.

I was driving home with the groceries, my mind on nothing more than the road ahead when, out of nowhere, I remembered Jane in tears. She was a teenager, probably fifteen, and something had gone wrong in school, some squabble with a friend. That evening, at dinner, she had burst into tears at the table, sobbing uncontrollably, unable to speak or explain what was going on. That was the only time I could ever

.

remember her crying and here it was, this reminiscence ghosting in from nowhere. And I felt unbearably sad, at the memory and at the fact that there had been nothing I could say or do then to make things better for her. And sadder still at the realisation that there never would be anything I could do about any of the troubles in her life. Everything was beyond resolution.

It was as if this was the first time I'd come face to face with that fact, as if – in recognising it – I was admitting that Jane was truly dead. But, of course, it was more than that, deeper. It had as much to do with my inability to undo or, at least, to come to an understanding of, the things that had never been finally resolved between us, good and bad.

Not that there were lists of unresolved issues, no yawning void left in the wake of my daughter's death. But the fact that anything I might say from here on would go unanswered was a bleak and frightening prospect. It reminded me of just how isolated I was and would be. This wasn't something that could be resolved by lifting a phone or writing an e-mail. This was a question to which there were a thousand possible answers but the veracity of none was verifiable.

Passing Jane's bedroom, I saw a form on her bed, the autumn sun spilling in from the early morning window. It was Ros. I realised I hadn't touched the bed, had left the sheets unchanged in the three weeks since her death. Was this where the dog slept when I wasn't about, was this where he came in the dark of night, padding away from my bedside when he knew I was asleep? Was he waiting or accepting what could not be changed? Did he have a sense of something that was beyond me?

Another morning, a day or two later, I was out walking as the sun was coming up. I scuffed my foot on the wintry road and a pheasant lifted from its hiding place, clattering into the air, its wings clacking hard to buoy it above the ditch.

By the time I got back home, the sun was fully up, streaming into the house, lighting my study with a lemon glow. Taking some drawings from my desk I laid them out on my worktable, the first time I'd looked at them in almost a month.

They were for a small office building in a town about thirty miles away. I had reached a point where almost everything was in place but now I had an idea. I wanted this building to reflect something of what was going on in my head and heart. I wanted this building, in some way, to be a reminder to me of Jane. No one else would or need ever know, but I'd know. I'd be aware of how personal this work was. It was a way of getting my mind focused.

And then I went to the cabinet where I kept photographs and sketches, clippings from newspapers, doodles, bits and pieces that I might someday use. In the bottom drawer, there was a pack of photographs of Jane, some colour, some black and white. Leafing through them, I found the one I was looking for and propped it on the worktable. And then I started drawing, sketching, letting my hand do the thinking, working on something that I could refine in time.

I worked for hours, drafting, redrawing, balling drafts into the wastepaper basket, looking from sketch to plan to photograph. Trying to find a way in which to fit my idea into the blueprint. I worked hard, discovering now and then that the sun had moved around the house, looking up to find the shadows had moved from one side of the room to another. And all the time, the sketches were changing, a dip here, a sweep there, a curve that suddenly reflected what it was that I wanted to achieve.

·

I was back working on the plan and the light was sinking, the afternoon drawing on towards an early dusk. Flicking on the table lamps, bending low above the desk, watching the curves reproduced on a draft design, standing back to compare, satisfied that I had done what I set out to do.

And then I was lifting the phone, calling the client.

'I have those drawings for you,' I said.

'There was no rush, honestly. I told you that, what with everything that's happened. We could have waited. It's just a building.'

'I know. Thank you. But I have them done.'

'Great. And how are you?'

'Back working. Day by day, you know.'

'Yes. Of course.'

'So I'll send them to you, tomorrow.'

'Great. I look forward to seeing them.'

'I've made some changes, to the front. See what you think. I really like the changes. It'll be a signature building.'

'Sounds very exciting. I'll give you a call when I've had a chance to look over them.'

'Thank you.'

'And take it easy. Don't push yourself too hard. We can wait. Everyone can.'

'Yes. Thanks.'

I put the phone down and looked from photograph to plan and back.

A photograph of Jane's shoulder, taken from behind, with a blue sea and a blue sky. Taken in Greece the summer before last, the arc of her golden skin, dipping and rising and dipping again where her arm fell away. Her tanned flesh against the cobalt of the world beyond, a sweep of bronze, strong, assured and tantalising. And there, on the plans, that same sweep of lines, part glass to catch the blue of sky, part metal to recreate this photographic image. Most of all, this was a plan that would represent, for as long as the building stood, that moment in my daughter's life and I would know.

It never crossed my mind that the client might not want it or that the plan might be rejected when it was submitted. I had no doubts but that what I had designed was practical and beautiful and that others would see the beauty in it, without ever knowing the inspiration.

And then I put the photograph away, turned off the lights and went to make myself some dinner.

Larry arrived at the door one morning. I invited him in. We drank coffee together. He gave me back Jane's phone.

'We have to keep the rest, clothes and so on, until after the trial. But I thought you might like to have this in the meantime. There are photos and things on it – we had to go through it, just to check.'

I told him about Blackbird and the way the phone ringing had perplexed him the night he found Jane.

'It happens,' Larry said. 'I've had it happen when I've been keeping an eye on a body, waiting for the pathologist before we move it. You're sitting there on your own, beside someone who's dead, and the phone starts ringing and you can't answer it and you know it could be that person's parents or partner or someone trying to find out what's keeping them or where they are or what's happened. It's a very strange sensation.'

Most nights I read myself to sleep and I often woke still propped against the pillows, a book fallen onto my lap. Sometimes it was the rising of the sun that woke me but, more often, it was something else. Some stirring inside myself, an unease reminding me that sleep was simply a necessity and, when it became all-consuming, it would presage the arrival of the eloquent presence of death.

One night, at the end of October, I woke in the deep darkness of the small hours and knew immediately that I wouldn't sleep again, not that night. There had been other nights like this when I had come, suddenly, awake, aware immediately of the thundering of my heart. And always I had listened for some other sound, something out of the ordinary that might have woken me, but all I ever heard was the breathing of Ros at the foot of the bed or, if he had gone to sleep on Jane's bed, the absolute silence of aloneness.

This night, it was a Friday night into Saturday morning, I got up and pulled on my jeans and a T-shirt and went down to the kitchen to make some tea. While the kettle rattled and clattered, I flicked on the radio. Leonard Cohen was singing, his voice almost conversational, talking for me, telling me, promising, regretting – all at once.

> … they hide, they hide in the world.
> I look for her always,
> I'm lost in this calling,
> I'm tied to the threads of some prayer.
> Saying, When will she summon me?
> When will she come to me?
> What must I do to prepare?
> When she bends to my longing,
> like a willow, like a fountain,
> she stands in the luminous air.
> And the night comes on
> and it's very calm.

I lie in her arms and she says: When I'm gone
I'll be yours, yours for a song.

As he sang, I could feel my head begin to lighten. For an instant, I thought I was going to be sick, nausea rising in me, up from my stomach and into my throat. Grabbing the edge of the sink, I held on tightly, my fingers clenched, a vice along the metal lip. As the nausea subsided, I could feel my energy drain with it and my T-shirt was soaked suddenly in perspiration. I believed I was going to pass out. And the voice was there, still singing, still catching my attention, speaking me a truth that was intended just for me.

'… but she says go back, go back to the world.'

I wanted to cry, as a way of acknowledging this sudden and desperate sense of isolation, but I couldn't. And then the room was swimming, the electric light becoming suddenly brighter than I had never seen before, radiating a burning heat. The air was swirling in surges of yellows and reds and violet blues, sweeping over, past and then through my body, catching me in a lightning storm from which I suspected there might be no escape, sucking me towards unconsciousness.

My knees began to fold and I held even tighter to the sink, wanting to plunge my face into cold water but unable, even, to turn the tap. And still the colours went shooting, back and forth across the room, dancing in a welter of intensity.

Something was trying to burn everything away, not some malevolent external force but some frantic, reckless sadness that had been massing in my heart for weeks, something deeper than loss and much more bitter. I believed that if I stayed in that room I would die, my body would collapse, my head would shatter, my brain would dissolve, everything would be lost – memory, possibility, even that knowledge of loss that, seemingly, was all I could be sure of now. I'd be left with nothing and I'd have nowhere to go in search of recollection. I'd be sentenced to the hell of not knowing, not remembering, being without the possibility of any connection, ever again, with Jane.

Unlocking the back door, I ran from the house, staggering out into the darkness, across the empty garden, falling onto the damp, black grass, shrieking out some creature noise that said nothing intelligible and yet screamed of hurt and despondency and oblivion and the bitter, brutal awfulness of loss and desolation.

Lying there, mouth gaping, aware of the sounds I was making, watching, through the kitchen window, the commonplace glimmer of the ordinary electric light bulb. I could see clearly now that there were no colours, no churning, no spinning, pulsing rainbows, nothing of that kind. Only the passion inside me remained and the only way I could release all this passion was by giving vent through sound. Horses might have been stampeding from my mouth, hooves thundering in the guttural consonants that were as senseless as everything that had happened. But the sounds were coming. I could feel them leave my throat and launch from my lips, I could hear them in the black garden.

Then Ros's tongue was cold against my face. He must have heard my wails and followed me into the garden. A moment later, there were footsteps on the gravel and Kate's voice above me.

'Are you all right?'

'I wanted to cry,' I said.

'What?'

'I wanted to cry but there was nothing.'

She knelt beside me on the dew-punctured grass.

'It's ok. Just take it easy. When you feel able, we'll go inside. All right?'

'Yes.'

She helped me to my feet and Ros walked ahead of us, into the bright, quiet kitchen where everything was as it should be. No swirling lights, no shooting bolts of colour, nothing untoward.

'Sit down,' Kate said. 'I'll make some tea.'

Ros lay at my feet, his eyes meeting mine, unblinking.

'What happened?' she asked.

I told her. About waking and coming down and hearing the song on the radio and feeling unbearably alone and feeling unwell and the sensation of the burning colours and shooting lights and of running into the damp, dark garden.

'You're stressed out,' she said.

'Maybe, but the strange thing is that I feel a lot more relaxed now. Tired but cleansed. Like I've let something out and it's gone. A lot of the frustration, the uncertainty, all that stuff. It's as if it went away with the sounds, as if I screamed it out of my system.'

'Perhaps you did. But you still need to take it easy, get away, talk to someone.'

'I wasn't actually seeing things, Kate. It's not a vision or hallucination, not some kind of supernatural experience. It was in my head. It needed to get out. It needed some way of expressing itself, that's all. Nothing more, nothing sinister, I'm not going mad or anything.'

'I know that.'

'No, you don't. You think it best to humour me. But I know what I'm feeling and I know why this happened. It's not because of some imaginary ghost. It was about me and getting something out of my system. Literally.'

Kate was back at lunch-time, arriving with scones and soup, moving quietly around the kitchen while I finished some work in the study.

We sat at the table. Outside, the day was bright and cold, the birch trees picking up the freezing sunlight and softening it, sheaves of bark curling in reds and pinks as the sun moved across the low sky.

'So, you're all right?' Kate asked.

'Yes, I'm fine. Honestly.'

'Good.'

'Like I said, it was about me, about what was in my head. Nothing else.'

She nodded.

'There's something I want to ask you, something I've been thinking about all morning,' I said.

'Yes.'

'Last night, when I was in the garden, you arrived out of the blue.'

'Yes.'

'It was the middle of the night. Where did you come from?'

Kate avoided my eyes.

'It's a serious question. Where did you come from?'

'I was at the gate.'

'What do you mean?'

'I was sitting at the gate, in the car. That's how I heard you – in the garden. Your voice.'

'You were sitting at the gate?'

'Yes.'

'Why?'

'I just was.'

'In all the years I've known you, Kate, I've never seen you *just* being anywhere.'

'Sometimes I come down and sit in the car, at the gate, just to make sure you're ok.'

'What do you mean *sometimes*?'

'At night. Just to check that everything is all right.'

'That I haven't set fire to the place or hanged myself from the front door, stuff like that?'

She smiled a wan smile but I could see that she was uneasy.

'And you just happened to be there last night, in the depths of the night?'

'Yes.'

'How long had you been there?'

'This is beginning to feel like an inquisition,' Kate said.

'I just want to know.'

'A while.'

'A while?'

'All right,' Kate said quickly. 'A few hours. I come down some nights and sit in the car at the gate, just to make sure, just to put my own mind at rest. When Brian is asleep. Sometimes I drive down and park out there and keep an eye on this place, on you, because I worry about you, I'm concerned about you, about what you're going through. And one night, I fell asleep in the car and it was almost dawn before I woke up, so I've taken to setting the alarm on my mobile. If I had my way, I'd be in here at night, making sure everything was right with you. And now you're thinking I'm stone fucking mad, aren't you? You think I've lost it. You think I'm the one you should be worrying about.'

'No,' I said. 'I don't. I'm touched by what you've done. You should have said – I mean if you wanted to sit here at night.'

Kate laughed a dry laugh.

'I'm sure the last thing you'd want is someone coming and going here at night. You need your own time and your

163

place to yourself. You don't need some lunatic drifting in and out of the house in the small hours. And neither does Ros.'

She rubbed the dog's head and he wagged his tail noisily on the wooden floor.

'I won't describe you as a lunatic,' I said. 'If you stop thinking of me as one.'

'I don't but I was worried. It's been a month. I keep waiting to see some crack in the façade.'

'Meaning?'

'Meaning that since Jane died, you've been going through things but you haven't allowed yourself to be angry or bitter or anything, not on the outside anyway. It's all going on inside you. You need to let it out. You need to be angry.'

'Anger isn't what I'm feeling.'

'Well it should be.'

'Perhaps it should, but it isn't. And you can't worry yourself about that, honestly.'

'Well I'm angry. I want to kill those bastards. I want to rip them limb from limb and see them burn in hell. I want to take their eyes out on the end of a hot poker. Literally. And I want you to feel that way too. I want you to hate them as much as I do. They took your daughter, they killed her, and, if they'd had the chance, they'd probably have taken my daughter and killed her too. You can't just drift around in a haze, you need to get that out. You need to say what I'm saying, feel the way I'm feeling.'

'I'm not you, Kate.'

'I know you're not me. But you're Jane's father. Keeping all this inside is dangerous. Don't you see that? It's not natural. You should be boiling with anger. Instead, there's this awful, dark, desperate nothingness around you. It's not good. It worries me.'

'I have a kind of peace here,' I said. 'I don't know how long that will last. I have no doubt the anger will come. But, for now, I have this feeing of still having something of Jane's personality around the place. And I want to keep it for as long as I can.'

'Of course you do,' Kate said, and her tone had changed to one of calmness. 'And you're right, I have no place telling you how you should feel. Of course, you're right. But the reason I sit in the car at night is because I feel there's all this stuff that must be inside your heart and it has to come out in some way. The quietness and the composure worry me, they seem like a mask for something much darker. Last night was almost a relief.'

'As it was for me.'

'And, anyway, I want to be near you. I often feel the need for that, especially at night. But that's not something new, is it?'

'No.'

'And it's not something you need to worry about.'

'It doesn't worry me, Kate. I only wish I could reciprocate but, at the moment, I can't.'

'I shouldn't even have mentioned it, but it's confession time, isn't it?' she smiled.

'I suppose it is. The thing is, when the anger comes, and I know it will come, I have no idea how I'll react or what it'll do to me. It may well destroy me.'

A morning, early the following week, a heavy frost had settled through the night and the hedges were like whitethorns in spring. I was walking the narrow lane that runs along the edge of the bog, in the overhang of the willows and silver birch that belt the peatland from the farmland beyond. The sky above me was blue and cold. Suddenly, rounding a bend, I was aware of the sound of falling rain from the grove of trees to my left.

The road was dry, the sky clear and yet I could plainly hear the *pit*, *pit* of water showering in one particular place. I stopped to listen. Ros went on nosing in the stiff grass, following whatever it is that dogs follow when they become obsessed with scents we can't fathom. And still it continued, water falling through branches.

Stepping off the lane, I moved through the trees, following the sound, weaving my way between and under the lanced and wintry branches, closer to the sound of the falling rain. Then the sun was beaming down, through a break in the trees, lighting a clearing of moss and fallen leaves. And the sodden upper branches were melting and dripping like showered rain onto the frozen branches below, the noise of water tumbling onto wood and leaves and fallen leaf mould was all around me, a brilliant singing, shining waterfall in the shelter of this band of tall, unmoving trees. I stood in the centre of the clearing, water surging all around me and I wanted, more than anything, to share all this with Jane, to bring her to this glade the following morning or the next frosty, sunlit morning so that she, too, could experience the wonder of the place, the time, nature's baptism of a sleeping forest.

And I knew, now that winter was imminent, the summer streams would make themselves known, the leaves stripping away to uncover broken mirrors, glimpsed in unexpected corners of the wood. And days like this, or other days when the bulky trunks of growing trees suddenly recognised the sun, even the winter sun, bringing to them the long-forgotten wonders of a blue sky, would come and go, while I'd still want to share them with someone who was lost forever.

The first day of November was a Thursday. A deep, dull day and then the sky cleared late in the afternoon and the night came down under the remnants of a shrinking moon and I sat watching it from the study window, the lamps unlit. Watched it rise and hang above the garden as though it would never move again, as though the world was frozen in this moment.

Eventually, I turned on the lights and went and made some dinner, read the paper as I ate my meal, washed up, read and answered my e-mails, did the things that people do when their lives are ordinary or when things so awful have happened that they long for ordinariness.

Midnight found me back, sitting in the darkened study, watching the moon, which had, somehow, moved across the sky while all of these things were happening. Now it was the second day of November, All Souls' Day. I had waited thirty-eight days. Now it was time.

Pulling on my coat and scarf, I whistled Ros from his sleep and we set off walking. Down the avenue and through the gateway, left along the empty road that was taking its shape in the half-light of the pared-back moon. I walked fast, Ros trotting beside me, crossing the roadway to climb a gate that was closed and padlocked now, a gesture from the farmer.

Ros struggled between the lowest bar and the ground, flattening himself, wriggling through and taking his full shape again on the other side. The field opened out before us, the field in which my daughter's body had been found. Acres of stubbled earth folding away in the grey light, wisps of mist lying close to the ground, like knots of rotting corn. Ros skirted along the headland, snuffling for rabbits. I hesitated, unsure whether to follow him or to cut straight across the field and over the brow and into the dip to the lower level. I realised I had no idea where I should go. All I knew, from my conversation with Blackbird, was that Jane had been left at the low end of the field, away from the road. Close enough to the lower gate that opened into another field for him to see but far enough away from it for him not to be seen. I knew where the lower gate was, diagonally across the field and well out of sight of the road, and so I set off in that direction. Ros continued along the headland, snuffling and snorting. When he realised I hadn't followed, he came galloping across the open ground, circling me, jumping and racing.

The roadway was a hundred yards behind us now, the field sloping gently down and away. In another fifty yards, it would fall quite suddenly onto the lower level, melting into the ditches that separated it from the next field and the next.

Would I know? Would some instinct draw me to the place I had avoided for the past six weeks? Or would I find myself wandering aimlessly, frustrated by my own lack of urgency in coming here? Would I, eventually, have to ring Larry or find Blackbird and ask them to show me where my daughter's body had lain through that long night?

Ros had calmed down by then, walking at my heel, his running and racing done. We breasted the brow of the slope and my eyes scanned the lower end of the field and, as they did, I froze. Sixty yards from me, in the angle between two ditches, thirty feet from the headland, a dark form lay on the stubble, huddled rather than stretched. I waited for it to move, waited for the figure to rise from the ground, but it didn't. Whoever this was, man or woman, they lay unmoving. Ros stood at my side, ears pricked, growling in the low, slow way he did when he was truly alarmed.

'Easy,' I said quietly.

He looked up and then away again, waiting for another word.

What was I to do? Walk away from a figure that might need my help? Turn my back on someone because their stillness frightened me? Yet this was a nightmare. I was in the very field in which my daughter had died and now it appeared I had found another body.

The dog eased forward a couple of yards, stopped to check that I was still there and eased forward again. Then, suddenly, he seemed to lose interest and he was off, loping easily across the field, down by the prone shape, not even stopping to investigate, on he went, to the lower headland, to the ditch, pushing through the brambles in search of something else.

I followed, still cautious, and then I saw what I should have seen from the brow of the hill. The form on the ground was a mass of rotting wreaths and flowers, their plastic wrappers flattened and discoloured, the cards that had carried messages faded and bleached by weeks of rain and autumn sunlight. This was the remnant of a shrine to my daughter, this was the place where her body had been left.

Standing there, I remembered what Kate had said, about the importance of anger, but, still, I felt none. I had no urge to imagine which stalks had bent or broken under her dead weight. I didn't visualise Blackbird kneeling by her nor Larry and his colleagues searching around her nor undertakers lifting her into the open mouth of a hearse. None of this was of any concern. Whether it was fate or accident or intention that had brought her body to this place was of no consequence. I had seen the place and I might or might not ever walk this field again but, either way, I had no sense of any element of Jane, body or soul, remaining in the place.

I whistled and Ros burst through the undergrowth, breaking out into the field, stopping to check where he might find me and then he came, crashing through the mound of dead flowers, scattering them as he passed, and I laughed, and imagined Jane laughing, too, telling Ros he was a lunatic and, for that moment, I was touched by the memory of joy.

I found a fallen branch in the wood, the leaves long rotted, the timber dyed a blackened colour by the rain. It looked sturdy but, lifting it, I was surprised by its lightness. And I thought of Jane's body in the ground, growing lighter by the week, less and less the young woman she had been. How long would it be before the outer form began to disintegrate, before the body was no longer recognisable as the form of the person it had been?

Occasionally, something happened that caught me and made me hold my breath, just for an instant, some occurrence that made my heart pound. Working late one night, bent over some drawings at my desk, the light of my work lamp making a pool around me, and with Ros asleep in a corner of the room, I was lost in the figures and shapes before me. I heard a soft tap on the window and it set every nerve in my body on edge. I listened. Nothing. Walked to the window and put my hand to the glass, squinting out into the November darkness, no one there. Turning to go back to my work. Another tap, light as a touch but definite. Switching off the light, I sat at my desk, watching the window. For a long time, there was nothing, no sound, no movement. And then it came again, soft, a gentle call for attention. Ros sat up looking from the window to me and back again, ears cocked.

I stumbled across the darkened room and hurried through the kitchen, picking up a torch as I went, the dog at my heels. Outside, the night was cold. Rounding the corner of the house, I walked quietly to the study window and stood in the darkness, listening.

The dog had lost interest, rustling along the avenue, scratching and scrabbling in the grass. And then the wind lifted, just for an instant, and I heard the sound again. Flicking on the torch, I caught a frosted rose head swaying, touching the windowpane, barely but enough to make the smallest of sounds. Was I relieved or disappointed? In that moment, I didn't know. I felt foolish that I had assumed on the supernatural when I had no belief in it whatsoever.

As the days and weeks of that month passed, there were times when the tracks of wild animals across the stubbled fields appeared like promises that I should follow, signs I should heed, suggestions that might beguile me, but they didn't. They were what they were – fox trails, badger tracks, rabbit runs. They would lead me to nothing more uncertain than a ditch or a stream or a stand of trees.

If something were to come to me, some sign from somewhere or something beyond this life, it would find me, rather than leading me on some vague meander in search of who knew what.

I had another visit from Larry, to tell me the two men who had been charged with Jane's murder would be appearing in court again. They'd be remanded in continuing custody but the report would probably be in the papers.

'How are you?' he asked.

'I'm getting there. I'm back doing a bit of work.'

'Keeps the mind occupied.'

'Yes.'

'Otherwise, are things ok?'

'Yes.'

'Good.'

'When will this come to trial?'

He shrugged his shoulders.

'Spring sometime, late spring, early summer.'

'Right.'

'It takes time.'

'Yes.'

'The wheels of justice et cetera.'

'Of course.'

I woke one morning to the insanity of sparrows in the gutter outside my window and, for a second, I thought it must be spring, last spring or next spring, whichever would be better than deep midwinter. And then I remembered, it was the end of November and whatever light there was out there was drenched and discoloured. I closed my eyes again, pulling the bedclothes about me, burrowing into the folds of the duvet, turning my back on the day and the dawn and locking myself away.

Another morning, I lay on Jane's bed. Just that. Not thinking. Not trying to connect with anyone. Not remembering or forgetting or regretting. Simply lying there, staring through the Velux window at the greyness above. For four hours, I lay there, drifting in and out of sleep, watching the sky change and clear and cloud and clear again.

And every day Kate called and every day Ros gave me away by racing to the door and barking joyously at the sound of her car on the avenue or her footsteps on the gravel. And every day, I knew she wanted to suggest I see my doctor and every day she bit her tongue and resisted the temptation to lecture me. Instead, she brought me food or shared the food I had prepared. She talked or listened or, more often, savoured the silence with me. Sometimes she went walking with me and we talked about Elizabeth and Susan, but it was always I who brought up their names.

'I don't mind, you know,' I said. 'You can't exorcise them from conversations because Jane died. There's no reason to feel guilty about them.'

'You're right, but it's still difficult.'

'You can't let me make all the running in deciding what we talk about.'

'I know.'

'But you do.'

'Yes.'

'Why?'

'I'm afraid of saying something inappropriate.'

'You've been doing that all your life.'

We both laughed.

'That's the first time I've seen you laugh in ages,' Kate said.

'I know. But who am I telling? You know better than anyone.'

She nodded.

'I've been thinking about Christmas,' I said. 'A woman stopped me in the supermarket last week and said, "Christmas will be a lonely old time for you." That's all she wanted to say, just to remind me that I ought to be miserable, in case I'd forgotten. And then she went off about her business, feeling up the avocadoes. She'd done her desolation deed for the day.'

Kate giggled.

'It's true,' I said. 'I bet she sets out to make someone miserable every day and her heart must have leapt when she saw me in the vegetable section. A murdered girl's father! Bingo.'

We walked on.

'So? Christmas?' Kate asked.

'Robert wants me to come to them. My mother wants me to come to her. You're going to invite me, I know.'

'Yes. That goes without saying. What would you like to do?'

'Not a notion,' I said. 'I thought about America. But do I want to spend hours in Dublin airport with my mother, hours on a plane with her, the days in America with her? If I go, she'll go.'

'She might not.'

'You kidding? Can you imagine her missing the chance of a ringside seat at the circus that's my life these days? She'd swim the Atlantic for that. *Great Expectations* meets *Jude the Obscure*!'

'So?'

'So, I might stay at home. Literally. But she'll want to be here. And you'll feel obliged to bring us to your house because you'll feel sorry for me. Or her!'

'But what would you like?'

'To be at home on my own, I think, or in America with Robert and Jenny. One or other.'

'Then that's what you should do.'

'If only it were that easy.'

'It could be. If you tell people.'

'It takes energy, Kate. Something that's in short supply right now.'

'I know,' she said. 'I know.'

.

One night I rang Elizabeth.

'I was thinking about you,' I said. 'I just wanted to say hello. To see how you're doing.'

'I'm all right,' she said. 'How are you?'

'Hanging in there. Good days, bad days.'

'I'm ok during the day,' Elizabeth said. 'I don't like nights. I don't like walking home from college. Mam and Dad told me to take taxis, they sent me money, but I don't want to do that either. I don't want to be running and hiding for the rest of my life.'

'You won't be. It's early days.'

'Yes.'

'Don't expect too much of yourself.'

'No.'

'And anyway, that money is better spent on CDs or videos or a few drinks or something.'

We both laughed.

'I just wanted you to know I was thinking about you, we all are. You need to live. Anything else is giving in and, like you say, you don't want to do that.'

'Thanks.'

'Good.'

'I'll come down and see you the next weekend I'm home,' Elizabeth said.

'If you feel up to it.'

'I was going to last weekend but, I don't know, I couldn't. Not yet.'

'That's fine,' I said. 'It's not something you have to do. When the time is right, you'll be welcome. Meanwhile, you stay well and keep looking ahead. Ok?'

'Ok. And thanks for ringing.'

'You're welcome.'

'I pray for Jane,' she said quietly. 'Every day.'

·

'Good.'

And then she was gone.

A Saturday morning, the second in November, I was sitting in the kitchen, a cup of coffee steaming on the table, the newspaper spread out before me. The doorbell rang. Ros barked, I cursed.

The man standing at the door looked vaguely familiar. He was in his late forties, sandy haired, wearing a jacket, open-necked shirt and corduroy trousers.

He smiled, uncertainly.

'Good morning,' I said.

'Good morning. I'm sorry for calling so early and on a Saturday but I had to come.'

'Right.'

'I'm Jerry Brown. I teach maths in the school. I didn't teach Jane but I knew her. To see.'

'Yes, of course. Now I recognise you. Come in. Please.'

I ushered him through to the kitchen.

'I was just having a coffee. Will you have one?'

'Thank you.'

Folding the paper, I threw it onto a chair.

'I'm sorry. I'm interrupting your morning.'

'Not at all. The day is long.'

We sat facing each other across the table. Jerry was silent.

'Would you like some toast or a biscuit?'

'A biscuit would be good. Blood sugar.'

I took a packet of chocolate biscuits from the press and put them on the table. He ate one and then a second.

'I'm sorry. I'm very nervous,' he said.

I nodded, assuming he had come to sympathise, something he'd probably been putting off for weeks.

'I was in the field, not the same field, the next field, the night Jane was killed,' he said suddenly, the words coming out loudly, too loudly.

'Sorry?'

'I was in the field across the ditch from where Jane was killed, on that night. I saw the lights of the van.'

'Right.'

'And I drove away. I panicked and drove away.'

'I see.'

'I've been wanting to tell you since it happened, but I kept putting it off, trying to put it out of my mind but I can't. I had to come and see you.'

'I appreciate that.'

'I haven't talked to the guards. I will if you want me to. I want to tell you why I was there, the full story. I have to tell someone. I did talk to Maura about it.'

'Maura?'

'Mrs Collins. The domestic-science teacher in the school.'

'She's a friend of yours. Obviously.'

'She was there, too.'

'Right.'

'I'd better tell you the full story. May I have some more coffee?'

'Of course,' I said, pouring him another cup. He took a third biscuit from the packet. I noticed that his hand was shaking.

'We, ah, Mrs Collins and I have been involved with each other for a number of months. We're both married. I should say that at the outset.'

'That happens,' I said, trying to put him at his ease.

'Yes,' he said. 'But it doesn't make it any less stressful.'

'Of course not.'

'Do you know Mrs Collins?'

'No,' I said. 'Domestic science wasn't Jane's forte.'

'Of course. Music was her thing.'

'Yes.'

He took another biscuit and smiled.

'Blood sugar,' he said again.

'Help yourself. That's why they're there.'

'We'd been seeing each other since before the summer holidays. It was just one of these things that grew out of ... circumstances. It wasn't something we had planned.'

'Right.'

'Through the summer, it was more difficult to see each other. Not easy to find reasons during the holiday time and then we, my wife and I, were away in Scotland. And Maura, Mrs Collins, was away too, in France, and both at different times. My wife and I went away in July and Maura and her husband went in August, the full month, so when she got back and we returned to school, we took every opportunity to see each other. It was as much need as opportunity by then. You know how something unattainable becomes suddenly essential?'

'Yes,' I said. 'I understand.'

He nodded, took another biscuit and drank from his coffee cup.

'If I'm being too circumspect please say so,' he said.

I nodded.

'But I'm hoping, when I've finished, that you'll understand why I did what I did and why I feel as I do.'

'Of course.'

'That night, Tuesday, 25 September, Maura and I met at the school. We were ostensibly going to Dublin to attend a union meeting but, of course, that was a ruse.'

I looked closely at the man sitting across the table from me. Was he mad? Was this some kind of twisted lunatic? I knew who he was, I'd seen him in the school at various events, but that didn't mean he wasn't mad. And, yet, his eyes were clear and he was leaning forward, eager to get the story told. I believed he truly wanted to tell me everything, hoping in some way that it would lift whatever weight was on his shoulders.

'We drove to the outskirts of Dublin that night, important to get away from the area, not wanting to be seen. One never knows who might see and say something. So we drove to Dublin for a time, went for a coffee and then we drove back. We were anxious to be close to home before we parked. Park up is what New Zealanders call it. We had a teacher from New Zealand once, she told me that.'

'Right.'

'There's a lane that runs down into the low field, behind where Jane's body was found. You can drive into the low field, when you get to the end of that lane, it opens onto the headland, no gate.'

'Yes. I've walked that lane.'

'That's where we drove. It's private.'

'Of course.'

'It was half past eleven when we got there. I was driving. Once we'd parked, we got out and sat on the bonnet of the car. But it was chilly and Maura said it was too cold to lie in the field so we got back into the car, the front seats, and began kissing.'

I assumed this was all I was going to hear but he went on.

'The strange thing is that virtually every detail of what was said and done on that night is retrospectively burned into my memory. As if it had been lying dormant until I heard of Jane's death and realised that we had been so close to her. And then the detail just reappeared, like a fish surfacing for air. But this fish has refused to be submerged again. I can only hope that telling you all this will help you decide what you think I should do. And will help me to exorcise the details from my brain, allow me some peace of mind. And I will be guided by what you say. Absolutely.'

I was about to interrupt, to tell him that the detail he was giving didn't alter what I thought, or didn't think, but he didn't give me time. Instead, he ploughed ahead with his story and I had no choice but to listen.

'I should tell you at this point,' he said quietly, 'Maura has a penchant for a certain kind of music. She knows the lyrics of virtually every song from a particular period in the seventies. It's extraordinary really. Almost total recall. And she has a fondness for quoting certain lines when she's in the throes of passion. Now I have no real interest in that music, but it does form an integral part of what I'm about to tell you. I just felt you should know that.'

'Thank you.'

'She was kissing my hand and she said, "Should have told her that I can't linger, there's a wedding ring on my finger." She quotes that line often, it's her little joke about our marital status.'

'Bay City Rollers,' I said.

He looked at me, startled.

'How on earth did you know that?'

'Pop trivia is one of my interests,' I said.

'You'd like Maura then.'

'I'm sure I would.'

'But it's best that I not introduce you. I haven't told her I was coming to see you. Unless, of course, you would like to meet her.'

I shook my head.

'I took off her jumper and blouse and while I was undoing her bra strap she was laughing and shaking her breasts in my face. She said, "Now you've got the breast of me, come on take the rest of me." She can be quite witty like that.'

'Yes.'

'Then she put her hand inside my trousers, she was giggling, "Get it on, bang a gong."'

'T.Rex.'

'Amazing. You two really would get along.'

For an instant, I forgot that this strange man was telling me about something that happened fifty feet from where my daughter's body had been dumped. Instead, I imagined myself sitting with two very bizarre people in a car, leaning forward in a kind of poetus-interruptus from some virtual back seat, identifying lines from thirty-year-old songs.

'Then she climbed into the rear seat of the car and when I tried to follow her, she kept pushing me back into the front seat and saying, "You can get it if you really want but you must try and try, you'll succeed at last." So, I opened the driver's door, jumped out and opened the back passenger door before jumping in beside her. She hadn't expected that. She was surprised. And delighted.'

'I'm sure she was.'

'We went on kissing and touching. Maura likes a great deal of foreplay. That's why we were there so long. Had she been someone who liked something more immediate we might have been gone before the van came down the field. But we weren't. Once, at a teacher's conference, we had three hours of foreplay. Anyway, that night, in the field, she asked if I enjoyed licking her nipples. I told her I did. "You be tellin' me yeah but you don't mean it," she said. It was another of her little games, tantalising. Sometimes she asks me questions simply to create an opportunity to quote a line that's running in her head. "Let your yeah be yeah and your no be no." I pretended to be disappointed and I backed away but she tackled me. We were wrestling. I don't mean seriously, playfully. And she said, "Everybody was kung-fu fighting, huh." That was, and is, my cue to move on to the next stage of love making. The more animal part.'

'Right.'

'That's the part I find most difficult because the attention turns to me. Maura believes the penis deserves the same level of foreplay and preparation as the clitoris. She doesn't accept that the male needs much less priming to be ready.'

'Can I stop you there, for moment, Mr Brown.'

'Jerry.'

'Jerry. Do you think it right that I should be hearing all this? I don't need to.'

'I need you to hear it, if you don't mind. It is part of the process I need to go through. Part of the penitential process.'

'All of this?'

'You have lost a daughter. A little humiliation is a small price to pay for my selfishness.'

'If you think so.'

'I do and I appreciate your forbearance.'

'You're welcome.'

'I'm relating the details because each time Mrs Collins and I have been together since, I've been haunted by the memory of what was happening as we were engaging in the sexual act. You understand?'

'Yes.'

'Maura likes me to ejaculate on her breasts. Something on which my wife is not at all keen. Never has been and has made the fact perfectly clear to me, since the beginning of our relationship. And while I very much enjoy this, Maura has always insisted that it not happen until she has climaxed. In the early days of our relationship, my enthusiasm overcame my better judgement with consequences for me.'

He smiled ruefully.

There is a point in a bizarre conversation where you can either walk away and put it out of your mind or you can accept the peculiarity of the situation and go with it. I had reached that point but, weighing up the options and despite the circumstances that had led to this man's arrival at my door, I reckoned it would be difficult to walk away from a conversation that was taking place in my own kitchen. So I gave myself over to accepting that it would be easier to hear the story through than to try to bring it to a conclusion before he had finished.

'She also likes to treat my penis as a pendulum, swinging it with her finger tips, very gently mind you, as part of the foreplay. "Swing your daddy," she'll say. "Take him higher, send him up to heaven." And she did on that night, too. It's a very exciting time for me because I know we're reaching the point where nothing will stop her. She straddled me then, she likes to be on top. She was in a mellow mood. Had she been in a more intense mood it would have been different. Sometimes she'll be quite forceful and say something like, "Can you feel the force?" Over and over. It's like a sexual mantra, but it works for her and I know she's thoroughly enjoying herself. When she had finally climaxed, she hunkered down and I knelt above her, waiting to hear her hum, "I could move a mountain when your hand is in my hand." And then she said, "But it's not your hand, is it?" And I said, "No, Miss." And she grasped me, tightly but not too tightly, and then I knew I could come. The whole thing is a little play, as it were, a piece of sexual theatre. Of course, it varies from night to night, different songs, different lines from the lyrics, but that's how it was on that night. As I said, it's as if it retrospectively burned its way into my memory.'

I waited, but he was silent.

'I see,' I said, not knowing what else there was to say.

'Then we relaxed, lying together in the back seat of the car, a rug pulled over us, our bodies still entwined, my hand on her damp breasts. I was waiting because sometimes Maura likes to have sex a second time. That's when we noticed the lights of the van coming down the other field, moving along the headland. For a moment, I panicked, we both did, thinking it was someone driving into the lower field. We scrambled into our clothes. We simply wanted to get away. Then the lights of the van swung around, it must have been turning, and the brake lights flashed twice. I scuttled into the front seat and started the car and drove away without turning the lights on. Maura was still in the back seat, still in a state of relative undress. Had I known, had I realised, I would have gone to Jane's assistance. Obviously, it would have altered our lives, mine and Mrs Collins', but it would have saved Jane's. And that is far, far more important.'

Something in the tone in which he spoke that last sentence was impossible to ignore. It was the tone of a man who was deeply and absolutely sorry for something he believed he should have done, a man who was haunted by the *if* of his inaction. All the unnecessary detail, all the personal disclosures were nothing when weighed against the sadness in his voice. And, looking across the table, I could see that same sadness in his eyes. He might be eccentric, even mad. He and Maura Collins might engage in some very strange role-plays but that didn't alter the fact that he had come to me looking for direction.

'That's it,' he said.

I nodded.

'No doubt you think I'm a stark raving lunatic. You probably believe the detail with which I've outlined certain elements was unnecessary but, to me, there is, as I've said, a matter of responsibility and reparation in this confession.'

'You don't have to confess to me, Jerry. It's not necessary.'

'I might have saved your daughter's life.'

'I don't think so. There was another witness to what happened. It seems quite certain that Jane was dead when her body was left in the field. There was nothing you could have done that would have altered the circumstances. And you couldn't have known what was going on.'

'I could have stayed, investigated.'

'And nine hundred and ninety-nine times out of a thousand you'd have found a courting couple in the van. Or poachers. Or guys wanting somewhere to drink beer or smoke dope. You have nothing to feel guilty about, either of you. There was nothing you could have done. Believe me. Nothing would have altered for Jane if you had stayed. Nothing.'

'Truly?'

'Truly.'

'Should I go to the guards, report what I saw?'

'It won't change anything,' I said. 'For Jane or for the case. All it might do is complicate your lives, you and Mrs Collins. I don't wish that to happen, nor, I'm sure, do you. And nor would Jane.'

'Thank you,' he said, taking another biscuit from the packet.

'Would you like some more coffee?' I asked.

'Just a hot drop.'

I poured while he sat munching his biscuit.

'The thing is,' he said, 'when I'm with Maura, I don't see a woman in her forties. I see the young, wild-headed girl who danced to those songs in her late teens and early twenties. It's the thing we do, isn't it?'

'It is.'

'We live somewhere else so much of the time, past or future. The present can be a terrible place.'

'Did you not tell him to feck off?' Kate asked, when I told her the story that afternoon.

'I couldn't.'

'Why not?'

'I just couldn't.'

'And you don't think he should go to the guards?'

'No. Honestly, I don't. It won't change anything.'

'Still, at least you know there's someone, actually two people, out there madder than you.'

I smiled.

'And no mention of Meat Loaf? "Paradise by the Dashboard Light"?'

'Too subtle.'

'Do you know the worst part?' she laughed.

'What's the worst part?'

'Susan has Mrs Collins for domestic science, and I have a parent-teacher meeting with her next Tuesday. I'll be sitting there looking at this woman with big hair and I'll be doing my best to keep a straight face and not to give in to the temptation to throw in some song lyric from the seventies.'

Robert rang, as he had done at least twice a week each week since Jane's death.

'I spoke to the mother this morning. She's happy to come over here for Christmas. How about you, brother?'

'I've thought about it.'

'And?'

I hesitated.

'You won't be saddled with looking after her,' he said quickly. 'You know that. Jenny has volunteered to do the chaperoning.'

'Does she know this?'

'Yes, she does,' he laughed. 'It's all taken care of. The mother flies out here on the nineteenth. Goes home on January second.'

'And have you been talking to Kate about all this?'

'What the heck put that in your head?' he laughed again.

'Something very organised about all of it. All the ends neatly tied up. Tell me this, complete truth now, have you booked a ticket for me?'

'Would I be so presumptuous, knowing you as I do?'

'And will you be hurt if I don't go?'

'No,' he said quietly. 'It's not my place to be hurt. I have nothing to be hurt about. I love you.'

'So, you'll understand if I don't go.'

'Yes.'

'Thanks.'

'Do you have any definite plans?'

'I think I'll stay here,' I said. 'I don't want to move Ros to Kate and Brian's place. I think he's confused enough already.'

'He's a dog,' Robert said.

'Do you remember the mutt we had when you were twelve and I was ten. The sheepdog, Shepper?'

'Yes.'

'Do you remember he got into a fight with another dog and got bitten on the jugular vein and bled to death.'

'Of course I do.'

'Do you remember where we buried him?'

'Yes. In the patch just beyond the rhubarb at the end of the garden.'

·

'And do you remember what happened two nights afterwards, when we were lying in bed, talking?'

'We heard him barking in the yard, the way he always barked. And we jumped up and ran to the window but there was only the moon shining on the yard and his empty kennel.'

'Robert, that's the only time in my life, ever, including when Beth was killed, including when Jane died, that I've been sure, even for a moment, that something made a connection with me from wherever it is that life goes to when it's gone from here. That mutt barking two nights after he died.'

'Point taken,' Robert said. 'Point taken.'

'Thanks.'

'We plan on getting home in the spring, probably April.'

'I'd like that a lot. More than I can explain.'

'Good. You look after yourself, brother.'

'I will. And you.'

That same night, another phone call, I heard the voice but not the first few words – rather I was hearing a young woman, and I was listening to Jane.

'Hi, can you hear me?' she asked.

'Yes.'

'Sorry, I thought for a moment that I'd lost the line.'

'I'm hearing you. Where are you?'

'I'm in Dublin.'

'Dublin?'

'Yes. I just finished in college, we had a late lecture.'

I was silent.

'I was hoping to come down on Sunday, by train, to visit Jane's grave. Is that ok? I just thought I should let you know.'

And then I was back to reality, knowing it couldn't be Jane, recognising the voice. Alice, Jane's college friend.

'Of course. It's Alice.'

'Yes. Sorry, I thought you knew. It's a bad line.'

'Of course, yes, please do come. I'll meet you at the station. What time?'

'Half-twelve, but it's not necessary to put yourself to that trouble.'

'It's no trouble. I'll meet you. We'll have lunch. We'll go to the cemetery afterwards. I look forward to seeing you again.'

'I haven't had Jane's name put on the headstone yet.'

Alice and I were standing at the graveside. She had brought three bunches of freesias, probably cleared her out of pocket money for the week.

'It's a nice stone,' she said. 'Very plain. Jane told me about it the first time we talked about parents. I hadn't known till then that your wife was dead. Jane said when she was young, she'd always thought the headstone was ugly. She said she'd wanted you to put up a huge, shiny, white marble cross.'

'Yes,' I said, laughing. 'She got it into her head that it should be big and brassy with a photograph of Beth on it, in colour of course. She was very disappointed when this "bit of a rock" – as she described it – appeared.'

'It's a beautiful stone. The first time I came to stay at your house, during first term in first year, two years ago this month, actually, Jane brought me up here, to see the grave. I remember her saying she was glad you hadn't listened to her when you chose the stone.'

'Oh, I listened.' I laughed. 'You couldn't not listen to Jane at that age, she never stopped talking. I listened and then I ignored her.'

'You were very close. She was lucky to be so close to you.'

'We both were.'

'I feel such terrible, awful, deadly sadness,' Alice said quietly. 'Whenever I think about her. Sometimes I purposely put her out of my mind, just to save myself from going through that sadness. It's just that I can't stop crying when I think about her. And then I feel guilty for trying to keep her out of my head.'

'We all do the best we can. We all avoid the things we can't deal with. That's why I haven't even thought about having Jane's name put on this stone yet and probably won't for a long time. I never imagined I'd see my child buried here before me. She knew how much you loved her and how much I loved her. She'd understand why things are the way they are with you. And with me.'

Alice smiled, her face tear-streaked.

'She would.'

'Yes, she would.'

In mid-December, the week before she was due to fly to America, my mother came and stayed for two nights.

'Would you like me to go through Jane's clothes, help you sort them out?' she asked.

'Not yet. I'll do that in time.'

'You should be careful of morbidity. It can set in.'

'It's less than twelve weeks since Jane died.'

'I cleared out your father's clothes two weeks after he died.'

'Was it that long?'

The irony was lost on her.

'We keep people in our hearts, not in a wardrobe.'

'I'll remember that.'

.

190

'And I've no doubt that Robert will be thoroughly disappointed that you didn't take up his very kind offer. It was you he was thinking of, it was for your sake he organised the tickets, not mine. You were uppermost in his mind.'

I rang Robert that night, when my mother was asleep.

'You did book a flight for me.'

'Who told you that?'

'The mother. During one of her rants.'

'And you believed her?'

'Yes.'

'More fool you.'

'Bullshit, Robert. You didn't tell me you'd booked a ticket. I asked you and you denied it. Now you're out of pocket.'

'A straightforward question,' he said. 'Where do you really want to spend Christmas? Now, a straightforward answer.'

'Here.'

'I am not out of pocket, then. Matter closed. All right?'

'All right.'

'Do you think I could get my friendly local farmer to throttle the mother when he's throttling the turkey?'

He paused.

'Bollocks, shit. I'm sorry – that was thoughtless and tasteless. Shit, I really am sorry.'

'But it's a good idea,' I laughed. 'You could ask him. Nothing ventured, nothing maimed.'

'You're not going to America, then?'

'No, but I think you knew that before you asked. You and that brother of mine.'

Kate grinned, her mouth crooked and beautiful.

•

'So can we expect the pleasure of your company?'

'No. I'm going to go west at Christmas,' I said. 'Not as far as the States but west to the sea.'

'Where?'

'Somewhere. Wherever I land. Somewhere that has wind and sea and big tides and breaking surf pounding the rocks.'

She looked frightened, her brow furrowing, the lines tightening around her eyes.

'But you'll be back? Won't you?'

'The sea is for watching, for listening to, not for drowning in.'

Her face relaxed.

'I'm sorry.'

'Don't apologise,' I said. 'I would never do that to you. Ever. Life is precious. I know that now. More than ever.'

But I didn't go to the sea. I had intended to, I had even made a booking for a hotel on the Atlantic coast but, on Christmas Eve morning, with my bags packed and presents delivered to Kate and Brian and the girls, a holly wreath on Jane and Beth's grave, the water turned off and Ros settled on the back seat of the car, I couldn't do it.

There was something about the house as I made a final check before going, a feeling of desertion, a tiny voice that said don't leave me. Not some ghostly imagining, simply the sound of doors closing on empty rooms, the noise the wind made as it piled up against the walls, the empty echo of my footsteps on the stairs, reverberating off the bedroom.

I went outside, took my cases from the boot and opened the car door. Ros came tumbling out, jumping and barking, racing inside, ignoring the post van on the avenue.

'You're heading off?' the postman asked. 'For the few days' break?'

'I was, John, but do you know I think I've just changed my mind.'

'A thing a man is entitled to do.'

'Happy Christmas,' I said.

'And a peaceful one to you, in spite of everything. And thanks for the envelope you left for me yesterday.'

I parked the car at the back of the house. As far as anyone who knew was concerned, I had gone away for Christmas and, to all intents and purposes, I was on the west coast. Whatever part of me was here in this house was not a part that wanted social contact. Whatever the day would bring would come from within me.

I went to bed early on Christmas Eve. I slept well and woke early on Christmas morning. After breakfast, I drove with Ros to a woodland five miles from the town, somewhere I wouldn't be seen.

The forest was deserted and we walked up between the trees, out of the cold wind and into the shelter of a hundred years of growth. The air became still, the wind catching in the high branches above us but allowing us a sanctuary of calm.

I thought of the hundreds of times Jane and I had walked here, from a time long before Ros had come into our lives. We had come out here for picnics when Jane was a child, we had ambled and chatted on long afternoons of sunshine or winter days just like this one, we had taken Ros out here for his first Sunday run. We had sheltered from rain, run through the cobble-locked sunshine, watched the first flurries of snow between these trees. Collected chestnuts, lifted sycamore saplings, watched badgers edging through the dusk, seen foxes with their young, collected arms of bluebells and sat quietly in the shelter of one tree or another listening to the breeze or the birds or the silence.

And I thought of a late evening many years ago, traipsing slowly down the hill, Jane on my shoulders, worn out from the day's adventure, already nodding off even before we had left the sultry dusk of the forest behind, her head lolling from side to side as I talked to her, trying to keep her awake till we got to the comfort of the car.

All those mornings, afternoons, evenings were gone now, but not beyond recall.

I imagined some passer-by or distant observer watching Ros and I, seeing a man and his dog out for a Christmas-morning stroll. And they might have imagined a waiting house, a busy family, a Christmas tree winking and nodding in a sitting room, food cooking in a warm kitchen, presents as yet unopened, carols playing from a quiet radio.

They'd have seen a man striding quickly through the clear air, his dog stopping to nose in the undergrowth then racing to catch up, to push ahead before some other scent caught the animal's attention and he wandered, again, off the forest path. They'd have seen the man walk on, eyes ahead, not waiting for his dog. Intent, they'd have thought, on getting back to his home and his family.

We did two rounds of the hill, breasting the summit a second time and moving down into the sheltered side, away from the east wind, turning right instead of left, down to the edge of the tree line, stopping to look out over the empty fields and across to the mountains beyond. And then we were off again, Ros moving well ahead of me, racing and chasing, back to the main path and the car park.

A couple were getting out of their car as I opened my car door to let Ros in.

'Happy Christmas,' the woman said.

'Happy Christmas to you.'

'It's a lovely morning. Not too cold for the time of year.'

'No it's not. Nice for walking.'

'Your dog enjoyed the run.'

'Oh, he did, this is his favourite spot.'

The woman smiled and again at Ros.

'Well enjoy the day, I hope you get everything you were hoping for!' she laughed.

'And you. Enjoy the walk.'

'We will,' the man said. 'Happy Christmas.'

'Thank you.'

When we got home, I parked the car at the back of the house. The phone was ringing as I opened the door. The caller ID was Robert's.

'Hi,' he said when I lifted the receiver. 'I wasn't sure you'd be there but I thought I'd try.'

'It's only ten o'clock here,' I said. 'That means it's all hours with you.'

'I know,' Robert said. 'Early riser. I assumed you'd be there. Despite the fact that you are supposedly on the other side of the country.'

'Changed my mind,' I said.

'Thought you might.'

'Why?'

'Because it's what I'd have done, too.'

'So how's the mother?'

'Settled in. Not as bad as I'd feared.'

'Missing me, I bet.'

'She has mentioned you in passing, yes, bemoaning your absence.'

'I'll ring you later, from the hotel in the west, of course! I'll talk to her then.'

'Do that.'

'What time is best for you?'

'Anytime after seven your time. She has me taking her to ten o'clock mass, we'll be home by eleven.'

'Ok.'

'Are you all right?'

'Yes, I am. Fine. Just back from a walk with Ros. Going to cook something and relax.'

'Have you thought about dropping up to see Kate and Brian and the girls?'

'No, I haven't, but I might.'

'Yeah, of course, you know best yourself. I'm in danger of turning into our sainted mother.'

We both laughed.

'Thanks for ringing,' I said. 'You're not a five o'clock riser, never were!'

'The house is quiet. Seemed like a good idea. Anyway, I was thinking about you.'

'Thanks. Seriously. I'm doing fine. Don't ring Kate and tell her I'm here. Please. If I feel like it, later, I'll go up and see them.'

'I won't. Word of honour.'

'Thanks.'

'I love you, brother.'

'And I love you.'

It was sometime after three that afternoon. My dinner was cooking in the kitchen. I was sitting in the study, reading the previous day's paper. It was still bright enough to read without electric light. Then I saw Kate on the avenue, her figure moving between the trees. Ros was asleep beside my desk and had neither seen nor heard her. I didn't believe Robert had phoned her. She had probably come out for a walk while dinner was cooking and decided to check that everything was safe and well at my house.

I sat completely still and she passed the study window without looking in. The dog went on sleeping, exhausted from the morning's walk.

Kate disappeared around the side of the house. Obviously, she'd see the car there. I'd tell her we'd gone west by train. I could move, now that she was out of sight, go upstairs and hide till she had left but if I did Ros would wake, too, and hear Kate and bark.

She was coming around the other side of the house, heading back for the avenue and the road beyond and home. But, as she passed, she hesitated, as though she had suddenly become aware of my eyes on her back. Stopping, she turned and looked through the study window. Dusk was thickening but I could see her clearly and it was obvious that she could see the outline of my figure in the shadowed room. She stood, unmoving, and I sat where I was, the newspaper on my knee, the dog still sleeping at my feet. She lifted her right hand and it froze in midair. I waved back, a small gesture, my fingers slowly opening and closing, my elbow still on the desk beside me. And then she smiled, a warm grin that accepted my presence without any need for explanation, before turning away, walking slowly down the avenue without another glance, fading into the falling darkness, only the warmth of her smiling face remaining in my mind's eye.

Flicking on the desk lamp, I walked into the kitchen and checked the food cooking in the oven. It would be another half-hour before it was ready. I set a place at the kitchen table and lit the stove. If I was at home, I was at home and there was no point in pretending otherwise.

I rang Robert, spoke to my mother, didn't lose my temper, had a few words with Jenny and then it was time to eat. The day, I thought, was passing. Another few hours, a couple of inane TV programmes and it would be over.

In a certain frame of mind, and under certain circumstances, most of us are capable of reading significance into events that are, at the very least, banal or, at best, coincidental. In the weeks after Jane's death, I had been careful, with perhaps the one exception of the rose tapping on my study window, not to make any associations between random events and my daughter's death.

I was aware of the danger of making such connections. One small coincidence can suddenly open up the possibility of a plethora of similar connections and, before there's time to look at them coldly and logically, the mind offers tricks and the heart follows willingly. It's part of the human condition, that urge to believe, the desire to be convinced that the need we have for the people in our lives has an importance that outweighs anything else.

The memory of our childhood dog's dead barking in the empty yard was and is clear to me and I believe I heard it but, as a child, I accepted it and took it for granted. I didn't search for literal or metaphorical paw marks or listen for further signs of some continuation of life. I had heard what I had heard and that was sufficient.

As we grow older, however, we begin to analyse and to search for reasons and explanations that tie in with our own aspirations. We cannot accept that the things that are of consequence to us are as nothing in the width of the world. Of course, we want to feel close to the ones who were close to us in the past and, as a result, we have difficulty in coming to terms with loss. We scrabble about, trying to find ways of postponing the inevitability of acceptance. We look for signs and omens and we grasp at any passing notion that appears to make our loss more important than anyone else's. And, when all else fails, we rummage through memory and try to find what we need in there.

Not that I have any resentment against memory. The reason I was spending Christmas Day alone was because of memory, because of the association between this house, that wood and the memories they hold of my daughter's life.

Association is a comfort but the notion of haunting is a disturbance. We all see things out of the corners of our eyes, catch the faint lingering perfume of a loved one at unexpected times, respond – as I did – to a sound or a coincidence but the important thing for sanity is to see these for what they are – reminiscence, happenstance, evocation. Nothing more.

So the fact that, late on a Christmas night, I wandered back into my study and picked up a pile of books that had sat on a table beside my desk since Kate had done her tidy up and airing weeks before was simply chance.

I had been watching a TV documentary and had seen something that reminded me of a book on Gaudi which I had meant to read. I knew it was somewhere in my study, in one or other of the dozen piles of unread volumes that were stacked precariously all over the place. In lifting this pile off the table, I found the CD that Jane had left for me on that last day when she'd come into the room. I had never got around to playing it, indeed it had slipped out of my memory. And now here it was, uncovered by chance, late on this Christmas night.

But that's all it was, not some present coming magically through the ether, not something that had miraculously moved from one place to another in order to be found. And I reminded myself of that fact when I saw it, dusty and bedraggled from its weeks beneath the pile of books.

It was a CD that Jane had duplicated, the cover photocopied in black and white. Inside, on a slip of paper, she had written: *Recommend Disc 2 to begin with. Track 1 is my favourite. Jane.* The CD was a collection of work by Jacqueline du Pré.

Taking the two discs from their plastic case, I found CD 2, slipped it into the CD player, turned off the lights and sat listening, pleased at this unexpected opportunity to hear something so important to Jane, something she had wanted me to hear and something that chance and untidiness had kept from me until now.

The piece of music was simple, quiet, immediately memorable. The piano and cello in gentle cadence, deep and slow, with a rising movement that never threatened to became too dramatic. It was a simple, reflective piece and it reminded me of songs my father had sung when I was a boy. It was sadly beautiful or beautifully sad, it didn't matter which. The piano kept time while the cello sang the melody, unaffected but totally affecting. Picking the cover from the table, I read the track listing in the shaft of light from the open kitchen door. *Sicilienne. Written by Maria Theresia Von Paradis.*

And so I played it again and again and, as I did, I wondered whether I had some recollection of Jane playing it on her violin, the strains floating through the summer dusk from her open window while I watered the vegetables. It wasn't important whether I had heard this piece or whether I was mistaking it for some other tune. She had left it for me to hear and now I was hearing it, three months after her death, sharing one of the few things left for us to share.

What did matter was the fact that I would never hear her play it again. I would never stand as I had so often done, listening to wonderful music in the evening air. I would never pause at what I was doing and enjoy the sound, simply because it was beautiful. I would never have the chance to marvel at my daughter's talent, never get to tell her again how wonderful she was and how much I loved her.

part

•

four

I COLLECTED MY MOTHER from the airport on January 2nd. Her plane had been delayed and darkness was falling as we drove out onto the motorway.

'You enjoyed the trip?' I asked

'Well the travelling wasn't what I had hoped. Why are planes so often late? I can't think of a time I've travelled that either the outward flight or the return flight or both haven't been delayed. If buses and trains and boats can run on time, why not planes? It's extraordinarily inconsiderate.'

'No one died,' I said.

There was an icy stillness to match the arctic air outside.

'And Robert and Jenny are well?'

'Yes.'

'That's good then.'

We drove in silence, on through the toll booth and south for home.

Only when we were clear of the city and she was certain that I wasn't going to lose my way in some industrial, urban wasteland where we'd both be kidnapped and held in a damp and dingy warehouse did my mother open up.

'Robert was very hurt that you didn't go over for Christmas.'

'Did he say that?'

'He didn't have to. I knew it. I know him well enough to see through the politeness. I understand him, I have an empathy with him that I have never managed to achieve with you.'

I shrugged.

'Why do you do this?'

'Do what?'

'You know what.'

'If I did, I wouldn't be asking,' I snapped.

'Remove yourself from your family, retreat into your own world. It's not something new. You did it when Beth died. You retreated. You made Jane a virtual prisoner, just the two of you against the outside world. It wasn't healthy then and it's not healthy now. Humans are social beings. And we are family but you react against both concepts. It's a most unwholesome trait and not one you got from your father or me.'

'Firstly,' I said, turning to her, knowing that by taking my eyes off the road I would annoy her even more, 'I have many, many friends and always have had, right back to when Beth and I married.'

'Keep your eyes on the road, please.'

I glanced at the empty carriageway ahead and then back at her.

'Secondly, how I chose to deal with my family situation after Beth died was my decision. I was living with a child who had just lost her mother. I had just lost my wife. Those same friends rallied round and made my life easier. They were and are good friends. You have no right to breeze in and dismiss them and my life like that.'

'Well you hurt your brother by not accepting his invitation and by leaving him with a plane ticket that was wasted money. Plane tickets do not come cheaply, especially at Christmas time.'

'I put a cheque in the post to Robert yesterday.'

'Money cannot buy a family.'

Turning the wheel sharply, I brought the car skidding to a halt on the hard shoulder.

'Listen,' I said. 'You have no right to use this kind of emotional blackmail on me. None. Yes, I've made mistakes in my life and done things I'd have done another way if I'd had a second chance, but I have always, always, always had one aim in mind and that was to give Jane a good life and a happy life and a secure life. Now it turns out that I couldn't do that, I couldn't protect her from everything. And if I could do it,

I'd be killed fifty times myself, as gruesomely, as painfully, as horribly as you could ever imagine. Nothing would have been too awful for me if it had saved her. But I couldn't do that. It was beyond me. I said that at the fucking funeral. Or were you too busy to listen?'

'Language,' my mother said, her face reddening.

'Bollocks to language. I'm talking to you about what I feel, about what's in here.'

I thumped my chest.

'There is no need to shout at me.'

'I am not shouting,' I said. 'I'm telling you a few home truths that you seem to have missed. I explained everything to Robert about why I wasn't going to America.'

'Well, it seems odd to me that you could go to an hotel somewhere and be with strangers rather than spend the holiday season with your family. We are the only blood relatives you have now, you do realise that? The only ones.'

I put the car in gear and pulled out onto the empty motorway.

'I realise that all too well,' I said quietly. 'I was at my daughter's burial. And, as a matter of interest, I didn't spend Christmas in *an* hotel. I spent it at home with my dog and my memories, and Robert knew that and accepted that and I didn't have to justify it to him. He accepted it, just as I accept that he knows how to live his own life. Each of us accepts the other, faults and failings included.'

We drove on, neither of us speaking, and when we reached the point where the motorway junction arched left for my house I kept driving, straight into the night.

'You missed the turn,' my mother said.

'No, I didn't.'

'I understood I was staying over with you tonight, to break the journey.'

'I think it best that I drop you to your own house.'

'Well I have been travelling all day. I'm not a young woman.'

'It's an hour more than it would be coming to my house. And, to be truthful, I think it best that we spend as little time as possible together at the moment. Neither of us appreciates the other's position on this. So it seems best that I drive you home.'

'There's nothing in the house.'

'I'll stop and get you what you need at the next petrol station.'

'You'll regret your harshness.'

'Possibly. But I also regret your harshness and I think we've both said enough about this for the moment.'

'Well I hope you treat your friends with more understanding than you do your family.'

'I treat my friends and my family with the same respect that they give me. You decided I should be in America for Christmas, just as you decided how I should live my life and how I should raise Jane and how I should behave when she died. You don't leave me room to be myself or to make my own decisions. And if *my* decisions don't fit in with your perception of what my life should be then you assume that I'm wrong. Well, that's not how I see it and, until you accept that I am my own person and not the person you think I should be, there's no point in our spending time together.'

'I see.'

'Good.'

I bought enough groceries to keep my mother going for a week, checked every room, turned on the central heating, put two hot water bottles in her bed, made tea for us and sat at the table with her, making small talk.

Finally, I told her it was time I was going.

·

'You could stay if you're tired.'

'I'm not tired,' I said. 'Anyway, Ros is locked in. I need to get back to let him out.'

'That dog gets more attention …'

The sentence remained unfinished.

'You get a good night's sleep,' I said, kissing her on the forehead. 'I'll ring you in the morning.'

'I'm sure I won't sleep.'

'I'm sure you will.'

'Listen,' Robert said when I called to tell him what had happened. 'She did the same over here. Told me we should have gone back over to Ireland for Christmas. She thrives on making people feel like shit. When Jesus hung on the cross and wept, he was thinking of our sainted mother and the moral blackmail she would sow and reap.'

'Very poetic.'

'Poetry is often just the truth dressed up. Or down.'

It was in the frozen foods aisle that I saw Brian pushing his trolley. It was the third day of January, about four in the afternoon. Outside, the rain was surging down the huge glass walls of the supermarket.

'Happy New Year,' I said.

I had called to see Kate and Brian on New Year's Eve afternoon but hadn't seen them since.

'And to you,' he said. 'Let's hope it's a better one than last year. I suppose it has to be, doesn't it?'

I nodded.

'You got your mother home safe and sound?'

I gave him a short version of the journey from the airport.

'Sounds fun.'

'How are the women in your life?' I asked.

'They're down visiting Kate's dad in Limerick. They'll be back home tomorrow evening. I couldn't go, I had to work yesterday and this morning.'

'Someone has to do it.'

He laughed and then, looking over his shoulder and checking that the aisle was empty, he spoke very quietly.

'I don't know if I'm supposed to tell you this yet or whether I'm supposed to tell anyone but no doubt you'll hear it from Kate, anyway. We're going our separate ways.'

'What?'

'We're splitting up.'

'Jesus. When did you decide on this?'

'It's been coming for months. We talked about it a lot over the Christmas. We talked to the girls.'

'It's that final?'

'Yes.'

'Would you like to talk?'

'Sure.'

'Not here,' I said.

'I don't know,' Brian smiled. 'Frozen foods! Seems an appropriate enough place.'

'Stop off at the house. I'll make something to eat.'

I was standing at the sink, peeling potatoes. Brian was sitting at the kitchen table, dicing carrots.

'Last time we were doing this kind of thing, here, was when Jane died.'

He nodded.

'It just goes on.'

'Yes.'

'I don't even know if you want to talk about this. If you do, that's fine. If you don't, that's fine too.'

'It could have happened anytime. Back when the kids were young I was sure we were going to break up. I didn't even believe the kids would keep us together. I kept waiting for Kate to tell me it was happening. And then, when they were growing up, it seemed like we had fallen into a pattern that might just keep us together. It wasn't love, maybe it was habit, but habits are hard to break and I didn't think we'd break the habit of being together. But we've managed it,' he smiled sardonically.

'I'm sorry.'

'You know, it's more the shock of the practicalities than the emotional fracture that's freaking me. I mean it's not as if either of us is in the first throes of love. But you get used to where you live and how you live and the people you live with.'

'Yes.'

'But it's not life and death. I realise that. You know, in a strange way, I think Jane's death may have pushed Kate to thinking this through to a conclusion. I haven't said that to her. I wouldn't. And probably I shouldn't say it to you but I think that made her recognise the frailty and the shortness of life. I think she's been looking more closely at her life since then, realising things are not as she'd like them to be.'

'And you said that you've told the girls?'

'Yes. On Christmas Day.'

'And?'

'Sadness but no tears, funnily enough. No real surprise. I think Kate may have talked to them about it. Kate was the only one who cried. Isn't that strange?'

I said nothing. I was remembering her walking around in the garden outside on Christmas afternoon, walking on her own in the aftermath of that decision and I was seeing her hand waving that small, self-contained wave that told me nothing. And I was thinking of the fact that we had spoken only once in the eight days since and that had been my flying visit to say hello on New Year's Eve. No phone calls, no communication, no chats across this kitchen table. No inkling of what was happening in my friends' lives.

'I'm really so, so sorry,' I said, at last. 'I should have been here for you both to talk to. I should have been paying more attention.'

'If I didn't see it coming, how could you?'

We had almost finished our meal when Brian said, 'I think Kate has been carrying a torch for you for years.'

'Me?' I hoped my surprise at his recognising this would appear as surprise at the very notion.

'I think so. And, hey, I'm not blaming you for this. I'm just telling you what I think. But it's just one aspect of the whole thing. It's not why it happened. That goes down to our growing away from each other. Nothing new in that, it happens all over the world, every day of the year. See, that's what I mean about being able to disconnect the emotional part from the practical part. I don't have any hang-ups, I don't have a vision of the heartbreak of two people drifting apart, even though I'm one of them. And that's because there isn't any heartbreak in the romantic sense. It's down to the who, what, where and when of reorganising our lives. I don't even believe either of us is in any hurry to move out, though I might be in for a nasty surprise when Kate gets back tomorrow. Thing is, we've been married for twenty-two years but it feels a lot longer.'

'So have you talked about the practicalities at all?'

'Kate has talked about moving out. She says there's no question of our selling the house. That's really as far as we've got. I think the rest will come in the summer.'

'And the girls?'

'Susan says to do whatever we want to do once we keep paying her fees! Elizabeth just said, "Worse things happen."'

'Is Elizabeth doing ok?'

'She's hanging in there, still seeing a psychologist in the college. She says she's doing all right. She says she'll be better when the court case is over.'

'I can understand that.'

'I hope you didn't mind my saying that, about Kate having a thing for you.'

I smiled.

'It isn't an issue. I just felt I should say it, in case some-thing happens in the future, between you two. Stranger things and all that.'

'Thank you.'

'How long have we been acquainted?' Brian asked.

'Best part of twenty years.'

'Do you think we really know each other, you and I?'

'Not really,' I shook my head.

'Why is that?'

'I think our lives always kind of ran in parallel.'

'That's what I think, too. With Kate there in the middle – my wife, your friend. Actually, let me rephrase that, Kate in the centre with me, her husband, on one side and you, her friend, on the other. But she was always there between us, she's the planet around which we orbited.'

'That seems a fair assessment,' I nodded.

'Anyway, we'll see what comes of all of this. "Let's hope we continue to live."'

'Paul Simon, the *Live* album.'

·

'Spot on.'

'But true, nevertheless.'

I rang Kate the morning after she got back and she came down to the house. We hugged in the hall and I thought, again, of Christmas afternoon, of that small gesture of recognition that deserved a greater appreciation than the tiny signal with which I'd acknowledged it.

'I'm sorry,' I said.

'Nothing to be sorry about. It's been coming. You can hardly have been that surprised.'

'I meant about Christmas Day. About you in the garden.'

'That's ok. I wasn't really in much of a mood for talking and nor, I'm sure, were you.'

'No.'

'You didn't go away in the end.'

'Got as far as the car and couldn't go.'

She nodded.

'Would you like a coffee?'

'I'd like to go for a walk. That way we can both look straight ahead when we talk. Not have to catch each other's eye.'

'Is it like that?'

'I don't know.'

Ros took off ahead of us, up through the trees, following the same path we'd taken on Christmas morning.

'I had a long chat with Brian. We had dinner together.'

'He told me. He was delighted.'

'With the dinner?' I joked.

'That too.'

'It all seems to be running smoothly. For both of you.'

Kate stopped and turned to face me. She laughed out loud, a hard, bitter laugh.

'Have you any idea?'

'I didn't mean life is going smoothly. I meant you both seem to be dealing well with it. Like adults.'

She laughed again, the same cynical laugh, and her eyes filled with tears.

'You've cut yourself off from everything, haven't you? I can understand that. What can't touch you, can't hurt you, but the problem with that is that you lose touch with all the other emotions, too.'

And then her mood seemed to change. Taking a deep breath and wiping her eyes, she slipped her arm through mine and we walked on together.

'Hey, I'm not here to lecture a man who's lost his daughter. I never meant to do that. It's not my place.'

'No, you're right. I have cut myself off. My mother would agree with you.'

'Jesus, thanks,' she laughed. 'Now I know I'm in valued company.'

'So, talk to me, Kate.'

'Yes, sir. You know how far back this goes. And it's not just about you and me. It's about Brian and me, but mostly it's about me. I'm not happy. Haven't been for years. And, yes, when Jane died it made me think a lot about things. About the girls, about not making life any more difficult for them but, in spite of that, I kept coming back to the fact that staying with Brian wasn't going to make life any safer for them or any happier for any of us. I kept thinking of what you said at the funeral. About the fact that we can't always be there for them. We can only be there for ourselves for as long as that's possible.'

We walked on, our feet sweeshing the dry leaves the wind had piled along the path. The sky above was grey, unmoving, and the trees were perfectly still. A small flurry of snow began to fall.

'Who'd have believed it?'

'Happy Russian white Christmas, in advance.'

'Thank you.'

Ros crested the hill and disappeared down the other side. We followed, our heads bent into the thickening snow, down again between the sycamores where it was drier, where the snow was tumbling only into the empty pockets where trees had fallen or been felled. Down to the lower headland and along a path that nestled in the shelter of a battered blackthorn ditch.

Beyond it, the fields were being dyed white and the sky was pouring out its winter gift. Ros ran out through a break in the ditch, rolling in the fresh snow, burying his nose in its softness, snorting and rooting, chasing and barking like a mad thing. And then he looked up, lost for a moment in the mesmeric sky that was falling all around him, searching for some sight or sound of us. It took him a moment to get his bearings, to locate the trees through the silent, sheeted blizzard. And, when he did, he came romping through the whiteness, leaving paw prints in the field, bursting through the ditch, shaking himself and jumping about us, as though he hadn't seen us in years.

Kate and I sat on a tree that had come down in the November storms, peering out from the shelter of the forest at the sloping, waxen fields. The ivy on the fallen tree had withered and died, upholstering the bark in a dry russet that whispered when we moved. Ros curled up in the arm of a dead branch and, assuming we'd be there for a while, closed his eyes.

'Strange world,' Kate said. 'So much beauty, so much sadness.'

'I've thought a lot about Christmas afternoon. Not just since Brian told me about you two. I've thought about me sitting inside, about you standing outside, seems like the story of our lives, Kate.'

'Of our non-life together,' she smiled and rubbed the side of my face with the back of her hand.

A breeze began to pick up, blowing parallel to the side of the wood, drifting the snow.

'This thing with Brian and me splitting isn't about you and me, it's important that you know that. It's not some desperate attempt to put pressure on you or to take advantage of you by worming my way into your life. Even if you asked me to, I wouldn't live with you now.'

There was no hint of irony in her face.

'Do you mean that? Literally?'

'Yes, I do. I love you but you know that. That goes without saying. But how could anything come of this now? It'd be like dressing in a dead woman's clothes and pretending to be someone else. That kind of thing just doesn't work. This is for me and it's about me.'

'I understand that. I'd never have thought otherwise.'

The snow was falling thick and fast across the fields, an impenetrable gauze blocking out the world.

'We may be snowed in here,' Kate laughed.

'For now at least.'

'That's not a bad thing, is it?'

'No.'

Everything beyond the hedge was a giant screen on which shadows played, nothing was clear and nothing had any definite or lasting shape. For a moment, there was a tree in the distance and then there wasn't. A glistening gate faded and reappeared and faded again. There was no sky and, if we had stepped through the frayed and shabby winter hedge, we would immediately have been lost in the blinding paleness of a landscape devoid of features.

'I wonder if Jane is out there somewhere?' I asked and the words surprised me almost as much as they surprised Kate.

She put her arms around me and hugged me to her.

'How could she be?' she whispered. 'She travels with you everywhere.'

The wind turned momentarily, lifting a sheet of snow and slapping it against our faces and then the wind turned again and lifted it back across the hedge and the flakes were lost in the spinning accumulation beyond.

'I would love you to fuck me. Here. Now,' Kate said quietly, her face still pressed against my head. 'But I'm only saying it because it won't happen. I won't let it happen.'

'No.'

'Isn't it a form of madness to spend fifteen years reliving the dream of one shag?'

'That's not all the last fifteen years were about, between us. Not everything hinged on that one day. Not for me, I know. And not for you, I'm sure. You don't believe that's all that was to it?'

'Don't I?'

'Well, do you? Can you sit here and tell me there's been nothing of importance or value between us?'

'Friendship.'

'Brian and I have a friendship,' I said. 'Are you telling me that's the same as what you and I have?'

'Well tell me what else we've had?'

'Closeness, dependence on each other, love for each other.'

'Easy to say.'

'You don't think I love you?'

'I don't know. You're fond of me. And, anyway, it's not the issue. I don't want you thinking any of this is about you and me. It seems to keep on coming back to that and it's irrelevant. The nature of love is to change.'

'Says who?'

'In my opinion. In my experience.'

'Not in mine.'

'Good for you.'

'Why are you so angry with me?'

'I'm not angry with you. I'm angry with me. For God knows how long, I've loved you and, in all that time, we've had sex once but that hasn't stopped me loving you, in spite of everything. In spite of my husband, my children, your daughter. Do you know how jealous I was of Jane? Of the fact that she was so close to you. There was no room for anyone else when you two were together. And the fact that she died means there never will be. Ever. So I'm not fooling myself. I'm not trying to be something to you that I never can be. That's what I mean about a dead woman's clothes. And part of me wants to have you inside of me and part of me would run a hundred miles.'

'I'm sorry.'

'*For my heart is with you altogether, though I live not where I love. When I sleep I dream of you, when I wake I take no rest, every moment's thinking of you, my heart is fixed in your breast.* But that's not enough, you know. I used to think it was but it's not.'

'No. I know.'

'Course you do. And the horrible thing is that you can grow tired of someone who's living, you can finally see their faults, but the dead are dead forever and the fondly remembered but mislaid moments become a shrine.'

'It's not that simple,' I said.

·

'Is it not?'

'No.'

'Perhaps you're right.'

'I think I am.'

'Who am I to contradict you? All I know is what I feel. I'm not an expert on the nature of definition. It seems to me that things happen and memories remain and you learn to live with what you have and dream of what you need. That's how I thought life was always going to be. But I've begun to see things otherwise.'

'So what will you do?'

'Don't know. Isn't that strange? After Brian and I had made the decision, after we'd talked to the girls about it, it felt like we'd done enough for now, like there was no need to do anything else. The information was out there and that was all that was needed. We haven't talked practicalities, beyond agreeing that we won't sell the house. It's the girls' home. It's our home, too. I'll get a place when I can, somewhere near enough to keep in touch. And I'll have to get a job. But all that will come. The funny thing is, I used to dream of doing this, years ago. Of having my place, having the girls there, seeing you, having you come to dinner with Jane, having you call to see me during the day, all that stuff. Now it's possible and the excitement seems to have gone out of it. Sometimes I don't think we recognise all the bruises we carry from the beatings we've taken from life.'

'I think you're right.'

We sat together, looking out into the emptiness of the falling snow, waiting for it to ease. I knew that when it did, we would leave this place and wend our way to the car and sweep the flakes from the windscreen and drive back home, the car heater warming us, back to our other lives and all the things that needed doing.

.

But I wasn't ready for that. I just wanted to stay in that time, nestled together on that fallen tree, taking warmth from the body beside me, watching the falling snow and not really caring what was beyond the snow because, for now, I didn't have to face it.

On the last afternoon of January, I decided I wanted to choose a photograph for Jane's memoriam card. It was as simple as that. I was sitting at my desk, talking to Larry.

He had called to tell me that the trial date had been set for early autumn.

'I'd have preferred it earlier, for your sake. It'll be a tough time, I know,' he said. 'But we'll get you through it and then things will start to change.'

The rays from the setting sun had made a rainbow between the empty trees and the garden was flooded with a glorious light.

'I must get Jane's memoriam card organised,' I told him.

He looked at me as though I hadn't been listening to what he'd been telling me.

I smiled.

'Just what you said about things starting to change,' I said. 'And that burst of sunlight. The year is moving on. I'm not talking about leaving things behind but I am talking about what I need to do. I'll deal with the trial when it comes, Larry, I just want to do the things I want to do, without thinking about them. And it feels like it's time to do this. Does that sound odd to you?'

'Nothing sounds odd to me. You're the one in the middle of it. I'm very much on the outside when it comes to the feelings involved. I have a job to do. What I feel doesn't really come into things – if it did, I couldn't do the job. And I feel a good feeling when I see someone starting to move his life along. I'm not here to judge anyone. Other guys get well paid to sit on the bench and do that.'

'Spoken like a true sceptic.'

He shrugged and smiled.

'Was Jane like you?' he asked. 'Personality wise?'

'I think it would be more true to say I took whatever personality I have from her. She was the dominant force in this house. Jane first, the dog second, me third.'

'Join the club,' he said and we both laughed.

'We need a system,' Kate said.

'A system is most important,' I said, mimicking her accent.

There was something light and flirtatious in the air. It was as though spring had suddenly removed something awful and replaced it with something bearable. It was the kind of laughing conversation Jane thrived on, the banter, the lack of direction, the possibility that it might lead anywhere or everywhere.

'If you don't stop taking the piss, you can do this yourself.'

'No, I value your advice and I wouldn't want Jane being ill-served by an unfashionable photograph.'

It was Saturday afternoon, the first of spring. Kate and Brian and Elizabeth and Susan and myself were seated around the kitchen table; a cardboard box of photos lay open between us.

'So what's the system, Mum?' Susan asked.

'Well, I think you need to put aside the pictures you definitely don't want considered,' she pointed at me. 'Then we can all go through the ones you think are possibilities and let you know what we think.'

'That's what you call a system?' Brian sniggered.

'It's a Mum System. Half-assed,' Susan added.

'You, of course, may have a better one.'

'We could divide the photos and each of us could choose our favourites and then pool those,' I said.

'Actually, and it pains me to say this, I think Kate's idea is better,' Brian said. 'Your way means a picture can get discarded without any check.'

'Tell you what,' I said. 'If someone makes coffee, I'll get started on the photos and by the time the coffee's ready, I'll have a load of pictures for you guys to look at.'

'If you had them on computer, of course, we could have a slide show. You're a Luddite,' Susan said.

'True. So I reckon you've nominated yourself for coffee making. And Mr Ludd will get cracking on sorting what's here.'

So many photographs, back to childhood. Photographs of Jane in Beth's arms, in her grandparents' arms, Jane in a babygro, Jane taking her first steps, birthday parties, her first day at school, on holiday, with Elizabeth, with Ros when he was a pup, at the seaside, with Elizabeth and Susan, halfway up a mountain, laughing, pouting, posing, caught unawares.

'I can't do this,' Elizabeth said suddenly; she was shaking. 'I really can't do this.'

Kate and Brian put their arms around her; none of us spoke. Instead, we sat in simple silence, listening to the choking sobs, watching the tears and snot congeal on Elizabeth's face, seeing her wipe it away with the sleeve of her jumper, seeing her eyes sink suddenly into her head as though some terrible sight had almost blinded her.

She took a deep breath, in an attempt to control her sobbing, and then another. I watched her shoulders stiffen and then shudder and then strengthen again.

'I know you want this to be like it used to be,' she said at last. 'I know you want us to think of happy times, but it doesn't work. It's a pretence, for all of us.'

Over her shoulder, through the kitchen window, I could see a pigeon picking its way across a flowerbed and then another appeared from behind a shrub and they moved between some potted plants, dipping and picking at the hard earth, moving deliberately in step.

'Sometimes it's easier to do these things together,' Kate said.

Elizabeth shook her head.

'All I keep seeing is someone … I don't know, someone I knew who's gone. I can't do it, I'm really sorry but I can't. I remember most of these pictures. Jesus, I'm in half of them. I'm sorry.'

'It doesn't have to be done now,' I said.

'You need to do it,' Elizabeth said. 'But it can't be a party. I don't think we should all be here. You should do it or maybe just one of us with you, but not me. I can't.'

'I think we'll head home,' Brian said. 'Might be the best thing to do at the moment.'

'I'd like to see them,' Susan said quietly. 'I haven't seen most of them before.'

'Well if you'd like to stay, I'd be glad of the company. I know how you feel, Elizabeth, and I didn't ask you all here to make things worse, but you know that.'

'Yes, I know that,' she said. 'It just isn't possible for me.'

'Sure. It may have been a bad idea.'

After Elizabeth and Brian and Kate had gone, I sat with Susan at the table.

'I'm closer in age to Jane than she is,' she said. 'Liz just kind of always had to be the one to pick and choose who was to be her friend. I got left with the rest.'

'Jane was very fond of you.'

'I know that. But Liz always made sure I knew she was her friend first and foremost.'

'Right.'

'It's a sisters' thing, I don't expect you to understand,' she shrugged and laughed.

'So, do we have a system?' I paused. 'That sounds awful but there are hundreds of pictures here. If I start getting upset over each one, I'll never choose and I want to choose. I want to get the card done soon. I feel the time is right.'

'You don't have to explain to me,' Susan said and her face was absolutely serious.

'Thank you.'

'I'd like to see them,' she said quietly.

'So?'

'I think Mum was right. You have to go through them all and then pass them to me and I'll make two sets, the ones I like and the ones I don't. We're looking for one with only Jane, right?'

'Right, but it could be taken from a group photograph.'

'Then it'll blow up like something crap probably.'

'Possibly.'

'Well, let's see how it goes.'

And so we began. For a time, we worked quickly. I discarded anything that hadn't been taken in the past three years. I discarded anything that wasn't absolutely in focus. I discarded most group photographs. But, as soon as Susan began to examine the pictures I passed to her, the questions and comments started.

'Who's this? Where was this taken? Wow, that's a gorgeous top. I don't remember Jane's hair being like that.'

'You're so like your mother,' I said.

'You like my mother, don't you?'

'She and Brian have been great friends to me.'

'I know that. But you like her? She certainly likes you. We all know that.'

'Do we?'

'We do!'

'And your point is?'

'My point is? I don't know what my point is,' she giggled.

'Kate and Brian are both friends of mine.'

'Yes.'

'Not just Kate.'

She burst out laughing.

'Come on. Who are you kidding? Mum is nuts about you. There's a difference. Dad doesn't fancy you at all.'

'Do you know how weird it is to sit here, listening to a young woman suggest there might be something between me and her mother? Not just suggest it, encourage the notion.'

'Well, it's pretty fecking weird to be sitting here going through these photographs but we're getting there. It's all relative. You're not my father, are you?'

I laughed out loud.

'I just wondered. I've often wondered. So has Liz. Stranger things have happened. I'm just asking. I'm doing you a favour here, so you can do me one by answering honestly.'

'I am not your father. I am not Elizabeth's father.'

'These things are possible. I know my mother would shag you if she could, so she might have done in the past.'

'Have you ever thought of becoming a writer?' I asked. 'You have a very vivid imagination.'

'I don't think so. Anyway, I believe you. Now, where was this taken?'

She waved a photograph in front of me.

'Greece. The summer before last.'

'She loved that holiday.'

'Did she?'

'Yes. She said it was the best time of her life. She said it was beautiful and she was really happy there. She said you two loved it.'

'We did but I didn't realise she was so positive about it.'

'Well she was. You should use this on the card.'

'Jane isn't even looking at the camera, her eyes are looking down. And there's a window frame in the shot.'

'It's her.'

I took the photograph from Susan. It showed a young woman, her right arm on the half frame of a white window. Her left hand pressed against the glass. She was looking down and to her right, her wind-blown, sea-washed, blonde hair falling over her left eye. She was wearing a sleeveless blue T-shirt and her face and arms were suntanned and lightly freckled. Her mouth was set in a serious line. It was a moment I'd caught from the garden of the whitewashed cottage we'd rented in Greece, an instant at the end of the day, the sun going down behind me, the light dying. Jane hadn't even known I was taking the picture.

When I'd shown it to her on the camera screen, she'd said, 'I look very serious.'

'Yes,' I'd said. 'And you look a lot younger than eighteen.'

And then she'd winked and smiled and walked away to shower.

'So what do you think?' Susan asked.

'Look through the others again.'

'What do you think of that one, though?'

'Some people would find it odd. My mother, Beth's parents, a lot of people. Most people. It's not your usual memoriam-card picture.'

'Isn't that good? The last thing Jane would have wanted is a photo that has her all dressed up for dying.'

I laughed out loud.

'You're a funny young woman.'

'Well she hated that kind of thing. The formality. The bullshit. She'd have loved this. She'd have picked it herself.'

I nodded and Susan smiled, holding the picture up, waiting for my verdict but too excited to wait very long.

'So what do you think?'

'I think you're absolutely right. I think this is the one. Absolutely.'

'Is Elizabeth ok?'

'She's fine. She and Susan have gone to Dublin for the day. So let me see the photograph? Susan says it's the one you have to use.'

I took an envelope from the kitchen shelf and handed it to Kate.

Taking the picture from the envelope, she smiled.

'Different but, then, she was different. It's a gorgeous photograph. She'd definitely be happy with that. Have you chosen any words to go with it?'

'Yes.'

'And?'

'"Golden slumbers kiss your eyes,
   smiles awake you when you rise:
   sleep pretty wantons do not cry,
   and I will sing a lullaby."'

'That's The Beatles.'

'Funnily enough, it's not. It's a guy called Thomas Dekker. Died in 1632. The Beatles just borrowed it.'

'You're a fount of knowledge.'

'Most of it useless.'

'Some. Not all,' Kate smiled.

'And you're sure Elizabeth is all right?'

'She's getting there.'

'It probably was a stupid idea, the picture-picking thing. It must have seemed odd to her.'

'It was a nice idea. I think she thought so, too, till she got here.'

'I'll talk to her later. Show her the photograph. See what she thinks.'

'Do that.'

'Susan was very entertaining. She's much more outgoing. I haven't had such an enjoyable conversation in a long time.'

'Thanks.' Kate laughed.

'What I meant is that she's very challenging. Keeps you on your toes.'

'That she does.'

'She's very like Jane, in her manner, her sense of humour.'

'True.'

'Strange that she and Jane weren't closer, that Elizabeth was the one who was closer to Jane.'

Kate shrugged.

'People are odd. We don't always choose what's best for us. Sometimes we make the wrong choices. Sometimes we do things for strange reasons. I think Susan has modelled herself on Jane anyway. Even though Jane was a year younger. Susan'll be twenty-one in August. She was always impressed by Jane, especially by the way Jane always seemed to be so focused. Susan pretends to be, but she's not. She's ditzy at heart but she covers it well. Elizabeth is more her own woman, perhaps that's where the attraction lay.'

'Perhaps.'

Kate looked again at the photograph and then put it back in the envelope.

'Photographs and memories,' she said.
'Jim Croce,' I said. 'ABC/Dunhill.'
Kate nodded but she didn't smile.

I took the photograph and the Dekker lines to the printer the following afternoon.

The woman at the desk was polite and helpful.

'I want the photograph on one side, just that and then these lines on the reverse.'

She nodded.

'Just that?'

'Yes. I think so.'

'Jane, isn't it?'

'Yes.'

'I was terribly sorry to hear what happened. It was horrible,' she said.

'Thank you.'

She hesitated a moment.

'You'll probably want to put her name and dates on, too, or an age. That's your choice, of course.'

'Yes, of course. I'd forgotten.'

She took a pad from a drawer and passed it to me.

I wrote Jane's name and age in block capitals.

'So the photograph on the front and the name, age and verse on the back?'

'Yes.'

'Would you like it as a card or a bookmark?'

'The difference is?'

She took some samples from a drawer.

'The bookmark,' I said immediately.

'And how many would you like?'

'I have no idea.'

'It depends on whether you're sending them to everyone who sent cards. I'm sure you're not. They're normally for friends and family.'

'Can you do a hundred then?'

'Of course. And if you need more, you can come back and I'll do more.'

'Thank you.'

'Did you want acknowledgement cards, for those who wrote, people who sent cards and things like that?'

'I've actually written back to everyone who wrote,' I said.

'That must have taken a lot of time and effort.'

'It seemed the right thing to do.'

'Of course. It's a beautiful photograph. She was a beautiful girl,' the woman said. 'Must have been a sunny place. Not here, not last summer anyway.'

'Greece,' I said. 'The summer before last.'

'Again,' she said, 'I'm really sorry. It was a terrible tragedy. An appalling thing.'

'Yes.'

'I'll have the cards for you on Friday morning. Would you like envelopes for some of them?'

'Yes. Say fifty envelopes.'

'Fifty envelopes and one hundred bookmarks and I'll have the photograph here for you to collect then, too.'

'Thank you. Can I pay now?'

'Of course, but you can wait till Friday if you wish.'

'No, I'd rather pay now.'

The woman totted some figures on a calculator and gave me an invoice. I wrote her a cheque and she gave me a receipt. And that was it.

Stepping out into the street, I found myself shivering. It wasn't the wind or the falling evening sky that put that coldness in my bones. It was something deeper and harder, something profound that had come out of the banal conversation I'd had with the woman in the print shop. It was the reminder, again, of that holiday in Greece, of the sunlight, of the days and the tempting quietness of the night. It was as if, suddenly, after all these months and everything that had happened, after all the conversations and solitary reminiscences, this one commonplace exchange had finally informed me, like a notice coming through the post, that my daughter was dead, that all the laughter and all my recent straining after normality, all my attempts at pretending that nothing essential had changed, were suddenly and patently revealed for the dismal pretences that they were.

The strength had bled from my body. It felt like I was going to pass out. Taking a deep breath, I edged slowly along the footpath, my shoulder brushing the shop walls, drawing support from their solidity. I knew I needed to find somewhere to sit down and I needed to get off the street. I thought of going back to the print shop, asking for a chair and a glass of water, and then I realised there was a coffee shop across the street. Checking the traffic, I crossed slowly and stepped into the café.

The place was deserted and I was glad of that. I sat heavily into the window seat. A waitress came immediately with a menu and put it on the table. She was a woman about my own age, with spiked red hair.

'Are you all right?' she asked. 'You look very pale.'

'I just need to sit down. Thank you.'

'You should have some sugar,' she said, pushing the bowl towards me. 'And a drink. I'll get you a soft drink.'

She was back almost immediately, a glass fizzing in her hand.

'Drink that,' she ordered.

I did as I was told.

'If you feel you're going to faint, just put your head down. Do you feel you're going to faint?'

I shook my head.

'You're sure? I'll stay here with you if you do.'

'Yes, thanks. I thought I was for a moment but I'm ok now. Honestly.'

'You weren't struck by a car or something were you?'

'No,' I said. 'It's just something that I remembered, something that happened a while ago. It just suddenly hit me. It's hard to explain but I'll be fine.'

'Your colour's coming back. Is there someone I could ring for you?'

'Honestly, I'm fine.'

'Tea then? And a sticky bun?'

'Sounds just the ticket. And thank you.'

'And put lots of sugar in the tea.'

'I will.'

When I got home, I sat at my desk and rewound everything that had happened through the afternoon – the trip to the print shop, the conversation about the card, the consideration of the woman who worked there, stepping into the street, the coldness, the weakness, the coffee shop like a refuge, the kindness of the waitress. She had refused to take any money for the drinks and cake. The slow drive home and Ros at the door, barking as he always barked when I drove my car into the yard. All the details were in place, everything intact. Nothing that was any different from any other conversation of three hundred conversations I'd had with people in the last five months.

But something in my mind had snapped on the street, something had informed me that my acceptance of everything that had happened was no longer acceptable, something inside me was rising up against the loss. It wasn't as if I suddenly wanted to kill the men who had killed Jane, nothing as predictable as that. I still had no place for them in my consideration and I doubted I ever would. To allow them any attention would be to give them a recognition that was more than they deserved and that was something I wasn't prepared even to consider. They were dirt and I would wipe them from the soles of my shoes as quickly as I could. I wouldn't even countenance their being in the same mental space as my daughter.

When the time came for the trial, I doubted I would even go. I didn't want to see them, I had no curiosity about how they might look or react, I didn't want to hear their mumbling explanations, I didn't want to know about their family circumstances or the hard lives they'd had, I didn't want to listen while one tried to blame the other. None of it was of any significance, it was all peripheral detail and knowing any or all of it would change nothing. Whatever they said would be no more than words spouted in an attempt to baffle or cloud or confuse or explain, as though there could ever be an explanation for what they'd done. Their hearts might bleed or they might decide on a resolute stoniness – it didn't matter to me. These two people had never been of interest to me and never would be. The consequence of what they had done was the thing I had to deal with, the event itself was something I could never imagine myself even considering.

'Now there's something strange,' Jane had said.

'What's that?'

'The Greek for "yes" is pronounced *neh* and the Greek for "no" is pronounced *okhee*. That could be very confusing.'

'Could be. You'll have to be careful.'

'Me?'

'Well you're the one boning up on the language. You'll be the interpreter.'

'That could be dangerous. Try me.'

She tossed the phrase book across the room.

'Please?'

'*Pahrahkahlo.*'

'Good morning.'

'*Kahleemehrah.*'

'How are you?'

'*Poss eesteh.*'

'Yes.'

'*Okhee.* No, *neh. Neh.*'

'Very good. You're getting there. I'm sure they speak English anyway.'

'That's a typically patronising, holiday-maker attitude. Worse than that, it's an oppressive, dictatorial, presumptuous attitude. It reeks of empire.'

'Right.'

'It says I can't be bothered making an effort so let them do all the work. They're only Greeks.'

'Listen,' I'd said. 'I was the one who refused point blank to go to Greece in the seventies, when my parents wanted to take Robert and me there on holiday. He was thirteen and I was eleven and we knew our own minds, even then. We insisted that we wouldn't go while the Colonels were in power, us and Ralph McTell. So less of the sweeping generalisations.'

'Did you really refuse to go?'

'Yes we did. My mother was all on for it. We said no, not while the country was under the heels of a dictatorship.'

'Really?'

'Yes, really. It was mostly Robert's idea but I stood behind him. He'd been reading up on it in the papers.'

'Cool.'

'I didn't think you'd be so easily impressed.'

'Oh I am,' Jane had laughed. 'You never mentioned that before.'

'There you are, you don't know everything about me yet.'

'So what happened?'

'The parents went. Left us with my aunt. Thought we'd be miserable. We had a brilliant time. The sun shone here and they had thunderstorms. Justice was done and, better still, it was seen to be done.'

I didn't tell Kate about the episode in town. What was the point? She'd fuss and worry. She'd make an appointment for me to see Frank Morris without even telling me. And Frank, in turn, would explain how the grieving process took apparently strange twists and turns but that these were to be expected and that I needed to manage my reactions and not isolate myself and then he'd ask why I hadn't been to see him. And, between them, they'd devise a plan to get me through the next eighteen months. And they would.

And so, for a week, I took Kate's calls, had coffee with her twice, walked Ros every morning and afternoon, worked hard on plans I was drawing for a house, kept myself busy and determined to put distance between myself and whatever it was that had happened on the street.

The night before I was due to collect the memoriam cards, I dreamt of Jane. It was a dream of recollection and the things that happened in it were just as they had been in reality. We were in the car, driving to the airport, packed and ready for our Greek adventure, three weeks on a small, quiet island.

It was four o'clock on a morning in early July. The motorway was empty, light beginning to sip the half-darkness of this summer daybreak in 2006.

'You may find it boring,' I said. 'We can always move somewhere else.'

'Somewhere that has discos and guys my age?'

'Yes.'

'Thanks but no thanks.'

'Three weeks is a long time to be in a quiet place with mainly your father for company.'

'Three weeks? It's been fifteen years since mum died. Don't you think I can make it through another three weeks?'

'Well I'm just saying.'

'Thank you. But I'm looking forward to it.'

'Me too.'

And then I woke, to the sound of Ros padding along the landing and jumping onto Jane's bed, as he did every night now, and I lay there in the darkness, wondering where that particular memory had come from and why tonight? I tried to remember the quality of Jane's voice in the dream. The words were clear but I wanted to delight in the tone, not just to be reminded. I wanted to actually hear it again.

I knew that if I slept there would be some other dream or no dream at all. When she came in dreams they were exceptional moments, always short, always exactly as they had occurred in life, always reminders of what had been, rather than flights of imagination.

Early the following morning, I collected the memoriam cards from the print shop. Afterwards, I went and ordered breakfast in the coffee shop down the street. Only then did I open the small parcel of envelopes and bookmarks. And there was Jane, beyond the Greek window, blonde hair falling, eyes downcast, freckled face, mouth set in a serious line. And, on the other side, the words and dates. Midsummer's day 1988 and a date I wished I could forget in the autumn of 2007. A hundred photographs of my daughter, a hundred copies of a poem, a hundred birthdays, a hundred days of dying.

And then a waitress was at my shoulder, putting coffee and scones on the table.

'Thank you,' I said.

'You're feeling better?'

I looked up: it was the same red-haired woman who had looked after me earlier in the week.

'Apologies,' I said. 'I didn't recognise you when I ordered.'

'You didn't order from me,' she smiled. 'Just that I saw you and thought I'd bring your breakfast.'

Glancing at the table, she saw the cards spread out before me and recognised them for what they were.

'I'm sorry,' she said. 'I didn't mean to intrude.'

'My daughter.'

I handed her a card.

'Christ! I remember this. Was it last autumn? The time has flown. I'm sorry I didn't know when you came in the other day.'

'I'd just ordered these cards,' I said. 'I think that's what had me feeling the way I was.'

'Well it would, of course it would.'

Looking up, I saw there were tears in her eyes.

I motioned to her to sit down and she did.

'I'm terrible for this,' she said. 'The slightest thing gets me going. They're always laughing at me at home. Anything starts me off. And you don't need this from a total stranger.'

'No need to explain,' I said. 'It's good to know there are people who care.'

'She's beautiful. I love the photograph. It's a real picture, not one of these posed ones you always see staring out from cards. Like the person knew why it was being taken. And they're always at bloody weddings. Every time I have a picture taken at a wedding, I squint or make a funny face, so they can never use it on my memorial card.'

I laughed loudly and then the waitress laughed too.

'I'm going to leave you to your breakfast. Again, I'm sorry.'

'I'd like to give you one of these,' I said, offering her a card. 'If it doesn't seem too strange a thing to do. Every time I look at them, I'll remember coming in here, the other day and this morning.'

'Thank you,' the woman said. 'That's really very good of you. And I'll pray for her.'

'And me?'

She grinned a crooked grin.

'And you.'

The following morning, while the frost flickered on the windows, I set to work putting the memoriam cards in envelopes and addressing them. I sent ten to my mother knowing that within forty-eight hours she'd be back to me, telling me she needed another ten or that I could have them back because she couldn't give that to anyone and that she'd get her own printed. But I didn't care.

After breakfast, I took Ros out walking and, on the way back, I stopped at Kate and Brian's house. Brian was in the yard, defrosting the windscreen of his car.

'Great to see the summer here again,' he smiled.

'Indeed.'

'Kate's inside, getting ready. She has a job interview this morning.'

'Has she?'

'Yep, in Donovan's. But it's not till twelve.'

'I brought these cards up,' I said.

I handed him one and he looked at it and read the verse and looked, again, at the photograph.

'That's the woman, no doubt about it,' he said. 'Can I keep this?'

'Of course. I brought half a dozen.'

'Thank you.'

Taking his wallet from his jacket pocket, he slipped the card inside.

'Now I'd better be going. Go on in. I'll talk to you later.'

'Yes. Take it easy, the roads are frosty.'

'I will.'

Kate was in the kitchen in her dressing gown. She looked tired.

'I believe you're job hunting,' I said. 'You didn't tell me.'

'It's just an interview.'

'Well I hope it goes well.'

'It's a pretty dead-end job in an office, as far as I can see. It'll drive me mad if I get it, and if I don't get it I'll be wondering why.'

'You'll fly it.'

'Not if there are half a dozen young ones willing to work for minimum wage and a percentage off the clothes they buy. The tide's going out, surely you must have noticed that with your own work. Everything's slowing down.'

'Hasn't hit me yet, but I've been playing catch up for the past few months.'

'Well take it easy then. Once you do catch up, there may be nothing left to do.'

'Thank you for that cheerful advice.'

'That'll be twenty euro.'

She poured two cups of coffee.

'I brought these over,' I said. 'For you and Brian and the girls. There are a few spares in there in case you think of anyone else. I gave Brian one outside.'

Opening the envelope, Kate took the cards from it and smiled.

'Beautiful,' she said. 'You were right to go with this.'

'Susan's idea.'

'Well it's the right idea. Thank you.'

She kissed me lightly on the cheek.

We sat drinking coffee. Kate nibbled on a slice of toast.

'So when did you apply for the job?' I asked.

'Last week. It was advertised in the paper. I'm sorry now that I did, but who knows what's coming round the corner?'

'Brian's job is safe.'

'Civil service, of course. But I can't be tied into depending on that forever. That's the problem. The jobs that I could have taken a year ago are gone. It's only this kind of crap that's left. And I wouldn't count on it for a pension.'

'Right.'

'I think it best I do something. Not just for the money, for sanity's sake.'

'It's that bad?'

'It is really. Yes.'

'I'm sorry.'

'Listen I have to get myself ready, shower, do my hair, all the rubbish that men wouldn't have to worry about if they had to apply for underpaid, dead-end, soul-destroying jobs. But I'll meet you for lunch. Should be out of this interview thing well before one. We can talk then.'

'I'll make lunch.'

'No let's eat out. Let's be normal and ordinary and eat in a public place. Ok?'

'There's a coffee shop across from the dry cleaners,' I said. 'Will you be able to find that?'

'I know it. I've been there a few times.'

'So have I.'

'Miracles will never cease. I'll see you there about a quarter to one.'

'Good luck with the interview.'

'Well, how did it go?'

'Too well,' Kate said. 'I had to tell them I didn't want the job.'

'Really?'

'They wanted me, but I didn't want them. Minimum wage. No insurance policy. No security. No prospects. They wanted me to do a job that they created for a seventeen-year-old with a short skirt and a low top. So I told them to shove it. Politely of course.'

'Good for you.'

'Yeah, but when I stepped outside the door, I felt stupid. Why apply and then turn it down?'

'What's the betting they ring you with a better offer if they don't get someone else?'

'We'll see.'

The red-haired waitress came to the table with menus.

'How are you?' she asked.

'I'm well thanks, and you?'

'Still here. Today's special is lasagne and we have baked potatoes as well.'

'Thanks.'

'Right. I'll leave you to choose. Be back in few minutes.'

'You know her?' Kate asked.

'Yes. I told you, I'm a regular here.'

'Since when have you been a regular in any restaurant in this town?'

'Since last week.'

We studied the menu in silence.

'You decided?' Kate asked.

'Yes. The vegetable panini and salad.'

'You should eat more.'

'Yes, Mother.'

The waitress came back and took our order.

'So what are you going to do about the job situation – if they don't get back to you, which I still think they will, if they have any sense?'

'Keep looking, I suppose.'

'Are you stuck for money? I can let you have some. I have more than I need.'

'Hold on to it. The building lark may be about to hit the dirt.'

'There's Jane's insurance policy. And really I am comfortable. The policy is not money I want to touch. I thought you could use some of it to pay the girls' college fees. It should go to something like that. It's not money I'd ever dream of spending on a holiday or a car or frivolous stuff.'

'Why are you always so hard on yourself, always so frugal when it comes to yourself?'

'I don't starve. I have everything I need.'

How stupid that sounded.

'Things,' I added. 'I have all the things I need.'

'Neither of us has everything we need,' Kate said quietly, as though she hadn't heard me.

'No.'

The waitress came with the food.

'Enjoy,' she said.

'The last time we were in a restaurant together was the day we went to the hospital to identify Jane,' I said.

'I was just thinking that, too. Great minds.'

'Yeah.'

'Are things any better for you now? In truth?'

'Yes and no,' I said. 'The day-to-day things are all running smoothly. That's why I mentioned the money. In fact, and please don't bite my head off, I've already put the insurance money into an account in your name. It's not my money, Kate, but it should be used for something that matters. Education, getting the girls started with house deposits, something like that. I know you'll think this strange, but you could use it, or Brian. If you need to get a step into a new life, either of you or both of you.'

'I don't know what to say.'

'I don't want you to say anything. I'll have the paperwork early next week and I don't want to hear any more about it. You use it as you think best. I could never use it and Jane would kill me if she thought I'd left it sitting in a capitalist bank.'

'Thank you.'

'Just one condition. No flashy red sports cars. Ok?'

'You're a strange man.'

'But I think you knew that all along. That's the attraction.' I smiled.

But Kate wasn't smiling.

'Have you any idea how hard this is?' she asked. 'Sitting here with someone I've loved since I met him, knowing there's nothing I can do to break into his life. Being the beneficiary of his generosity.'

'As I have been of yours –'

'Shut up and let me say what I have to say,' Kate interrupted. 'You really don't have any idea and I'm not blaming you. A year, two years after Beth was killed, I thought we were finding some common ground. I was prepared to live with you, to marry you, to be your mistress, whatever it took to be closer to you. But that never happened. One shag and that was it and that was worse than nothing because it was bloody enjoyable. Like I told you, I've been living in the blind hope of a day when Jane and my girls had left home and we might have a time and place to be together. I was cold about it. I cut Brian out of the picture. I just lived in the hope of you and me. Just us. No one else. And that might have happened. At least, that's what I told myself. But it won't happen now. I've accepted that, but you go on being a kind man, you go on being my friend and I go on being in love with you. And that's it. And when I was sitting in Donovan's office this morning, looking around and thinking I might be stuck there for the next twenty years, I realised that I have to get away. I can't go on putting myself through what I've been putting myself through. If I don't see you and hear from you regularly, I may have some chance of finding whatever is left of my life. So that's what I'm going to do. Move and then find a place and a job. Dublin. London. Somewhere that's miles from you. For far too long, I've been thinking the other way round – find a place, find a job and then move. But that'll never happen. If I go, it'll force me to do the rest. I decided that this morning. That was the best thing that came out of that poxy interview. It made my mind up. And, now, you come along with this offer of money, right on cue. So, no, there'll be no sports car and I will look after the girls but I'm going to use some of your gift to get away from you. How ironic is that?'

'It's pretty ironic.'

'For fuck's sake,' she said.

The woman at the next table threw a withering glance in our direction.

And then, before I could move, Kate was pulling her bag from under her chair, stumbling between the tables and barging past a woman with a buggy in the doorway and then she was gone.

It rained all that night. I know this because I was awake all night.

I hadn't rung Kate that afternoon or evening because I thought it best to give her time and space to deal with the things that were going through her head. I didn't believe there was anything I could say at this stage that would make a difference to her and, anyway, I didn't want to have some kind of stilted conversation, knowing that Brian might be sitting in the same room. Kate and I knew one another well enough to leave each other alone when the situation demanded it. One or other of us would sense an appropriate time to make a connection again.

The day passed and the next and it was Sunday night and Robert rang and we talked for over an hour.

'How are Brian and Kate and the girls?' he asked.

'The girls are fine, yeah. Brian and Kate are talking about going their separate ways. Kate's talking about moving somewhere. Nothing final yet, but it seems it's going to happen.'

'And does that affect you?'

'No,' I laughed and I told him a version of the conversation Kate and I had had in the coffee shop.

'Well, you know what I think?' Robert asked. 'If ever I saw a couple et cetera, but I'm not a matchmaker. Nor was I ever meant to be.'

'It's complicated,' I said.

'Sounds like it's getting less so.'

'Not really. If anything, it's getting more so.'

'Because your excuses are drying up,' Robert laughed.

'Something like that.'

'But that's not the all of it?'

'No.'

'Well, I can't advise you there. If it's something you want to talk about, I'm here. But you already know that.'

'Yes.'

'Or if it's something you'd rather talk to Jenny about?'

'Thanks.'

'Or both of us. I'm running out of combos here!'

I laughed.

'Speaking of which,' Robert said. 'We're hoping to get back there in late April.'

'Great. I look forward to it. Excellent.'

'Well, you know the number. Don't be a stranger.'

'No.'

As soon as I'd hung up the phone rang again. My mother's number flashed on the call ID. I let it ring out and then waited ten minutes before checking the message. Just in case, by some awful miracle, she was still on the line.

'It's me,' the recording said. 'I hope everything is well with you. I haven't heard from you since Wednesday. I hope you're all right. I'm sure you're busy but give me a ring for a chat when you get time. I like to know what's going on in my boys' lives.'

No you don't, I thought.

On the following Tuesday morning, I had a call from a woman at the bank. All of the paperwork had been completed. I just needed to get Kate to sign a form and the money could be transferred.

'That might take a few days.'

'No hurry,' the woman said. 'Whenever is suitable to you both. It's all here. It should only take five minutes.'

And still I let things sit. What was I to do? Ring Kate and say, I know you think I'm a bollocks but I need you to sign this form and take this money so would you mind swallowing your pride?

The remainder of that week slid by and, all the time, I was thinking about how I should say what I needed to say. The facts were clear and, at first, I thought it was simply a question of finding the right phrases. But there were no phrases that would make it any easier to tell or to hear.

And another weekend came around and I spent all of that cold, clear, crisp Saturday out on the hills with Ros. I brought food and water in a rucksack and we walked ourselves to a standstill and then we rested and ate and looked across at the last tatters of snow on the distant peaks.

Someone was burning gorse on the lower reaches of a mountain and the smoke was drifting towards us, across the valley, slowly but certainly. And so, too, I thought, the time was coming when Kate and I would talk, when she would say what she had to say and I would tell her what I could tell her. It was strange to think about it because, inevitably, when it was done, things would change forever between us and a small part of me didn't want that to happen. But, mostly, I looked forward to telling the truth.

Walking back to the car, wind burned and exhausted, I felt strangely revitalised.

Coincidentally, or perhaps it wasn't coincidence, when I got home there was a note through the letter box. *Sorry I missed you. Away with the girls tomorrow. Will call on day after. K x*

·

'We need to get to the bank to sign whatever needs signing,' I said.

It was Monday morning. We were sitting in my kitchen over coffee, each making uneasy small talk, as though nothing had happened, as though there was nothing in particular that needed to be said, each waiting to say so much.

'When suits?' Kate asked.

'Today, now, in an hour. Whatever fits in with your plans.'

'Now is fine. Just let me finish this coffee.'

'Sure. Take your time.'

'I've been thinking a lot over the past week,' she said suddenly. 'You need to stop letting things happen to you and make them happen for you. You need to be more passionate about life. And I'm not talking about shagging me. I'm talking about you and this way you have of sitting back and letting life wash over you. I've known you for twenty years and you've allowed yourself to just exist, you've lived without passion.'

'That's not true.'

'Yes, it is true.'

'I've had passion in my life.'

'Well I haven't seen it. Oh, you had it for Jane, same as I have it for Elizabeth and Susan, but that's for others, that's a different thing, that's protection. You don't have passion for yourself, you don't have obsession, infatuation, a fixation for a person, for people, for the possibilities of your one, wild life. I've never seen it in the way you live your life.'

'That doesn't mean it isn't there or hasn't been there.'

'Well, unless you're humping the red-headed waitress in the coffee shop, there's no sign of it. And, even if you are, you're keeping it well under wraps. Come on. I've seen you virtually every day in that time and there hasn't been anything that ever gave a hint that you really cared about something that was really important to you for yourself. It's never been there and that's not a healthy thing. It just isn't. You need something for yourself.'

Kate understood as much about me as any living person but she still didn't know me. I wanted her to accept that not everything in my life was admirable. But most of all, I needed her to comprehend the extent of the hollow that had been left in that life. If no one recognised the magnitude of what had truly caused that void then something deeply wonderful would have gone unrecognised and unspoken. And I knew in my heart that it is never enough simply to remember.

'I want us to go to the bank. I want you to sign the forms. I want the money transferred. Then I want us to sit down, not necessarily today but sometime soon, and I want you to listen. I have things that I need to tell you, things you need to hear.'

'As have I,' Kate said.

'I really want to get all the paper stuff finished, it's been sitting in the bank for days. And then I'll talk all you want. I promise. Ok?'

'Ok. Let's do it, let's go. If it's that important, I want to hear it. I presume it's not a marriage proposal?' Kate smiled a weak smile.

We went to the bank, signed the papers and went for a coffee. And then I had a call from a client who was having problems with a planning application on a house I'd designed for him. It was a situation that needed my attention.

'Tomorrow,' Kate said, as I was leaving the restaurant. 'Today wasn't meant to be the day. I didn't honestly ever feel it was. Tomorrow will be better.'

'You sure?'

'Yes. I have things I can get done myself, things that need doing. In fact, I think tomorrow is better all round.'

'Ok.'

'So, tomorrow?'

'Fine,' I said. 'Eleven? Twelve?'

'I'll come down around half twelve,' she said. 'And, again, thank you so much for the money. I won't blow it all on myself. You know that. The girls will do well from it, education wise, life wise. Seriously.'

'I know that,' I said.

'And if you ever need it, or part of it, back …'

'I'll never need it.'

I met my client, went with him to the site and then to the planning office.

'You don't have to do this,' he said. 'I really don't expect you to come and see the planning people with me. That bit is not your problem.'

'Part of the service,' I laughed. 'Let's see if we can sort it.'

'Well thank you. I greatly appreciate it.'

I didn't tell him that the last thing I wanted to do was sit around at home thinking about what I might say to Kate and how and what her reaction might be.

And so we drove to the planning office, saw some people, talked the problem through and sorted it out, more or less.

When I got home, I took Ros out and we walked for a long time, through the early dusk, into the early darkness and beyond. Finding our way back along the winding lane with difficulty, getting home just before the rain came.

Then I cooked and went back to work, toiling through plans until I found myself nodding over the drawings.

·

Kicking off my shoes, I shuffled upstairs, pulled the duvet around me and fell asleep, fully dressed.

And I dreamt that dream again. Me in the garden, Jane humming a tune beyond the hedge and then the tune became some scattered words and then the words became the sound of her violin, the low notes picking up the song. She sang while she played, the fiddle resting against her shoulder, her voice low and serious, singing for herself, not allowing me to hear it clearly.

'Was a man I learned it from,
living down Senora way.
I don't look much like a lover
but I say his love words over
often when I'm all alone,
mi amor, mi corazón.'

And then the words were gone again, the violin notes strengthening and rising, soaring confidently through the summer air, asking to be heard. And Jane was walking slowly between the shrubs, finding me, singing more slowly, the bow skipping softly across the strings, the music coming effortlessly.

'I haven't seen him since that night.
I can't cross the line you know
and he's wanted for a gambling fight,
like as not it's better so.
Still I often kind of miss him,
since that last, sad night I kissed him,
left his heart and lost my own,
mi amor, mi corazón,
Adiós mi corazón.'

The song was over. The bow held cruciform across the strings, Jane was smiling.

'Did you like that?'

'Yes. It's beautiful. I didn't know you'd learned it.'

'I did, for you.'

'Really?'

'Just for you.'

She smiled a reckless, inscrutable smile, that enigmatic grin that I loved.

'Thank you.'

'You're most welcome.'

And off she went, whistling some other tune, the fiddle tucked beneath her arm, the bow swinging in her hand, making a different kind of music.

And then I woke and it was dark, just before five. The dream was gone, but not the memory.

'I hadn't forgotten,' I said aloud.

I could hear Ros jumping from Jane's bed next door and padding through the darkness to my bedside.

'Good boy,' I said patting his head.

He yawned, lay down and settled himself on the wooden floor.

'I hadn't forgotten,' I said again, more quietly, but no answer came, nor did I expect one.

I smiled. If Jane could have sent a smiling memento this would have been it, but there were no channels through which to send those reminders and nowhere from which to send them. The only prompts were the ones I had planted in my memory from a time before she died. There were no secret messages. Whatever teasing was being done was an echo of the same teasing that had gone on while she was alive.

But that didn't stop me talking to her. I did it all the time, around the house, when I was working, in the dead of night, in the garden, on the hillside, in the car. And I always listened for a reply. And sometimes it came from some words she had once spoken and sometimes it came in a remembered laugh or a sigh of disbelief or, best of all, in that grin and the laughing eyes and the beautiful smiling shrug that told me I was a hopeless case but she loved me anyway.

The house settled again and I heard the ticking clock recede as I closed my eyes, certain for those moments that there was nothing I couldn't tell Kate, positive that she would understand and, anyway, if she didn't, it wouldn't alter anything. The past would still be as guiltless and as good as it had ever been. Nothing that had happened required an apology, there was no need for feelings of culpability or remorse.

This assurance came from somewhere in that past, bringing a sense of peace and conviction.

I knew it wouldn't last, that I'd wake in the morning dreading the conversation to come. But, in the meantime, everything seemed right and I found myself drifting away, listening to the shallow breathing of Ros and to the greater silence of the wide and empty night. That was all I remembered and then I slept, again, soundly.

Across the morning sky, the sun was hard and small and red. It sat among the thorns of the hawthorn hedge, trapped for now, looking as though it had lost the energy to climb or even colour the day. A clot of crocuses under the garden wall, well sheltered from the scratching wind, raised their heads in search of the possibility of heat and, finding none, they bent again to the ground, pulling whatever warmth they could from the memory of summer that was caught somewhere beneath the freezing earth.

Ros lay in the firelight from the wood stove. When Kate's car sounded in the yard, he raised his head but only to acknowledge her arrival. He had no intention of going out again. Our early morning walk had persuaded him against the great outdoors.

I ushered Kate in from the wintry garden.

'Just when I thought spring was in sight,' she said.

'Coffee's up.'

'Lovely. Thank you.'

We sat at the table, the stove throwing its roaring heat around the room. Outside, the sun was still struggling to free itself from the hedgerow, the small birds chattering and arguing around the bird feeders.

'Now,' Kate said. 'I bought you this. It's not from your money but it is a little thank you from me and from the girls, though they don't know it yet.' Taking a package from her bag, she placed it on the table. 'I know there's no point in asking you to open it now. But you can open it when you feel like it. Sometime. It won't go off.'

'Thank you,' I said. 'Thank you.'

'The other thing I want to say is that I'm going away this week, the day after tomorrow, in fact. I'm going to stay with a friend of mine in London, Sheila, you met her a couple of times. The girls know, Brian knows and now you know. That's everyone important in my life. I'm going for three months initially. My friend says there's lots of temping work there and that's what I'm going to do. See how I like it. See if I can live without all of you. The girls are coming over for Paddy's weekend. Brian is coming over for Easter. You can come and visit if you want but there's no pressure. And I want to tell you something else about the money. I've put most of it into two accounts for the girls, half and half to each. The accounts are in my name because I don't trust either of them not to blow the lot on shoes and bags and rubbish, but it means Susan can do her Masters and Elizabeth can look at what she wants to do. I just thought it important that you know that. If I need something I can get it but that's not the plan. Most definitely no sports car.'

'That's quick,' I said. 'The London bit.'

'Yes. Well I don't see any sense in hanging about. I think it's good, for both of us, for all of us. Hanging about isn't going to change anything. Not after all this time.'

'It still seems awfully sudden. You're sure it's the right thing to do?'

'I have never been sure, ever, in my life, that something was the right or wrong thing to do. I always found things out by doing or not doing. Mostly by not doing, so can this be any worse? Anyway, it's London, it's twelve weeks initially. It's not the Antarctic for three years.'

'True.'

'And I need to do it. Not for you or Brian or the kids, but for me.'

'I understand that.'

'Good.'

She sipped her coffee and I noticed that the sun had, at last, pulled itself from the intricacies of the hedge and risen a little into the vacant sky.

'So that's my news. Bet you can't match that.'

I smiled. Of course I could but I wouldn't. If Kate were leaving in forty-eight hours, I wasn't going to unburden myself of everything I had wanted to say. The last thing I wanted was for her to hear my story and then to vanish for months on end. So, instead, I told her part of the truth.

'It's about us,' I stammered. 'About the things between us.'

'There's this whole wide prairie between us, the one that you wouldn't let me cross,' Kate said quietly, without looking at me. 'Wouldn't or couldn't.'

'Couldn't,' I said

'Couldn't then.'

'But today I'm going to tell you some of the things that have happened on this side of that prairie.' I hoped my tone was light, hoped it might make what I was going to say more palatable. 'And I really hope that it gives you a better idea of who and what I am.'

'I think I know that already, half a lifetime or have you forgotten? Let me guess. You've been shagging the waitress from the coffee shop? No, I asked you that already. You're gay! You have a gay lover.'

She was laughing, not aware yet that I wasn't smiling, that I hadn't joined in the banter as I normally would.

'I'm sorry,' she said at last. 'You wanted to talk. It's just a fucking weird situation. Me sitting here telling you I'm leaving. You sitting there telling me you're going to explain things to me after all these years.'

'It started out with her needing me,' I said quickly. 'But it ended up with me getting bound up in the whole thing, not being able to differentiate between what was necessary and what I imagined was necessary.'

'What exactly are you talking about here?' Kate asked. 'I'm confused. Is there someone else, please tell me? Have I really not been seeing something that's been going on under my nose for months or years?'

'I'm talking about Jane, when she was small, and you and me then,' I said quietly.

She laughed again.

'Jesus, for a second there I thought you were telling me there'd been someone else all this time, some vivacious blonde who I'd never guessed at. I understood that about Jane, I always understood. I know that each of us would die for our children. I knew exactly what you were saying and feeling when you spoke at the funeral. I've known it for years, I've never really felt any envy, ever.'

'I realise that. You've been very open and understanding, absolutely, in what must have been a very strange and difficult place.'

'That's good,' Kate said and she reached across the table, putting her hand on mine and squeezing it. 'It's good to feel that strangeness, that's good.'

'Is it?'

'Yes. You once told me your life had been lived on the surface, emotionally, right back to your childhood.'

'I did.'

'So to feel this, to miss Jane this much, till it aches and cuts into you, is natural. I worried when you said you had no strong feelings about those bastards or any of that stuff. It's not that they're important. It's that you're important. It's that it's important that you allow your feelings to flood back into you, or even to flood in for the first time. And, of course, that makes me hopeful, too. I'd be lying if I said it didn't. No matter how strange and lonely it is, I'll always be there for you, you only have to say.'

She withdrew her hand and poured us both some more coffee.

'A long time ago, way back before Beth was killed, I fell in love with you,' I said. 'But I didn't do anything about it, I didn't even say anything. In the beginning, it was because I didn't know you well enough and I didn't want to wreak havoc in your life or mine, I suppose. And later I thought I couldn't, I truly didn't believe I could balance the two parts of my life, being here for Jane and being there for you. I weighed up the consequences of what might go wrong. Always of what might go wrong, never of what might work out. I gave no consideration to what might happen or to how things might be resolved or any of that. I just lived, in the moment, for Jane. And, in a strange way, I suppose I allowed Beth to come between us, simply by her being absent. Had she been alive, you and I might have been together. Isn't that odd?'

'You're leading me round in circles,' Kate said. 'I'm lost. I thought we were up and down this road before. Are you telling me, after all these years, that you really loved your wife?'

'No. But I am saying I allowed her absence to linger, I tried too hard to be father and mother, even though I didn't think Jane particularly needed a mother when Beth was alive. I let Beth ruin something, even in her absence, that might have worked, would have worked, something that would have made all our lives better. But now it's too late. I believe it's far too late for us. I've gone beyond the place where I could turn back. Beth's death came between you and me and now Jane's death will do the same. I see things repeating but I can't change them. I don't have the energy or the ability. I know that must be an awful thing to hear but I'm trying to be as honest as I can.'

I wanted to look away, to cast my eyes down but, instead, I kept watching Kate. She rubbed her hand across her mouth then lifted her coffee cup but she didn't drink from it. Instead, putting it back down, she covered her mouth with her hand. And then she breathed out, a long, low breath that sounded like a sigh but wasn't. And she breathed out again and I realised she couldn't speak, that her voice had failed.

'Have I said enough? Do you want me to try to explain further or would you rather I didn't?'

Kate shrugged and opened her palms; her eyes were filled with tears but she wasn't crying. Her mouth moved but with the crooked, sluggish movement you sometimes see in drunks. Her lips were trying to fashion shapes and the shapes would formulate sounds and the sounds would be words but nothing came. No shapes, no sounds, no words. And for some terrible, empty, pointless reason, I remembered the day she and I had made love in the bedroom upstairs.

'I don't wish most things in my life could have been different,' I said. 'I want you to know that, but I do wish I hadn't caused you so much pain and I hope I haven't left you feeling you've wasted years.'

When Kate spoke her tone was even.

'It's a horrible thing to say, but I'm going to say it anyway. I thought, in my darker moments, that Jane's death might finally bring us together, that I might be able to save you from some of this trauma and bitterness and horror. But, then, I realised I couldn't. I wanted you for so long, so many years, not just physically, I wanted to be with you.'

'And I've dreaded telling you what I've told you,' I said. 'But I had to.'

'Why did you have to?' she asked. 'And I'm not being judgemental in asking that, I'm simply wondering.'

'You deserve to know and I needed to tell you.'

'Guilt?'

'To an extent.'

A log collapsed in the stove, flames eating it away so that it fell knocking another, tumbling against the glass door. Ros sat up, looked about him and then lay down again.

'So,' I said.

'Is that a question?'

'Not really.'

'Good, because I don't have an answer.'

Opening the stove door, I fed an armful of logs onto the blue embers. Ros rolled on his back and I rubbed his belly.

'I don't know what else to say to you,' Kate said. 'And I don't want to sit here saying nothing and I don't want to walk away from you because I know how difficult this has been, but I don't want you to think it's all ok either. I never felt jealous of Jane, I know I said I did, but now I think I may resent her. I think I'll be sitting in some office in London thinking, That bitch. Isn't that wretched?'

I didn't answer.

'Anyway, there's absolutely no point in our sitting here for three hours dissecting this. Get your coat, we'll take Ros for a walk.'

'Do you still make love to me, in your imagination?'

'No. Not because I don't want to but because I can't. I don't have the strength to go back to that, or the courage to face the emptiness that replaced the life we might have lived. It isn't just about the little sex we had. It's about everything.'

We were walking up through the woods and now the sun was nesting somewhere in the lower branches of the empty sycamores. We were heading for the fallen tree where we'd sat to watch the snowstorm. Neither one had said so, but we both knew it.

'I'm haunted by a woman who'll never be here and who'll never be gone,' I said.

'You'll learn to live with that,' Kate said, thinking, I realised, that I was talking about her.

We walked on, moving fast into the blades of the coldness, heads down, coats pulled high around our faces. Ros ran ahead and then stopped and checked that we were following.

'I'll miss this place,' Kate said, her breath coming out as mist.

On we went, between the trees, along the stooped back of the wintry hill and down towards the fields of sleeping rape. The sky was a still blue and the sun was a summer red but otherwise the day was more winter than spring. I remembered other days up here, when the six acres of bluebells were ringing in the Maytime air and to step between the evening trees was to walk into a glade of kingfishers, moving in a soft breeze, the scent of the flowers lying drenched under the lowest branches.

That was then, whenever then was. Last year and the year previous to that and a spool of years twisting back through this decade and the one before, back to the early eighties. Summer had merged into summer up here, blazing skies or clouds hanging like threats over the middle weeks of May but always the glow of bluebells and the scent, reminders and promises.

Cutting off the path, we crossed the ivied floor of the forest, moving back into the light, coming out on the rim of an outcrop above the fallen trees. In its shelter, two people were lying on the ground, kissing, their bodies tangled in a confusion of clothes and limbs.

'So which of us asks them to move?' I said quietly

Kate was frowning.

'We should go,' I said. 'We can walk or we can sit in the car or we can go somewhere else. If we stay, Ros is going to disturb them.'

'We'll do a round of the hill,' Kate said, moving away. 'They may have gone by the time we come back again.'

I followed her along the path, away from the sunlight and back into the shadows of the forest. She was walking fast, as though she needed to get away from what we'd seen.

'They were just a couple of kids,' I said.

'I think I know that.'

I followed in her footsteps till the path widened and I could walk beside her.

'We can go, if you like. We don't have to stay here. You don't have any obligation to stay and talk any of this out.'

'I know that, too. Let's just walk for a while.'

'Ok.'

We moved down the forest path, the hill on our left and the fields below us to our right.

'The theory is that it's easier to talk about difficult things when you're sitting or walking side by side, no eye contact,' I said.

'That was my theory but theories are purely theoretical.'

'Yes.'

'But if there are questions that you have, I'll try to answer them. If it makes any difference.'

'I've kept waiting, for twenty years, for something to happen and things have happened, marvellous things, exciting things and terrible, awful, horrible things. But whatever it is that I've been waiting for, the particular thing that would give a meaning to everything, that hasn't happened. And I don't think now that it ever will.'

We had reached the car park again but Kate continued on, hurrying across the open space and back into the sheltering wood.

'Maybe there are other things that you really want to tell me,' Kate said. 'This might be the time because I'm not sure we'll ever talk about this again.'

'I don't want to be another Jerry Brown,' I laughed.

'God forbid. I don't know what I need to hear and I don't know what you want me to hear. Let's keep walking and if that pair are gone when we get back to the tree we'll sit there and talk. If they haven't left, we'll just leave it until whenever, if ever. The thing is, whatever else you might tell me will be too much or too little because I don't know if anything you say will make anything any easier to accept. I mean, driving out here, I thought I could hack it. But then when we saw that couple, it just, I don't know, it just did something.'

'Meaning?'

'Meaning I thought of you and me and then I thought, What the fuck am I doing? What am I thinking? What the hell is going on in my head that I'm remembering one solitary shag with a man who just told me that there's no hope for us, ever. After twenty years of being his friend and wanting him and lowering myself to believing his daughter's death might be my best hope? I think about that and I'm disgusted with myself.'

'You've never been anything but kind and good to me and to Jane. Don't ever blame yourself for something as understandable as need. I loved you, Kate. I love you, you're the only woman in my life. I would love to be able to live with you, I would love to have the comfort of having you close to me. I'd love to have you making me laugh every day and I'd love to be there to make your life as happy as I could. But I can't do it, I just can't. This is how things are and always will be. Always.'

I was aware of the silence about us. The sun was now as elevated as it would be that day, peering down through the higher branches, its eye following us as we worked our way up the hill again. In the distance, between the pines, I saw two figures moving down the hill but they were too far away to identify as the couple we'd seen at the tree, so I said nothing. I listened hard for birdsong but there was none.

Ros rolled in a deep drift of fallen sycamore leaves and pine needles and then ran ahead again, sheaves of rust tracking in his wake. A tunnel between old trees mouthed silently at us, sloping to a barbed-wire fence and beyond that an empty field but we went on, rounding the hill, moving away from the path and across the shining floor of ivy.

There was no one in the shelter of the fallen tree and we climbed onto the vast, humped back of a hundred fallen years.

Before us, the fields were red in the light of the frozen sun.

'You know I really don't want to talk about this,' Kate said. 'I can't. It'll all make me cry and I don't want to cry. I want to walk away from it as if nothing had been said today. I want to be as hurt as I've been for years, but no more than that. I can live with that but not with any more.'

We sat together, the sun already dropping behind us, the forest's shadows lengthening across the sweeping acres. Kate tilted her head against my shoulder and I put my arm around her and yet there was nothing in the way of real closeness about us. The day began to fade gently away and I knew we'd walk back through the afternoon darkness and sit in the car and, if we spoke, it would be about things that didn't matter. We wouldn't talk again about what I'd said and we wouldn't mention Kate's going away and we'd part with a hug and a promise to talk the following day but we wouldn't.

I'd do my work, concentrating that little bit too hard on the drawings before me, and Brian would drive Kate to the airport, saying whatever needed to be said. They'd reassure each other that everything would be fine, Kate reminding him of this or that to do with the girls.

But neither she nor I would find a way across the divide between us. We were back again, petrified teenagers on opposite sides of a dancehall, wanting to move, rehearsing what we might say until the preparation became everything and the moment passed, regretting our inabilities but forever marooned. Not, it was clear, because we didn't want to move but, rather, because we were both aware that circumstances had taken us beyond any place we had ever considered or even imagined being and we must accept silence as an inadequate but unavoidable substitute for whatever anger or regret there was between us now.

And then Kate called me from the airport in London. She'd just arrived. I could hear the flight announcements in the background.

'You know the extraordinary thing is that if you wanted me to come back and live with you, even now, even after everything, I would. Isn't that crazy? I still would.'

part

•

five

AND SO THE SLOW PROCESSION of the days continues. February edging into March and couples calling with ideas for house plans on sites they haven't yet found or extensions to houses they once imagined perfectly adequate. It happens every spring, a seasonal instinct people have to find a new place to live or a new view on a familiar place. And it's always possible to tell where the enthusiasm lies and where there's acceptance.

A couple comes to me and it's obvious that the new house is the price of an affair. Another couple comes and the extension is in expectation of a child. And I share, for a couple of hours, in the dreams that are there, the aspirations that lie beyond the drawings and blueprints and bank loans. And I hope these dreams can come true because the rest of life is only what the world or circumstance can offer.

And Elizabeth and Susan come back from their weekend in London and we sit at my kitchen table looking at pictures on their cameras, the first time we've sat at this table since the day we chose Jane's memoriam-card photograph and I wonder if the irony is lost on them but I don't dare ask. We look at pictures of Kate and Sheila, pictures of Kate in Trafalgar, Kate laughing, Kate with her hair newly cut, the colour changed.

And after his Easter visit to London, Brian calls and tells me Kate is well.

'She says you should go and see her.'

'She's all right?'

'Seems to be. Loves her job. And no English accent yet, thankfully.'

'What has it been? A month?'

'Seven weeks.'

'She's doing well then?'

He gives me her address and phone number.

'Give her a call, she'd like that a lot.'

I wonder if it hurts him to be the go-between.

'I will. Sometime.'

We have little else to say.

'And how are you?'

'I'm pretty well,' Brian says. 'The girls are home every second weekend. Some things never change.'

He blushes.

'It's ok,' I said. 'And you're right, some things never do.'

In late April, Robert and Jenny arrive. We travel a bit, daytrips to Wicklow and to Kilkenny. They take my mother to Killarney and Galway for a week. I plead work and insanity. I stay at home but she comes back with them and I survive a long weekend in her company. We visit Jane's grave.

'I'm not sure that stone is weathering well,' my mother says. 'I think something more traditional would have been better. Black marble, perhaps.'

Jenny takes her walking, they look at other headstones, they compare and contrast, my mother is out of earshot.

Later, I tell Jenny she's a loss to the diplomatic corps.

The following night, after my mother has gone to bed, Kate's name comes up in conversation.

'I really hoped it would work for you two,' Jenny says.

'It did, for me,' I tell her. 'But sometimes what's ideal for one person is a cruelty to another.'

'I guess.'

'I could happily have gone on living here and having Kate as my friend.'

Jenny nods.

'Do you talk regularly?' Robert asks.

'I haven't been in touch since she left. She called me from Heathrow, the day she arrived. We haven't spoken since.'

'And no word from her?'

'None. She sent her number and address with Brian at Easter.'

'That's a gesture,' Jenny says.

Robert shrugs a question mark.

'It definitely is,' Jenny assures him. 'And a pretty obvious one.'

'I think you're right,' I say. 'But if I do get in touch, there's nothing new I can tell her, nothing that I haven't said. And I don't want to cause more pain because I know I've caused a lot of pain already.'

'Perhaps there will be something to say, in time.'

'Perhaps. Maybe.'

'But you owe it to Kate to at least keep in touch.'

'Yes.'

Two days later, I drive them to the airport and Robert hugs me.

'I love you, brother,' he says.

'And I love you.'

'And you'll come and see us in the summer,' Jenny says, and it's not a question.

'Sounds like I have no choice.'

'You don't.'

April flowers into May and I go on working. The mornings are bright now well before six. Ros and I have a routine. Getting up just after five, walking out to meet the day before the moon has gone down or the sun has come up. We get home by seven and we eat and I work until lunch-time.

In the afternoon, when the sun is hot, I'm out in the garden. Ros lies in the shadow of the roses or he stays in the house, choosing the coolest spot at the foot of the stairs, his nose on the hall tiles. Or sometimes I drive out to the woods and we walk there together. The earth is hard and dusty and the sun spills through the high branches of the sycamores, loching in unexpected places where the bluebells are a shade lighter and the primroses a dash brighter and the new leaves a shining, translucent lime.

And one evening, in the middle days of May, I sit on the fallen tree and Ros settles in the cooling glimmer of the fading bluebells. Through a frame of whitethorn, there's a field of young corn, the headland left in grass. And when I walk in that grass at the head of the field, I can stand in one or other of the dry, dust-brown tracks that run, initially, in perfect parallel through the field before they come together in the distance, finally spearing into another field, this one filled with vibrant yellow rape flower. Beyond that, a line of dark hedge cuts across that parcel of land from the next, another singing yellow space that seems to stretch into the distant foothills.

And far away to the west, across the dandelion valley, the mountains rise against tomorrow's sky, their shoulders catching the sinking sun. For fifteen minutes, they have an other-worldliness, glinting crimson, trimmed in scarlet and blinding lilac, before strange shadows begin curling slowly between the crevices.

And for those minutes, I'm back in Greece, sitting in the evening shadow at the gable of the whitewashed house, watching the sun's final descent into the Ionian Sea, observing it change shape from circle to semi-circle to sinking dome.

I drive back home, the western sky hanging indigo in my windscreen, the evening star stabbing the sheet of night and then the other stars all following. I have my memories and they are dearer to me than anything.

The following morning the mountains come back to me and I remember the battered, fractured hillsides of Greece. We go hiking there again, climbing at the break of daylight, before the sun has scaled the other face, and come out among the remnants of another life, the fallen walls of a lost village.

We sit in the midday shadow of a cave, drinking our water, eating deliberately, watching the land sink beneath the weight of the afternoon heat. Rocks and the stumps of long-dead trees waltz that crazy, chimeric dance that inanimate objects often do to the illusive, silent music of mirage. We giggle together as boulders shimmer and shimmy in the scrub below us, pointing to this one and that, waiting for them to grow shadows before we venture out again, moving slowly down the side of the sleeping hill, feigning surprise when we find the rocks have recovered their sturdiness. Down, down we go, moving gradually through the lengthening afternoon, back into the valley, where centuries of toil have persuaded grass to grow and crops to show their reticent heads, back to the cooling comfort of a shower and, later, to the simple food and unfussy wine of a local restaurant.

Those memories are my companions through the morning and, while I eat my lunch in the sunny garden, birdsong sirens in the noon heat. I cannot get you out of my head. I go on thinking of you all day and I don't have to fight off guilt or even sadness and I don't wish that anything between us had been different.

Is that where it started, in Greece, the summer before last? It's certainly where it manifested itself. I could say it's because we were alone so much of the time, out in the mountains, down by the sea, content in each other's company, reading the same books. And that would be true. So let's say Greece was the alpha point. You'd tell me that's a weak and lazy metaphor, you'd tell me you could do better and no doubt you could. You were the one with the firm grasp of the language, alpha to omega.

So let's just say being away from everything and everyone familiar was the catalyst. That much we agreed on, when we talked about it afterwards.

'But,' you said. 'It would have happened anyway because I wanted it to.'

It wasn't that day, the one when we'd climbed the mountain, but the one after. We'd been out all afternoon on a fishing boat, moving between islands, swimming in the deep, clear water, talking with the other tourists on board. It was after eight when we got back to the house and almost ten before we ate.

We'd arranged to meet an American couple, to whom we'd spoken on the boat, and their three children, two young men of nineteen and twenty and a daughter of fifteen. The meal was a huge success and we ate and drank into the small hours. The two young men made a reasonable job of some Everly Brothers songs and their sister recited Robert Frost.

The four of you sang together, 'Moon River' and 'I Will'. And then someone found a violin and you played and sang 'Wild Mountain Thyme'.

'I will build my love a bower,
by yon clear crystal fountain,
and upon it I will place
all the flowers of the mountain.'

Outside, a full moon was sailing above the warm, blue sea and I was so proud of you, proud of the way the restaurant had fallen silent, of the way the owner had come from the kitchen to stand, his hands on the back of a chair, listening, enthralled while you played and sang.

'You will come back tomorrow night,' he'd laughed. 'You will sing, the customer she come and I will pay the money to you. All of us will be happy.'

But he wasn't really joking. If you'd said yes, he'd have asked, 'What time?'

It was after two when we spilled into the narrow, quiet street, promising to meet the following morning before the Americans left for Carolina, and almost three before we were back in the house, curled up on the couch that filled the veranda, watching the man in the moon dip his toes in the sea.

'So did you like either of those American hunks?' I asked.

'Hunks? Is what they were?' you said. 'Not for me. Not my type.'

'You have a type?'

'Someone more mature,' you said. 'The older man. A touch of grey, distinguished. Someone interesting.'

'They were pretty good singers.'

'You can only sing for so long. It's the silences that count.'

'Really. That's a very philosophical statement from a nineteen-year-old.'

'That's me. Mature and philosophical,' you laughed. 'And you should know that well enough not to be surprised.'

'So definitely not your type?'

'Most definitely not. I'll stick with you.'

And you snuggled up beside me and kissed me on the cheek.

'You're my man,' you said.

It's evening now, a high summer evening and the season isn't a month old yet. You'd love this weather, you'd make the best of it. Never mind that your exams would be just around the corner. I'd hear you humming in the shadow of the maple tree. I'd hear you playing music from the other end of the garden.

But it's summer and even if you aren't here it doesn't feel that way. I begin to stake the peas and beans. Already they're climbing the imaginary poles for which they long. And so I plait them gently around the canes and string one stake to another and imagine the plants writing new sentences in the night, following the headlines of string, finding their own new letters in the short summer darkness.

And you follow me from chore to chore. Standing by me while I water the sandy drills of carrot seed. Kneeling by me while I weed the onion bed. Leaning on my shoulder, your fingers entwined, while I eye the length of each potato drill.

We walk away from the vegetable patch, down between the trees to where the garden opens onto the fields and the river beyond. You're wearing that rich-blue summer dress you often wore and your legs and arms are already tanned from three weeks of sunshine. Your face is softly freckled and your hair has lightened with the sun. You look as beautiful as you've ever looked and a branch of gratitude gently brushes my face. We pass slowly between the trees and then I feel your hand in mine.

And you kissed me again, on the back of my neck. Your lips stayed on my skin, following some imagined line of latitude until they found my mouth. Were we both a little drunk? Perhaps but not drunk enough to mistake what we were doing. Your tongue on my tongue tasted of summer, there was no hesitation. You were holding my face in your hands, kneeling above me and I could smell your sea-washed skin through your shirt.

And there was that moment when you stopped kissing me, when either one might have said something but neither did. And then I kissed you again and our mouths were open, waiting for the hungry taste of tongue on tongue, our faces pressed together, your forehead hard against my skull, your legs pressed against my leg, making a space for it between your thighs, moving but hardly moving, your body stiffened, every muscle tense against what was to come. And there was almost silence, only the whisper of your breath and mine. Your legs tightening, your breathing sharp and fast. I held you and it seemed our bodies would crush, one into the other, until you broke away, angling against my thigh, pulling my head against your dark skin, your breath coming out in an urgent vocabulary that was foreign to me. Your shirt was soaked in perspiration, my tongue tasting the salt of your skin and the salt of the sea, your legs even tighter, fastened with a desperate ferociousness about me. And then there was nothing, as though every ounce of energy were gone.

For a long time, neither one of us moved. I tasted the trickle of perspiration from your neck, I listened for the sound of the sea but all I heard was the slow, calming beat of your heart.

'Jesus,' you said, at last. 'Where did that come from?'

I knew you were talking of the paroxysm that had left you empty. And you laughed quietly while your body slowly folded about me, softening against the contours of my own.

It's as if, in recent weeks, I've found a place where we can be together. And even if it's only a place called memory, it has its own attraction and, for now at least, I live in the shelter of recollection. You move with me through the days. We take Ros walking, up the woods, we saunter along the familiar paths and, when the nights finally settle, we're here together.

I have no idea how long you will stay and I resent the occasional intrusion when somebody calls.

I sleep in your bed now, your perfume scents the pillow. I make a place for your absent body in my arms.

We woke late that morning in Greece, two sleepy figures on a sunlit veranda. A hurried shower, a quick breakfast, walking fast through the morning streets, rushing to be at the pier to see the Americans off. Later, we hired two scooters and curled up the narrow mountain roads, gaining confidence as we went, weaving between the pedestrians, stopping on a corkscrew bend to look back down on the shrunken harbour and the deep-blue sea beyond.

On the mountain top, we left the scooters and wandered through a monastery garden and into the small dark church. Standing at the back of the shadowed nave, you put your hand in mine and squeezed my fingers.

In the late morning, sitting over coffee outside the monastery café, I said, 'We need to talk about last night.'

'Do we?' You winked. 'We could just forget it happened.'

'Yes, we could.'

'Is that what you'd like to do?'

'Would you?'

You laughed out loud and leaned across and kissed my cheek and whispered, 'No.'

That night, after dinner, we walked down to the harbour and sat, watching the late trawlers return from their day on the sea. I wanted to kiss you, to be kissed by you.

Walking back up the dark, sloping street, you took my hand again.

'There's probably a time to talk about us,' you said. 'I'm not sure it's now but maybe it is, that all depends. I have no regrets about last night. It's what I've wanted for a long time. I don't need to justify it to myself. This is what I want for us.'

'Long term?'

'For as long as I can see into the future.'

'It changes so many things.'

'Not for me,' you said. 'If I'd had the courage or the chance, what happened last night would have happened a year ago. I wouldn't expect anyone else to understand, but I understand. I have no sense of discomfort about this. But you might.'

'I don't know what sense I have. Beyond reminding myself that it did happen. It's not something I can define or analyse.'

'But you want to?'

'I feel I should.'

'You see, I don't. I just go with it.'

And you pulled me to you in the darkness of a doorway, and kissed me.

I'm walking the long road across the bog, Ros chasing the scent of loping, scattered hares. And I'm thinking about Kate, and wondering if ever there will come a time when I can tell her about you and me. For now, I have no need. I'm content to live in this sudden rekindling of the life we lived for fifteen months, the secret, giggling existence of lovers. It has all come back to me from somewhere and, for as long as it lasts, I'm content with the memory and the sense that something of you has survived.

Once, we sat late into the night, talking around the details of our affair. You, insisting that analysis kills everything.

'I don't talk about my music,' you said. 'I can't sit down and explain my feelings about what I play. I just play it and it makes me happy, it excites me, it's a passion.'

'But if someone were to look at us, from the outside, they'd see something unhealthy and twisted and wrong. They'd accuse me of exploiting you and they'd say I'm destroying the potential of your life. They'd lock me up.'

'Just as well no one knows then,' you laughed.

'They are serious accusations.'

'I know that. And they don't bother me. I know exactly what I feel and regret and guilt and doubt don't figure among them.'

And you were laughing again, always laughing your way out of the tight corners of my questions.

I loved the intrigue just as I loved the firmness of your body. I looked forward to the weekends when you came home. Meeting you at the winter station was the highlight of my week. Hugging you on the public platform. Holding your hand in the privacy of the car. Sitting across the dinner table, hearing all your news. Dropping Elizabeth and Susan and yourself to town. Waking on Saturday mornings without you beside me or waking in the middle of the night when you slipped into my bed, always the uncertainty, always the fascination. You were my lover, but I was never sure of when or where you'd come to me. Sometimes a weekend would pass without our sleeping together.

I was enthralled by your beauty and vivacity. You were everything I had never had and I lived in the certain knowledge that this was happiness.

I finish another set of plans. A woman comes to collect them.

'How are you?' she asks, touching my arm lightly as she's leaving.

'I'm well,' I say. 'I'm really, really well.'

'That's good. I'm glad to hear that.'

'How does this make you feel?' you asked one night.

We were lying in bed.

'It makes me feel loved. And young.'

'Well you're hardly ancient. What are you? Forty-seven?'

'You know bloody well that I'm only forty-five.'

I wrestled you on top of me.

You kissed the bridge of my nose.

I kissed your breast and your neck and your tongue was inside my mouth and your legs were tight about me.

I know there is no acceptable explanation for what we were, father and daughter, and lovers, but I remind myself that you never cared what others thought.

'What other people do is not my business, I don't interfere and I don't judge. And what we do is none of theirs.'

Whenever you talked about *us* and *we*, my heart rose and, little by little, I stopped thinking of you as my daughter. You were the woman I loved.

Sometimes, I felt a sense of unease about us but only in the way we feel uneasy about the ones we treasure in our lives, only in the sense of knowing that everything beautiful comes to an end, a sense of unease but never of wrongness.

'I'm happy,' you said.

We were sitting in the kitchen, a Friday night, dawdling over dinner.

'No doubts?'

'None.'

'There may come a time,' I said quietly.

'May. Might. Maybe.' You shrugged. 'Who knows if any of us will live that long? I'm happy now.'

I live in the warmth of that love and, if I have one regret, it's that there is no one to whom I can talk about us. Instead, on these slow summer evenings, I stand in one place or another in the garden and wait for you to step barefoot between the flowers. Your dress is blue against the wildness of the hedge roses, your hair has lightened to the gold of sand, your skin is softly sunburned and you're carrying a bouquet of poppies.

Tomorrow morning, the red petals will litter the kitchen table but, for now, there is no world beyond this place and you and I are safe together.

You whisper, 'I love you.'

And I repeat what you have said, out loud.

A robin flits from stake to stake between the white pea-flowers, a blackbird bathes in the dusty earth, the evening is charged with the scent of woodbine and I know that I will always feel this way, so empty yet so grateful.